"Witty . . . Delightful . . .
A fun-filled read,
a well-constructed plot,
entertaining characterizations,
and affectionate vignettes"
Kate's Mystery Books Newsletter

And praise for the previous Faith Fairchild mysteries:

THE BODY IN THE KELP

"Great characters,
a wonderful plot
and a puzzle laid out
in the unfinished threads of a quilt."
Ocala Star-Banner

And the AGATHA AWARD winner:

THE BODY IN THE BELFRY

"Sparkles like a Yankee pond
on a bright autumn day"
Washington Post

"Faith is a promising sleuth . . .
A humorous and engaging addition
to the muder-in-the-village genre."
Booklist

"Literate, cleverly plotted . . . A charmer"
The Drood Review of Mystery

Avon Books are available at special quantity discounts for bulk
purchases for sales promotions, premiums, fund raising or educa-
tional use. Special books, or book excerpts, can also be created to
fit specific needs.

For details write or telephone the office of the Director of Special
Markets, Avon Books, Dept. FP, 1350 Avenue of the Americas,
New York, New York 10019, 1-800-238-0658.

Other Avon Books by
Katherine Hall Page

THE BODY IN THE BELFRY
THE BODY IN THE KELP
THE BODY IN THE VESTIBULE

HUBBARD
HOUSE

THE BODY IN THE BOUILLON

Katherine Hall Page

AVON BOOKS ◆ NEW YORK

ACKNOWLEDGMENTS

I would like to thank Dr. Robert DeMartino
for his invaluable medical advice.

All the characters, places and events of this book are fictitious, and any resemblance to living individuals or real places or events is strictly coincidental and unintentional.

Grateful acknowledgment is made by the publisher for permission to reprint "The Queens Come Late" by Norma Farber. Copyright © by Thomas Farber. Used by permission.

AVON BOOKS
A division of
The Hearst Corporation
1350 Avenue of the Americas
New York, New York 10019

"A Thomas Dunne book"
Copyright © 1991 by Katherine Hall Page
Drawings by Phyllis G. Humphrey
Published by arrangement with St. Martin's Press
Library of Congress Catalog Card Number: 91-21704
ISBN: 0-380-71896-0

First Avon Books Printing: November 1992

AVON TRADEMARK REG. U.S. PAT. OFF. AND IN OTHER COUNTRIES, MARCA REGISTRADA, HECHO EN CANADA

Printed in Canada

UNV 10 9 8 7 6 5 4 3 2

For my son, Nicholas

Do not do an immoral thing for moral reasons.
—Thomas Hardy, *Jude the Obscure*

PROLOGUE

This is the story of a house, Hubbard House—or, to be more precise, two early-nineteenth-century houses connected by a twentieth-century addition faithful to the period. Nathaniel Aldrich, the original owner, had amassed a considerable fortune shipping "West Indies Goods," to use the more genteel label of the time for rum, and he built a large house outside Boston in the countryside. He believed the air would be more salubrious for the large family he intended. But he had only one child, a daughter, and when she married, he built a replica of his house next door, unwilling to part from her. The only difference between the two houses was the staircases. Nathaniel's house, as it continued to be called forever after, was graced with a magnificent staircase spiraling up two stories from the rear of the large entrance hall. In deference to his daughter's fear of heights, the staircase in her house, Deborah's house, was a double one, proceeding in elegant, gentle stages from floor to floor.

The last Aldrich died, the estate was put up for auction, and Nathaniel and Deborah's houses became Hubbard House. The staircases remained untouched, but the enormous pier glass Nathaniel had placed across from the staircase to reassure his daughter as she descended the steps was sold to a couple from New Hampshire. Dr. Hubbard was afraid it might break.

It was after eleven o'clock at the Hubbard House Life Care Retirement Home. The doors were locked and most of the residents in the main building and outlying cottages were asleep.

Naomi Porter was dreaming she was at the Chelsea Flower Show in London. One of the Queen's gardeners was asking her advice about orchids. Her husband, Danforth, who had been such a whiz at double digging when they had had their own extensive garden instead of the small greenhouse off the living room now, snored dreamlessly at her side.

Leandra Rhodes was also asleep, but her husband, Merwin, was not. They had been married over fifty years, and he had always acceded to her demand that the light be out when she wanted to go to sleep. Lying in the dark, reviewing the day's events, had become such a habit that he eventually considered it essential. As soon as she had dropped off, he'd switch the lamp on and read. She never knew.

Fingers of light shone beneath other doors, but by the time the clock chimed midnight, everything was in darkness. This was New England, and old adages retained their currency. If one wasn't early to bed, one wouldn't be early to rise.

Those in the hospital annex slept more fitfully, aware perhaps of the ailments and frailties that had placed them there for a long or short stay. A ghostly figure in white slipped silently from one of the rooms, entered another farther down the corridor, and noiselessly shut the window. The curtains grew still at once. The room's occupant had tossed most of his blankets on the floor, and these were carefully replaced before the figure went to the door, opened it a crack, looked out, and then walked softly away.

Beyond the cottages in an apartment above the garage

housing the vehicles and equipment, which kept Hubbard House so faultlessly maintained inside and out, Eddie Russell was quite awake. The night was still young.

He was stretched out naked on top of his bed facing a large-screen TV and flicking through the home shopping channels with the remote. Images of jewelry, collectors' plates, fuzz busters, and cookware raced across the screen. He stopped at some earrings. A voice urged, "Just in time for those special holiday occasions. The office party, an open house. Filigree peacock earrings, eighteen-carat gold. Two inches long and one inch wide. Three layers of feathers that move as you move, and a French clasp to make sure you'll never lose them. Tonight only we're offering this exquisite item with a retail value of $455 for $183.18, plus $3.75 for shipping and handling. Or, if you prefer, the easy-pay plan—three payments of $61.06 each."

Eddie rolled over and reached for his drink—Chivas on the rocks. "Want some earrings, baby? They'd look great on your lobes." He nibbled the one nearest to him, then gave it a sharper bite.

"Eddie! You're hurting me," his partner squealed in delight.

"Come on, want some earrings? Take down the number and I'll get them for you."

"Oh, honey, you're so good to me."

Eddie smiled. "That's because you're so good to me."

The earrings were going to be a good-bye gift.

1

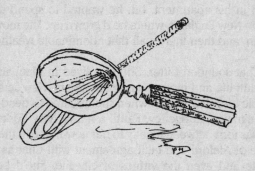

"I'm not going to tell you anything unless you do *exactly* as I say and do not get involved any further than is necessary for my peace of mind. I want you to promise, Faith."

Faith Sibley Fairchild considered for a moment. Her Aunt Chat, short for Charity, was using her most uppish aunt voice. The only way to find out why she had called all the way from New Jersey to Massachusetts—and before the rates went down—was to agree with Chat's no uncertain terms. But, Faith reflected as she dutifully swore, peace of mind could cover quite a bit of territory.

"I don't know if you remember my old friend Howard Perkins. He moved to a retirement home near you last month. I had meant to tell you, so you could go and see how he was."

This didn't seem like much to ask, and Faith was puzzled about the oath. Going to pay a call on Howard Perkins, whom she vaguely remembered as a dapper colleague of Chat's in the advertising business, wasn't even up there with the secret of the Rainbow Girls. Why all the cloak and dagger?

"No problem, just tell me the name of the place and I'll be happy to run over—today, if you like."

"I said 'was,' Faith. Howard died last week. He had a very serious heart condition and certainly should have stayed in his apartment, but he wanted to spend his last years in New England, where he'd grown up. The move was a strain, and then there's all that abominable weather you have."

Chat sounded bitter. She had lived in Manhattan all her adult life and moved out to Mendham, New Jersey—a sensible distance away—when she'd retired as head of her own lucrative ad agency. Faith, a native New Yorker herself, was torn between loyalty to her new home in the small village of Aleford and tacit agreement with Chat as to the climate and even the virtues of city life. She'd been in Aleford for more than three years, and she still missed New York. She wondered what Howard had done with his apartment. Like Chat's old one, it had been in the San Remo on the West Side. Not that the Reverend Thomas Fairchild, Faith's husband, would ever entertain the idea of even a pied-à-terre anywhere except in his own backyard, but Faith would always enjoy playing that absorbing and perpetual New York pastime "Apartment, Apartment, Who's Got an Apartment?"

"Oh Chat, I'm sorry to hear that. I do remember him. He was a lovely man."

"Yes, he was. We thought we might get married once, but we were such good friends, it seemed foolish to risk it." Faith thought she detected a slightly wistful note in her aunt's voice, which quickly vanished as Chat got back to business. "Now, I'm sure you're wondering what this is all about and too polite to say so. There was a letter in the mail from Howard today—another example, incidentally, of the scandalous way the postal service is being run. He mailed it several days before he died and I'm just getting it now. Anyway, I'll read you the relevant part:

. . . I must close now, Chat dear. It's time for dinner and I don't like to be late. The food takes me back to my boyhood—all sorts of old favorites I haven't had for years. I've put on a pound or two! There is one thing that is bothering me, though, and I don't quite know what to do about it. I plan to tell Dr. Hubbard eventually, but I want to get it all straight first. I'm sure he'll be able to handle the matter. I'm already fond enough of the place to want to avoid involving the authorities. I'll tell you all about it in my next letter. Human nature being what it is, I suppose I shouldn't have been surprised—even here at Hubbard House, surely an oasis, and that's why I must do something to keep it that way for my fellow residents—and yours truly too. I miss you. . . .

"Well, the rest you don't need. Poor Howard—he must have stumbled across some kind of scandal, who knows what. But I feel a certain responsibility to follow up on it. I'd hate to think that people were being mistreated in any way. I thought of going there myself and having a look around. I could pretend to be interested, however difficult that might be, but it might not be necessary if you could make a few discreet inquiries for me and find out what kind of reputation the place has."

"Hubbard House is nearby—in Byford—and I've never heard anything negative about it. Tom has made some pastoral calls there. I could start by talking to him and then speak to Charley, if you like. If there are any rumors, he'll know."

Charley MacIsaac was Aleford's veteran chief of police. While consuming bottomless cups of coffee and dozens of corn muffins at the Minuteman Café, he was also taking in at the same time whatever was happening—or not happening—in the town and surrounding environs.

"And don't leave Millicent out," Chat admonished.

"I was afraid you'd say that." Faith sighed. "But for you, anything."

Millicent Revere McKinley gathered her information from the vantage point of her authentic colonial clapboard house with a bow window (a nineteenth-century addition by a like-minded ancestor) affording a panoramic view of Aleford's Green and Battle Road, its main street. Millicent had regarded Faith with suspicion ever since Faith had rung the historic call-to-arms bell in the old belfry after discovering a fresh corpse therein. The body was warm, and Faith had surmised it was not impossible that the murderer was lurking nearby on the hill in the bayberry bushes. Although the event was long past, Millicent still managed to remind Faith whenever possible that the bell was solemnly tolled on only three occasions: the death of a president, the death of one of the descendants of the founding families of Aleford, and on Patriots' Day as part of the reenactment of the events of that famous day and year.

Millicent had also saved the lives of Faith and her son, Benjamin, and there was that burden too. Faith figured she'd spend the rest of her days in Aleford making amends. She longed for a chance to even the score—snatch Millicent from under the hooves of runaway horses, dash into her burning house to save the glass-enclosed mourning wreaths plaited from the tresses of Millicent's forebears, or have the legislature pass a bill establishing a state holiday honoring Ezekiel Revere, distant cousin of Paul and great-great-great-grandfather of Millicent, who cast the original Aleford bell. But Chat was right. Millicent would know what was going on at Hubbard House. The question was, would she tell Faith?

"And remember, if you turn up anything that looks serious, tell MacIsaac or your nice state police friend."

"Of course, Chat. Yet I'm inclined to think it's probably

that they weren't getting their evening snacks on time or one of the people working there was a bit rude, although there is that reference to 'the authorities.' "

"Exactly, and that's why I want you to be cautious. Now, call me when you have something to report. Love to Tom and Ben."

And with that Chat hung up abruptly, as was her custom. She could talk your ear off in person, but she hated the phone.

Faith walked back into the parsonage kitchen. It bore little resemblance to the one she had encountered when she had crossed the threshold as a new bride. Faith could only assume whoever had cooked there prior to her arrival had had no need of counter space, light, a proper stove, or a refrigerator. A properly equipped kitchen to work in was a question not simply of avocation for Faith but of vocation as well. Before her marriage, she was the Faith behind Have Faith, one of Manhattan's most successful catering businesses, lending her culinary talents to the glittering parties she had previously graced with her attractive presence.

Now that Benjamin was old enough to go to nursery school in the mornings, she had been looking for locations to start the business again. Husband, home, and child were fascinating in their own way, of course, but sometimes a woman needed more. In Faith's case, much more. She was blissfully happy watching infant Ben evolve into toddler Ben and now little-boy Ben, and there was no one she'd rather be with than Tom—usually. However, the four walls of the parsonage, quaintly vine covered though they were, were beginning to move in a little too closely. By chance she'd found a caterer right in Aleford, who called himself Yankee Doodle Kitchens and who was preparing to retire to Florida in February. He was happy to sell her his equipment and arrange for a transfer of the lease, but he would not relinquish the name. He might want to start it up again, he told her, and besides, people associated his work with it. Faith was afraid of that and quickly assured him she

5

would continue to use her old name, as her ecclesiastical mate didn't think it would cast any blasphemic shadows on his surplice. Faith, daughter and granddaughter of ministers, who knew exactly how much glass her house had always been made of, wasn't really so sure of that, but she had been well on her way to a national reputation with articles in *Gourmet, House Beautiful,* and *Bon Appétit* and wanted to capitalize on that publicity. She had also continued to market a successful line of Have Faith jams, jellies, chutneys, and all sorts of other good things to eat.

She took the bread she had been letting rise from the back of the stove, punched it down, and started to knead, filling the room with a strong aroma of cardamom and yeast.

It was that peculiar time between Thanksgiving and Christmas when all the women's magazines were running articles on how to avoid holiday burnout, suggesting everything from long baths with ice-cold slices of cucumbers over the eyes to transcendental meditation, in the same issues in which they were including patterns for gingerbread models of Chartres Cathedral, replicas of the Ghent altarpiece in needlepoint, and recipes for croquembouche for one hundred.

Faith was not feeling too stressed—yet. She'd been steadily filling her freezer with yuletide treats, and while she was not like those people who have selected and even wrapped all their presents by Labor Day, her Christmas list was almost finished. Shopping, Christmas or otherwise, was something she did as a matter of course all year. She was a strong believer that what went on the body, or what that body looked at, should be of the same caliber as what went into it. And some of her old habits had died hard, or not at all. She knew about Filene's and Jordan's, and had heard tell of a Bloomingdale's and a Barney's not too far from Aleford, but if it wasn't from Madison, Fifth, or SoHo, it wasn't the genuine article. And besides, shopping in New York gave her a chance to go to Zabar's for lox, whitefish salad, knishes, and all the other comfort foods of home she craved.

She glanced at the clock. Eleven thirty. Ben was finished at noon and Tom was picking him up, as he did when he didn't have another engagement. Ben's school was in the Congregational church located directly across the green from First Parish, the Fairchilds' church. The two churches looked like bookends with all the old houses bordering the green arranged tidily between them. A liberty pole with an enormous flag and various rough-hewn boulders with plaques marking significant events or individuals were the only things on the green itself. Even the path went around, but it was a true common, and in good weather those who worked in the handful of businesses comprising downtown Aleford ate their sandwiches there at lunchtime, and schoolchildren on their way home stopped for a game of Frisbee. Faith had often taken Ben, first to crawl on the blanket of grass and now to run.

Presently the back door opened and Ben tumbled in shrieking, with Tom close behind. "This time I really am going to catch you, Benny Boy!"

Ben grabbed Faith ecstatically around the knees. "I won, I won!"

Faith picked him up, gave him a big kiss, stroked his hair, blond like hers and beginning to lose its curl, then asked that timeless maternal question, "What did you do in school today, sweetie?" It received the usual answer, one that varies only among "nothing" and "I don't know" or, in Ben's particular case, total silence. She reflected how silly it was to ask day after day, but knew she would keep on and one day, perhaps when he was in high school, he'd sit down and give a blow-by-blow account of his every waking minute since he'd left her side and then she'd probably not be paying attention.

Tom held up a blood-red finger painting. "Look what Ben made. Isn't it wonderful?" Their eyes met. Neither of them had any illusions as to their son's precocity or lack thereof. It looked like millions of other two-and-a-half-year-olds' finger paintings. Ben was affectionate, cheerful, sometimes cooperative, and that was enough for them.

"Sit down and I'll get lunch. I had an interesting call from Chat this morning."

Tom would miss supper—much of a minister's life is spent not in prayer but at committee meetings—so Faith had cooked a big lunch, as she often did when his schedule was like this. They'd have something light when he got home, and she'd feed Ben early. With luck, he'd be asleep. Now they sat down to a casserole of boneless chicken breasts she had lightly poached in white wine and layered with zucchini and carrot matchsticks and blue cheese. The juice from the chicken and what was left of the poaching liquid that she had poured over it made a delicious sauce. There was also some nutty basmati rice and steamed pea pods. With the holidays, she was trying to keep on eye on their calories, although Faith was as slender as she had always been and Tom never seemed to fill up his tall, rangy frame. He was trying manfully now.

"This is delicious, honey. Ben, we are two lucky guys." Ben was daintily picking up each grain of rice left on his plate after he had impaled all the rest of the food on his eager little fork.

"So—what's the news? Why did Chat call? It had to be for a reason; she never calls just to talk."

Faith related the call and, as she did, wished she had jotted down the exact wording of Howard's letter. She'd call Chat back and ask her to read it again.

"Farley is over at Hubbard House now. You met him before he moved—Farley Bowditch. I've dropped by a couple of times to visit him. He seems happy enough and I've never seen anything that would suggest he should be otherwise. The place itself is beautiful. It was the Aldrich estate, and Dr. Hubbard has kept the grounds pretty much as they were. People go over to see the rhododendrons in the spring. They're planted along the drive and pretty spectacular." Tom glanced out the window at the overgrown, woody shrubs in the parsonage backyard. They looked particularly bleak in winter. "This year we really have to do something about those bushes. Cut them back, fertilize . . ."

"Yank them out and start over," Faith suggested. "But tell me more about Hubbard House."

"I don't really know much more. I've met Dr. Hubbard several times, and he seems to genuinely care about the elderly. People around here have a great deal of respect for him—and his whole family. They're all involved with the home. His son's a doctor too and his daughter's a nurse, I think."

"Sounds like 'Marcus Welby' *and* 'Father Knows Best.'"

"Now that you mention it, he does look a little like Robert Young, except Dr. Hubbard is taller—bigger all over, and he has that old Yankee voice, sort of a combination of marbles in the mouth and foghorn."

"Not unlike your father." Faith laughed.

Tom glanced involuntarily over his shoulder. The adage in the Fairchild house had always been "Spare the voice and spoil the child."

"I can't see that there could be any harm in asking around about the place—or danger," Tom added pointedly, referring to some of Faith's previous investigative endeavors.

"You know, Tom, I'm pleased that Chat asked me to help. Not that I'm about to trade my whisks and spatulas for a cape and magnifying glass, but it means she has some respect for my sleuthing abilities."

Tom's reply, which Faith recognized as a heavy-weather warning flag gliding up the mast, was cut short as they both suddenly realized that during their conversation Ben had slid down from his chair and was quietly and gleefully scattering an entire box of linguine over the pantry floor.

"Ben! What are you doing? No, no. That's very naughty! You help Mommy pick up all these spaghettis immediately!"

Tom surveyed the mess. On the Ben scale it was merely a two. Nothing like emptying the vacuum or the ultimate ten, crawling into Tom's mother's car and releasing the emergency brake—fortunately on level ground with several adults running frantically after him.

"Honey, I have to run. I have a meeting with the new divinity school student who's going to be working with us this winter. I'll call you later."

Faith came over and gave him a kiss. "You mean you actually prefer talking to another adult to cleaning up pieces of spaghetti from the floor? Naughty, naughty."

"Don't put ideas in my head. I have to work this afternoon."

Faith turned back to the linguine. Ben thought it was almost as much fun picking it up as throwing it down, and afterward Faith cleared away the lunch dishes and took him upstairs for a nap.

While he was sleeping, she planned her campaign. MacIsaac first, then Millicent. Not that she believed in delaying the inevitable, but since Millicent was going to treat her like a congenital idiot, she'd like to know at least one or two things about Hubbard House beforehand. That way she might not appear to be a complete fool—to herself.

She made a quick call to Chat, took down the exact wording of Howard's letter, and baked the Norwegian Christmas bread she had prepared that morning.

Faith loved the holidays—the traditions, the food, the getting and giving. She'd taken Ben down to New York last week for a look at the tree at Rockefeller Center, the poinsettias massed on the altar of St. Patrick's, and the windows at Saks and Lord & Taylor—even though he was still a little too young to truly appreciate it all. It was never too soon to start. For her these periodic trips to the city, especially at certain times of the year, were a kind of life-support system. Back in Aleford at the end of the long cord, she was willing to grant that New England was the perfect place to be at Christmas. They had already had the first snow, which melted quickly but brought a reminder of things to come. At this time of year no one thought of getting stuck in snowdrifts, backbreaking shoveling, chapped lips and drippy noses. Instead, memory brought the full moon shining like a beacon over unmarked fields of snow, snowflakes on mittens and tongues, sledding and snow angels, tall pines covered with white, and the feeling of sitting before the fire while the storm swept past the windows and down the chimneys.

But Faith wasn't thinking Currier and Ives. She was thinking Hubbard House.

Chief MacIsaac wasn't at the station. Deputy Dale Warren told Faith to try Patriot Drug—the Chief had mentioned he needed some throat lozenges, might be starting a cold. If he wasn't there, then, of course, try the Café. Faith thanked him and wheeled Ben in his stroller out the door and back up the street toward the pharmacy. Like most of Aleford, it had been there forever and no one save herself appeared to find anything humorous about the name, or the fact that besides what one would expect to find in a store of this nature, they also sold the odd case of tuna fish, lawn mower parts, seed packets in the spring, and shoes. Not shoes like those found in Svenson's Shoe Store up the street, where Ben sat on a wooden pony and tried on little Stride Rites with what seemed liked greater and greater frequency, but shoes with the labels cut out or slightly mismatched. If one of your feet was a seven and the other an eight, Patriot Drug was the place for you. It was also one of the few places in the country, no doubt, where you could still get old favorites—and possibly collectibles—in the Friendship Garden line, Dierkiss talc, and Muguet des Bois perfume. Patriot's policy was keep it till it sells. Faith peered in the door, noticed they were having a special on rather dusty cases of imported bonbons, but didn't see Charley.

He was sitting in his usual booth at the Café, toward the rear but on the side facing the street. His hands circled a mug of coffee, and an empty plate was pushed to one side.

"May I join you?" Faith asked.

Charley grinned at the two of them. "Anytime, Faith, and how are things with you?"

"Fine, but I hear you have a sore throat."

The Chief did not seem surprised that the information had already made its way around to Faith. This was Aleford, after all.

"Just a tickle, but these will fix it." He motioned to his pack of Fisherman's Friends.

The waitress, a pleasant woman named Helen Griggs who attended First Parish, came over to the table. "Have you decided yet, Mrs. Fairchild?"

Since Faith had either blueberry or corn muffins whenever she came in, which one was the only knotty question. She ordered blueberry, a cup of coffee, and a doughnut for Ben. He was usually so intrigued by this thing with a hole in it that Faith could count on a good fifteen minutes of uninterrupted conversation while Ben looped the doughnut on his finger and gnawed his way to the middle.

She told Charley about Aunt Chat's call and produced her copy of the passage in the letter that referred to Hubbard House for Charley's perusal. Charley took his time.

"There's basically two places people go to around here when they can't live at home anymore. Peabody House down the street, but that's pretty small, only room for eighteen and you have to be hale and hearty to get in. They don't have any medical facilities there beyond a nurse and an aide or two. Hubbard House is a bigger operation. You can start out in your room or cottage and then, if you need it, move to the hospital section Dr. Hubbard added when he set the place up. Must be about twenty, twenty-five years ago. Before that he was a GP, had an office here in town where that new dentist is now."

Faith and Tom were patients of the new dentist, who had been in practice in Aleford for only seven years, as opposed to the other dentist, Dr. Cook, who, from the look of him, might have flossed Sam Adams.

"Roland Hubbard was just about everybody's doctor. Delivered all the babies, a lot of them in their mothers' own beds, made house calls. You know, the kind of thing we don't have anymore."

Charley sounded bitter. Maybe his throat was worse than he was letting on. He might actually have to go to the doctor's office to get a culture. As for having a baby at home, Faith was very happy for any and all advances medical science might make. She doubted she'd ever want to trade the security of Brigham and Women's for her own roof, not to mention the mess.

"Why did he leave his practice?" Faith asked.

"His wife was very ill and he didn't have much time to see her, let alone take care of her. He thought if he opened a retirement home, he could be with her more, and he was. She only lived two years after Hubbard House opened, but from what I hear she was very happy about the idea. Maybe he knew he would need to be around more for the kids too. Anyway, that's how it turned out."

"I understand his son and daughter are both at Hubbard House."

"Yes, Muriel and Donald. Donald moved back to town and has a small practice in addition to Hubbard House. Muriel lives at the home."

"And you've never heard anything shady about the place?"

"Never. And over the years I've gone often to see a lot of friends. The only drawback to Hubbard House is what it costs. When my time comes, I doubt I'll be there, but I'm glad it's around for the people who can afford it and need it."

"Charley! All this is a long way in the future."

"The future has a way of creeping up on you, Faith. No, I won't go to Hubbard House. I'll go back to my people in Nova Scotia or just stay in my house here until they carry me out."

It must be a very bad sore throat. This kind of lugubrious talk was definitely out of character for Charley.

"Anything else that occurs to you?"

"Not really, but I'll let you know if it does. And I'll drop by there this week and have a look. Talk to a few people. It certainly sounds like this Perkins fellow found something out of kilter. Best thing to do would be to show the letter to Hubbard."

Faith wasn't so sure. Until she'd had a chance to find out a little more, she didn't want anyone at Hubbard House to get the wind up.

"Charley, I'd appreciate it if you didn't say anything about this to anyone—not around here or at Hubbard House."

"I know. It's your baby, but if it looks like anything serious is going on, you'd better let me in on the double. I still feel bad about the last time, and I want to be able to look Tom in the eye—you and little Benjamin too."

"I promise," swore Faith, thinking as she did so that two oaths in one day meant life was getting a bit more interesting than usual. She brightened up. "Next stop, Millicent."

"I'm surprised you bothered with me at all."

"You underestimate yourself, Chief MacIsaac—and don't think I don't know there's more you could have told me about the Hubbards if you weren't so honorable. Millicent doesn't have that problem."

Faith moved Ben from the booth back into his stroller and struggled with the belt that held him in. He wasn't in his subzero snowsuit, only the intermediate weight, yet

14

putting him in the stroller was already like trying to wedge a pillow into a case too small. She brushed some crumbs off him. It certainly wouldn't do to let one fall on Millicent's cherished threadbare orientals.

On the way over, she gave some thought to where she and Tom might end up in their twilight, golden, or whatever the current euphemism was, years. She looked about at the frigid landscape. Definitely someplace a little less bone chilling. Someplace with sun, blue skies, and good food. Someplace like Eugénie-les-Bains in the southwest of France.

Millicent let them in with her usual implacability. Faith could be her best friend or worst enemy for all her manner displayed. After dumping Ben in what she hoped was out of harm's way with the contents of the toy bag she had brought for the purpose, Faith got directly to the point. More or less.

"I wonder if you might be able to help me. My aunt, Charity Sibley, is retired and living in New Jersey now. She asked me to make some inquiries about a retirement home here, Hubbard House, and I thought you might have friends there or know something about it."

Faith had no intention of telling Millicent about Howard Perkins' letter, and Chat *had* asked her to make inquiries. Not that she thought she could fool Millicent into thinking that having an aunt who might move to Hubbard House was all there was to it. They knew each other too well. It was possible they could become friends at some point—perhaps at the third millennium. At present they tended to circle warily when they met.

Millicent had been looking Faith straight in the eye as she spoke. It was one of the methods she employed. Now she looked away, gasped slightly, and stood up. Ben was obliviously playing with some small Majorette cars four feet away from a spindly table supporting one lone china shepherdess. Millicent moved the table a foot farther away. She sat down, smoothed her skirt, and prepared to answer

Faith with the air of one who had just saved a rare piece of family Meissen from certain destruction. Faith knew exactly how "rare" it was, since she had turned it over to look at the mark when Millicent was in the kitchen getting coffee on an earlier call. It looked as if this visit was settling into the pattern of all those before. She was about to add something, something begging, but Millicent had decided she was ready to spill the beans—a few.

"Hubbard House hasn't been around very long, about twenty-five years I believe. Not like our own Peabody House, which dates back to the Civil War. Still, Dr. Hubbard is providing a wonderful service for people, certain people. Only the best people go to Hubbard House to die." Millicent looked Faith in the eye again as if to say this Charity Sibley, whoever she was, might have trouble getting past the gates.

"I have considered it myself, of course, but so far I am able to manage here quite well on my own."

Millicent must be in her early seventies, and Faith had no doubt she would still be going strong thirty years from now. She was a small, trim woman with a Mamie Eisenhower cut she had never wished to change. Her bangs were gradually giving way to solid white from iron gray, but everything else about her looked as it always had. She was one of those people whom it was impossible, even unseemly, to imagine as a child. Today she was wearing a blue sweater with intricate cables, a white round-collared blouse, and a matching blue wool skirt.

"I see you are admiring my sweater," Millicent said. "It's one of my own." Millicent was a demon with a needle, and most days saw her perched in her bay window, eyes front, while endless intricate sweaters, mufflers, and socks flowed into her lap.

"As I was saying, I doubt I'll go to Hubbard House—or Peabody for that matter—yet it certainly is lovely there. Dr. Hubbard bought the old Aldrich estate. There were two beautiful Adam houses side by side. Nathaniel Aldrich built

the later one for his daughter when she married. A nice custom, I've always thought. Dr. Hubbard joined the two together and built the hospital wing out the back. He also converted several of the outbuildings into cottages. It's very tasteful."

Faith tried to think of something to say that would get Millicent away from porticos and back to what was going on inside Hubbard House, but she knew it was futile to try to direct the conversation.

"Poor Dr. Hubbard. He was our doctor until he started the home, and our families were friends. His wife, Mary, had never been strong, and I remember Mother saying it was exactly like that old saying, 'Shoemakers' wives go barefoot and doctors' wives die young.' She did die young, and you never saw a man as upset as he was. If it hadn't been for the children, I'm sure he would have followed her. She was a Howell, but one of the ones from Pepperell."

Faith refused to be sidetracked by Millicent's encyclopedic genealogical prejudices. She didn't know what kind of Howell Mrs. Hubbard should have been, nor did she care.

"Tell me about Muriel and Donald," Faith interjected instead, eager to display some of her newfound knowledge.

Millicent was not impressed. "They're both very good children, always have been. Muriel runs things at Hubbard House. She got some kind of training in nursing-home administration after finishing her RN. Donald is a doctor like his father, and I'm proud to say he's my doctor. Of course with his work at Hubbard House, he can't take too many private patients," she added, squelching any hopes Faith might have had of joining the privileged few.

"Muriel never married, but Donald is."

Since she didn't elaborate, Faith had to ask, "To whom?"

"To Charmaine Molloy, I believe her name was. Not a local girl." And Faith had to be content with those damning

words, since it was clear Millicent wasn't going to say any more. She made a mental note to find out more about Charmaine. It wasn't one of the most popular girls' names one heard in New England, nor did it seem to date back to the days of Patience and Persis, which still cropped up now and then.

"My aunt is interested in the kind of atmosphere one might find at Hubbard House," Faith pressed.

" 'Atmosphere'?" Millicent's expression suggested this was either a frivolous or an inappropriate question.

"Not like mood music or oxygen." Faith was getting irritated; pulling teeth was such hard work. "As in what do they do all day."

"Of course. They do what most older people do. Read, take walks when the weather permits, socialize. Hubbard House also has some facilities for artwork, a loom I believe, and things like that. They also provide transportation on Fridays for the symphony, although many residents still drive. Whenever I've visited there, I've always been struck by how busy people are. That and, of course, how delicious the food is. They pride themselves on it."

Faith could imagine. But it did sound like a place where people simply continued the kind of lives they had lived before, with some changes necessitated by retirement and health restrictions. Friday afternoons in the same seats they had always taken at the Boston Symphony, the flower show at Horticultural Hall in the spring, an afternoon at the Atheneum, and perhaps time to look in at the Algonquin or Somerset club to see an old friend or two while the wife got her pearls restrung at Shreve's or a new frock at Talbots—since the unthinkable had happened and Stearn's was out of business.

"So it's certainly a place that has never had a breath of scandal." Faith played her last card.

"Scandal! I should say not. The Hubbards are one of our finest families and truly devoted to what they do." Millicent had answered too quickly and too emphatically.

There was something there, yet she clearly wasn't about to tell Faith.

Faith realized it wasn't going to be that easy to find out what had upset Howard Perkins. Hubbard House was impeccable, it appeared—but not impregnable. She loaded Ben's toys back into the bag, strapped him into the stroller, and thanked her hostess with what she hoped was the appearance of gratitude before wheeling him down Millicent's garden path.

It had been obvious from the start. There was only one thing to do if she wanted to find out what Howard could possibly have been describing—go to Hubbard House herself.

2

Hubbard House was just as impressive as reports had led Faith to believe—more so, in fact. Two imposing three-story brick mansions sat side by side on a high knoll. Wide verandas with graceful columns suggested something other than a pure New England influence—as if the architect had gone on a junket to magnolia country. But since it was Byford, not Natchez, the columns were severely Doric, and any Corinthian leanings had been held tightly in check. The nursing-care annex connected the two houses. It was also brick—old brick to match the others. It was set slightly back from its neighbors, and a screen of well-kept shrubs extended across the front. The long drive with its fabled rhododendrons bordered precisely trimmed lawns with benches and a belvedere where weary walkers could rest. There was a golf course in the distance.

There was nothing institutional about Hubbard House from the outside. It had been hard to find the entrance—the sign was so discreet as to be almost invisible. Faith followed a series of wrought-iron arrows and found the parking lot. For a moment she had imagined cars were banned.

Ben was going to a friend's house to play after school, one of those unexpected reprieves that suddenly make a mother's day seem long, empty, and luxurious. He spilled his milk twice at breakfast, but Faith merely smiled. "You're certainly full of joie de vivre this morning," Tom had commented, rolling his "vivre" out from the back of his throat in an appreciative approximation of Gérard Depardieu. A sophomore year in France had left its mark in the form of a permanent love affair with the country. Faith had debated briefly whether to tell Tom about her plans to visit Hubbard House. She decided to tell him after the fact, that being her usual modus operandi. Besides, she had told him about her conversations with Charley and Millicent and he had not said anything about stopping her investigation.

But when he had kissed her at the door and asked directly, "What are you up to today? More baking?" she had answered, "I'm not sure," and crossed the fingers of her right hand, which happened to be out of sight in her skirt pocket. Faith felt she was due the occasional absolution crossed fingers supplied because of her ministerial family connections. God knew what a burden that was.

Now she walked up the stairs nearest to the Hubbard House parking lot and noticed that there were indeed wheelchair ramps and an ambulance entrance at the rear of the nursing wing. She crossed the veranda to the main entrance and noted the big pots of evergreens, which would contain other things in other seasons. There were no rocking chairs, though. Clearly Dr. Hubbard wanted his porch free from any elderly connotations.

A large, gleaming brass door knocker hung on the front door, but Faith felt a bit awkward at rousing the populace. Instead, she turned the knob and pushed gently. The door swung open, and she walked into a beautifully furnished living room. Deep-blue wall-to-wall carpeting was covered by authentic-looking orientals. Wing chairs, Queen Anne high- and lowboys, and other appropriately aristocratic furniture filled the room. It was completely quiet, and Faith thought it was empty until she realized that a few of the chairs were occupied by individuals engrossed in the day's *Christian Science Monitor* or *Wall Street Journal.* There was a reception desk off to the side. A door directly behind the desk bore a plaque with OFFICE etched on it in small Gothic letters.

Faith moved behind the desk, which was bare except for a crystal bud vase with a stalk of white freesia in it, and knocked at the door. It was instantly flung open by a small woman of a certain age with pinky-red curls, a navy-blue suit, and a kitty-cat-bowed, fuchsia blouse.

She grabbed Faith by the arm. "Thank goodness you're here! I've been out of my mind trying to get someone. What with Mrs. Pendergast ringing me every other minute from the kitchen and Muriel from the annex, I haven't been able to call my soul my own all morning. Now, come straight along."

It took only two seconds for Faith to decide to keep her mouth shut and follow this woman. She couldn't have asked for a better entry to the workings of Hubbard House than to be mistaken for a worker, and it appeared the job was in the kitchen, so there wouldn't be any bedpans.

She trotted along obediently as the woman sped through the halls and down a flight of stairs, observing that the decor of the living room had been continued throughout, augmented by rows of hunting and botanical prints. It was almost too predictable. She also observed that the place was completely devoid of the smells Faith associated with nursing homes—Lysol, rubber sheets, isopropyl alcohol, yesterday's cabbage.

Her guide darted through a swinging door and Faith found herself in a cavernous kitchen, not fitted out as she would have arranged, but not bad. Presiding over the cuisine was a middle-aged woman of greater than average proportions on any scale. She was stirring something in a huge marmite on the top of the stove, and when she turned around to greet them, Faith was sure the "Mrs." was an honorary title. Faith had never seen a mud fence and had always thought it would be hard to construct one, but "homely as" immediately sprang to mind. Mrs. Pendergast had perhaps tried to compensate for the dun hue of all her features by choosing incongruous black eyeglass frames with rhinestones on the corners, which served only to emphasize the drabness of the rest of her appearance. Still, it suggested a lurking sense of humor—or something. They should get along all right. Two women with the same interest, although at the moment Faith was thinking more of plots than pans.

"Mrs. Pendergast, here is an angel of mercy! Just in time to help you," dithered the woman with the curls. "Now what was your name again, dear?"

"My name is Faith, Faith Fairchild." This was no time for aliases. Besides Farley Bowditch, there could be other former Alefordians who would recognize the minister's wife. She reluctantly shelved Deirdre Morgana, Letitia Carberry, and some of her other favorites for another day.

"Mrs. Pendergast, Mrs. Fairchild. I take it you're all set? Good, now I'll leave you two ladies to your work." After this burst of speech, she scampered out the door and Faith and Mrs. Pendergast stood eye to eye for a moment.

"Did Miss Vale tell you what was needed?"

"Not exactly," Faith responded. "Some kitchen help, I gather."

"Help is right. My lunch regular and her backup have both come down with this flu, and the volunteers so far stay long enough to learn what to do, then leave to finish their Christmas shopping or some such thing. I finally told Miss Vale that if she couldn't find somebody to stay for the next two weeks, they'd have to start sending out to McDonald's.

Oh, that got her, you can imagine. Most of these people think a Big Mac is a large truck."

Faith shuddered. She *was* an angel of mercy.

"Miss Vale"—for apparently that was the redhead's name— "didn't say anything about two weeks, but I'll help all I can."

"It's getting the food ready and into that contraption there"—she pointed to a dumbwaiter. "You don't have to do pots or dishes. The wheelchair boys and girls do those."

"Wheelchair boys and girls?"

"The college kids who work here and go get the people in wheelchairs who live in the cottages for meals or take others out for a spin around the gardens. They serve the meals and clean up."

"I think I'll be able to help you, but most days only until eleven thirty, because I have to be home when my little boy comes back from nursery school. And only weekdays, I'm afraid."

"That will have to do it and it may not be two weeks, but Dr. Hubbard is very particular about the food preparation, and if he thinks there's a chance of passing the flu around with the food, he'll have them stay home longer. Not but that I agree with him. Of course, I'm never sick myself."

It would take a mighty germ to fell Mrs. Pendergast, Faith thought, and found herself nodding solemnly—in tacit agreement, she supposed, or just to have some participation in the conversation that continued its one-sided course.

"Now, don't worry about the cooking. I do all of it. Have been for thirty years—the last fifteen right here. I need you to chop things, help me get organized, and dish it all out."

"Like a sous chef," Faith commented.

"I don't know any Sue chefs. Like another pair of hands is what I mean."

"Fine." Faith reached for an apron. "Why don't you tell me where to start." She was a firm believer that a woman's kitchen was her queendom. Still, it might be possible to introduce some flavor into the cuisine after a few days. The only cookbook she could see was an ancient edition of *Fanny Farmer,* and while it made for wonderful bedtime reading—caramel potato cake, and her own personal favorite, Canapés à la Rector: caviar on toast sprinkled with diced cucumber pickles and red pepper, divided into sections, by anchovy fillets—she hoped the inhabitants of Hubbard House weren't subsisting on macaroni and chipped beef and the book's other stick-to-the-ribs staples.

"We're giving them fish today—scrod and some greens and potatoes. The first thing you could do is start peeling these with this contraption while I trim the beans. The soup's all made and on the back burner." She gestured toward the stove. "There's always some who want soup first, or they can have juice. Then we give them a salad. And I've got last night's pot roast for those who don't want fish."

"How many people are there?" Faith asked.

"One hundred and fifteen total, but we never get that many for lunch. The cottages have kitchenettes and some people make their own lunch. And there's usually a few who are traveling or eating out. They mark their meal choices in the morning on those little sheets. There's sixty today and seven trays."

"Trays?"

"Yes, for the people in the annex. The wheelchair kids come for those first."

Faith worked quickly, but it took a while before the potatoes were on. She looked around to see what was next and clamped her mouth shut as she watched Mrs. Pendergast with an ancient canister of paprika, liberally sprinkling the fish before putting it into the oven to bake. They were assembling salads and Faith was about to start priming the pump to get information more relevant to her investigation than the merits of V-8 juice versus tomato when the door swung open and she heard the click of high heels on the kitchen tile.

"Do you need some more help, Mrs. P.? I have a spare half hour and it's all yours."

The voice belonged to a tall, languid-looking young woman with, depending on one's frame of reference and charitable inclinations, a long Modigliani or Afghan-hound-like face and black hair cropped close to her head. As she spoke, she took off the jacket of her suit, an Anne Klein Faith had considered herself last year, and rolled up the sleeves of her silk blouse. She wasn't beautiful, yet everything about her was—the way she walked, her voice, and all the separate parts: luminous gray eyes, smooth glowing skin. It didn't add up, but came close enough.

"I can always use help, Denise. Grab an apron from the closet and you can finish these salads with Mrs. Fairchild here while I scoop out the Grape Nut pudding for dessert." Mrs. Pendergast spoke in tones bordering on affection.

"Are you a new Pink Lady?" Denise asked Faith as she slipped on a pair of rubber gloves and grabbed a handful of lettuce.

"A what?"

"A Pink Lady. That's what we volunteers are called because of the pink dusters we're supposed to wear. I told them I was happy to come and do whatever they wanted, but nothing could induce me to put that thing on."

"I don't think I'm one. Nor," she added, "have I ever drunk one. I'm just helping here until the lunch crew recovers from the flu." Faith hoped Miss Vale wouldn't suddenly decide to fling a duster her way to wear in the kitchen. She'd have to be firm and cite Denise as precedent.

"Do you live in Byford, Mrs. Fairchild?" Denise asked.

"No, I live in Aleford, and please call me Faith. My husband is the minister at First Parish, and we have a two-and-a-half-year-old boy. How about you?"

"I live in Byford—for the moment. Try prying a teenager away from the friends he's made. I decided it wasn't fair for Joel to lose both his father and friends, so we're here for at least two more years."

"I'm sorry to hear about your husband. Was his death recent?" Faith asked, switching into the empathetic minister's wife voice she thought she ought to be cultivating. It was a slight shock to watch Denise explode into laughter. Hysteria?

"I should only be so lucky. No, the creep is very much alive and living in L.A. with wife number three, formerly mistress number three hundred and three, who didn't want wife number one's kid around. Wife number one didn't want him either. I'd been raising Joel pretty much alone anyway, and I wasn't going to back out on him. Plus we got the house, no problem, and actually both of us have never been happier."

"It sounds like you didn't exactly have a match made in heaven," Faith commented.

"I was just plain stupid and not young enough to have age for an excuse—but maybe not that stupid. I never had my wedding silver or towels monogrammed, for instance."

Faith laughed. She hoped Denise would be around a lot in the next two weeks. Besides being entertaining, she might have picked up what was going on at Hubbard.

"What do you do here—as a volunteer?" Faith asked, also wondering *why?*

"I started by driving some of the residents to temple for services on Friday nights—the rabbi had asked for volunteers from the congregation, and then when one of the people I drove, Mrs. Rosen, broke a hip and was recuperating in the nursing wing, I visited and read to her. One thing led to another and I became a volunteer. I love being adored and I don't have a whole lot else to do with my time. If I weren't so selfish, I'd go out and get a job, but I don't want someone telling me what time to be there and what to do."

Obviously she didn't need the money, Faith observed, looking at her neat little Patek Philippe watch and the

heavy gold necklace she wore. Her fingers were conspicu-
ously bare of rings.

"How about you, Faith, why are you doing this? Christian love?"

"Nothing so selfless, I'm afraid," Faith answered. "I
was on my way to visit a parishioner and Miss Vale mistook
me for someone coming to volunteer and brought me here.
But since Ben is in nursery school in the mornings, I can
help for a while." She decided not to tell Denise about
Chat's letter. Until she had more of an idea about what was
going on, she wasn't going to mention it to anyone even
vaguely associated with Hubbard House.

"That is so typical of Sylvia—Sylvia Vale—and yet
somehow she never puts a foot wrong. Here you are. The
problem's solved even though she was completely screwed
up about it."

The salads were done and only needed dressing,
which the residents put on themselves.

"Do you want us to do the bread, Mrs. P.?" Denise
asked.

"Yes, and I'll mash the potatoes, and then it will be
time to get the trays done."

"You should be doing this instead of me," Faith remarked. "You know so much."

"Not a chance. Remember I'm selfish. I don't want to
have to be here every day at a certain time. Besides, I have
a hair appointment tomorrow. With this cut, I have to go all
the time. It gives me another purpose in life, and it's almost
as nice as the old days in high school when my friend Linda
and I used to iron each other's hair, smoke cigarettes we
took from her mother, and gossip. Somehow my hairdresser Richard's stories don't seem as interesting as which
cheerleaders went all the way and whether the math
teacher was seeing Debbie Jackson outside school, but
Richard pampers me and I love it."

Faith was still searching for someone who could cut
her hair—if not exactly as she'd had it before her northern

migration, at least in some approximation. She didn't want Denise's cut, but she recognized the hand of a master. Before she could ask her where Richard wielded his scissors, Denise looked at her watch and exclaimed, "Have to run! 'Bye, Faith. Nice meeting you. 'Bye, Mrs. P. You've got a treasure here. Let her do some of the cooking. I think she knows how." She winked at Faith. "Joel and I love Have Faith's wild berry jam."

A faint whiff of Coco lingered after she left, mingling with the smell of the brown bread, Parker House rolls, and cranberry muffins they'd been putting into baskets. Mrs. Pendergast lumbered over.

"Put a few more muffins in each. We've got them to spare today. And you know these ladies always bring big pocketbooks to meals." She laughed.

Faith hadn't pictured the stately inhabitants of Hubbard House as the types who filched rolls from the dining room, but then it could also be yet another example of Yankee frugality—she could hear the soft murmurs, "Don't want them to go to waste, you know." She added some more to each basket and went over to help Mrs. Pendergast fill the trays. The tray slips were tucked under the silverware, and she saw that one of them was for Farley Bowditch. He must be in the nursing-care wing.

"I'm going to have to leave soon, Mrs. Pendergast, but I could bring this tray up on my way out. Mr. Bowditch is a friend."

"That would be fine. It isn't hard to find. You go back the way you came, but instead of taking the stairs, take the elevator and go to the second floor. We're in the basement of the annex. When you get out of the elevator, go straight and turn right. His room is in the middle of the corridor." She hesitated. "Do you think you can stand another day?"

"I think so." Faith smiled. "See you in the morning." Mrs. P. hadn't been a font of information—not yet anyway—but Faith was getting fond of her. She'd get even fonder if she could take over some of the cooking.

She picked up the tray. Farley had opted for the fish, and it lay in overcooked splendor on a Wedgwood plate with a blanket of red paprika and a morsel of parsley. She popped a cover on it to keep it hot and set off.

It was easy to find the nursing-care wing, but Faith decided to get deliberately lost on the way back. Of course she could always ask Sylvia Vale to show her around, but it was more fun—and instructive—to go alone.

Farley was sitting up in a chair by the window and was delighted to see her.

"Mrs. Fairchild! How nice of you to come, and you've brought my lunch, I see. Perhaps you would join me? The kitchen is so obliging and the food is quite tasty."

"I'm afraid I don't have time today, but thank you. Actually I'm volunteering in the kitchen for a while, as they are short of help at the moment."

"Ah yes, your culinary renown has preceded you, no doubt."

"I'm not sure about that. I'm peeling potatoes and arranging salads for now."

"All in good time, my dear."

"But please, don't let your food get cold. I thought I would bring it up and see how you were doing. Tom sends his best and says he'll be out to see you soon."

"How kind. Well, I'm fine, but Roland—that's Dr. Hubbard—is not happy with my get-up-and-go. He says it's gone and wants to keep a closer eye on me until we find it." Farley laughed brittlely, wheezing slightly.

Faith decided to use the Aunt Chat ploy. "I have an aunt who lives in New Jersey now who is considering Hubbard House, and I told her I would ask some of the people who live here what they think of it."

"Who better?" Farley agreed amicably. "The horse's mouth."

Faith expected him to continue, but he appeared to be distracted by a tomato, which had surfaced from the midst of the lettuce. "Oh, this is nice. Tomato *and* lettuce." She waited patiently as he guided the fork from plate to mouth, tensing slightly as the tomato quivered and started to fall. It was like watching Ben eat. The mission was accomplished, and while he was chewing she asked, "Are you happy here?" Time to be direct.

"Oh my, yes. Best decision I ever made—coming here. They take wonderful care of you and you meet such interesting people. Of course, I knew quite a few of them before, but we have stockbrokers, lawyers, teachers, even preachers here. A lady who writes books. A couple who raise orchids in one of the cottages. A vast assortment. Then there's the ghost."

"The ghost?" asked Faith, wondering if this was a pet name for someone, an old New England tradition associated with the house, or perhaps where Farley's get-up-and-go had wandered.

"I should say my ghost. Nobody else has seen it, yet it's real enough. Comes into this very room at night and shuts the window. Sometimes pulls my blankets up around me. So considerate. Roland says he wishes it would appear to more people. Would help cut down on staff." Farley laughed and wheezed again. "But tell your aunt not to be afraid if she hears about it. We're used to ghosts around here. My mother used to see her grandmother sitting on the porch swing the first of June every year. It was how we knew summer had arrived. I don't know much about ghosts in New Jersey, but you tell her she would be quite happy here. Don't know much about New Jersey either. Only went there once when my nephew graduated from Princeton. Didn't get into Harvard. Seemed like a nice enough place, but you tell her to come here. Probably better."

Farley was turning his attention to the fish, and Faith said good-bye with promises to return the next day. She wouldn't be getting any useful information from him, that seemed clear, but she always loved this kind of elderly gentleman. She looked back at him—sitting with perfect elegance in an old bathrobe from Brooks with a shawl draped around his shoulders. He could have been presenting his papers at the Court of St. James.

As she left, she noticed a nurse's station, which opened onto an atrium, at the end of the corridor and walked down for a closer look. It was well equipped, and even the gold-framed botanical prints on the wall behind it did not disguise the fact that this was a medical facility. She'd noticed the oxygen hookups and other hospital-room paraphernalia in Farley's room. It was all unobtrusive but state of the art. Whatever Howard Perkins had stumbled onto, outdated or shoddy medical equipment wasn't it. A door to the left of the nursing station opened and a woman who appeared to be in her late thirties came through, carefully locking it behind her. Before she did, Faith glimpsed a wall of glass cabinets—obviously the medication room.

The woman smiled at her. "Hello, are you looking for someone?"

"I found him, thank you. I've been visiting Farley Bowditch. I'm helping in the kitchen and brought him his tray. He's a parishioner of my husband's."

"Oh, then you must be Mrs. Fairchild. I'm Muriel Hubbard and I met your husband when he was here the last time. Farley loves company and it was good of you to come. And Mrs. Pendergast must be thanking her lucky stars. We've been having a terrible time with so many of the staff out, and it's impossible to get short-term replacements."

Muriel was a small but solid woman. Her brown hair, cut in a sensible, chin-length Dutch bob, was streaked with a few gray hairs. The bangs accentuated her broad forehead. Her glasses hung from a string around her neck, and she was dressed in a navy-blue skirt, starched white oxford-cloth blouse, and comfortable nurse's shoes. She exuded competence, security, and dullness.

"I'm glad I can help," Faith told her, "but I must get home now. I've already stayed later than I planned." Virtually nothing so far had gone as planned, Faith thought, her

mood elevating as it did whenever unpredictability surfaced in days that at present tended to march in step.

"Thank you again, and I'll look forward to seeing more
of you." She extended her hand and shook Faith's warmly.
Muriel was obviously a very nice person.

Faith dashed to the parking lot and drove home. The
phone was ringing as she opened the kitchen door. It was
Tom.

"Where have you been, honey? I've been calling you
all morning."

"I went out to Hubbard House to visit Farley Bowditch
and—" Faith started to explain.

"That's nice. I'm sure he appreciated it," Tom interrupted. "I'm going to be later than I thought tonight, but I
will be home for dinner." His voice sounded grimly determined. Something was up, Faith realized—not just from the
tone of his voice, but from the fact that her visit to Hubbard
House had scarcely been noted. She hoped it wasn't complaints about wording in some of the hymns again. There
were so many points of view these days, and Tom had been
going in circles trying to keep everybody in tune.

"Fine. I have to get Ben at the Viles'. He's playing with
Lizzie today. Then we have to do the food shopping, so I'll
be running a little late too. Is everything all right, darling?
You sound a little harried."

"I am. Leave a light in the window and get out the
scotch."

Faith hung up. This wasn't just hymns. A thought
stabbed her. Maybe the director of the church school was
ill and couldn't direct the Christmas pageant! This was
always a worst-case scenario and something her normally
unflappable mother had fretted about at Christmastime all
during Faith's childhood. Jane Sibley was noted for her
cool toughness in court, and there were hints of a possible
judgeship, but the intricate theological wrangling about
who was going to be Mary this year and my son isn't going
to be a shepherd *again* totally unnerved her. Let alone

getting them all down the aisle and in some sort of recognizable order at the altar.

But Tom would have said something, especially if he intended to drag her into it. She shook her head. He wouldn't ask her in any case. Pix would do it. Pix always did everything. In fact, it was odd that she wasn't doing it in the first place. Pix Miller was Faith's next-door neighbor, and the Miller family's intimate involvement in two murder investigations, which Faith had literally stumbled into, had forged a bond stronger than either the occasional cup-of-sugar type neighborliness or the "you planted your hedge over my property line" antipathy.

She drove to get Ben, and the job of tearing him away from Lizzie effectively blotted out any and all thought. Today was worse than usual. Lizzie's mother tactfully stood aside as Faith wrestled a screaming Ben into the car. "Don't wanna go! Wanna stay wid Lizzie! Nononononono!" and so on. She gave Arlene Viles a weary smile and backed out of their drive. The only thought that comforted her was that Lizzie would be worse about leaving when she came to play at their house. As she drove to the market, she thought she might suggest this phenomenon to Tom for some kind of sermon. What does it say about human nature that we derive so much comfort from not being last in line? No matter how badly your child might behave, there are always worse ones. And, a friend had told her once, no matter how fat you think you are and how much cellulite is dimpling down your thighs, there's always someone in the Loehmann's dressing room who looks worse. Faith was some years away from these comparisons, yet the point was the same.

Ben had calmed down as soon as Lizzie's house was out of sight, and now her only problem would be to convince him to sit in the cart and not try to "help" by pushing it for her. She grabbed a bunch of bananas as soon as she entered the store, put one in Ben's hand, and strapped him in before he had a chance to protest.

Tom was later than usual, and looking at his expression when he entered the kitchen, she could see that he was mad, not sad. So no one had died or contracted some serious disease. It was merely some pain in the ass—a congregation being like any other group of individuals.

She put her arms around him. "Come on, let's have a drink and sit in the living room while you tell me all about it. I fed Ben and he's watching a Winnie-the-Pooh tape—that gives us roughly twenty-two minutes of peace."

"Wonderful, darling—although whatever you've got in the oven smells so delicious, I'm not sure I can concentrate."

Faith had decided Tom needed some good, solid food—nothing nouvelle—so she'd prepared a pork roast with garlic, rosemary, white wine, and olive oil. There was curried cabbage, fresh applesauce, and a potato galette Lyonnaise to go with it. She poured herself a glass of Georges Duboeuf Beaujolais Nouveau and followed Tom into the living room. Ben was at the far end, mesmerized by Eeyore, and barely acknowledged Tom's kiss.

"All right, what is it? They've discovered the bordello we're running on the side in the parsonage? Or someone got a back issue of *Playgirl* and saw your centerfold? What?"

"Oh, Faith, I wish it were something funny. I really don't know what to do, or rather I do, and the next couple of months are going to be so damned unpleasant. And why now? You know how much I love Christmas."

Faith did know. Tom's family started getting the cartons of ornaments down from their attic before Halloween—just to check and see if any of the lights needed new bulbs. When the house was finally decorated, there wasn't a corner that had been overlooked. Some year Faith fully expected to find St. Nick toilet paper peeking at her from the roll.

"I also feel a bit petty about it. It shouldn't bother me so much, but he has a way of getting under my skin—and it's only been one day!"

Everything was suddenly clear. "So," said Faith, "you can't stand your new divinity school intern."

"I loathe him. So will you. He's arrogant, pompous, self-centered, stupid, and he smells."

"Well, at least you can tell him to take a bath. Hint around."

"It's not good old BO. It's some kind of horrible men's cologne."

"And what is this creature's name?"

"Cyle—as in 'Kyle,' but spelled with a 'C'—and you can bet it didn't start out that way. We met this morning to discuss what he would be doing, and he started interviewing me! Before I knew it, he was offering advice about my sermons, ways to keep the congregation alert, and suggestions for a new wing for the parish hall. I began to feel a knot in my stomach that is just starting to go away now." He took a mouthful of scotch.

"How long will he be here?"

"Until the first of March, and there's no only about it."

Faith was a little surprised at the intensity of Tom's reaction. Cyle must really be something. Tom was the least judgmental person she knew. Turning the other cheek, living and letting live—this was Tom. At the moment he was sounding more like her.

"I suppose what is actually troubling me is contemplating the kind of damage a person like this will do in the future. Imagine going to him for comfort. The sole thing that is going to make this bearable is for me to finagle my way onto his ordination committee."

"Why do you suppose he wants to be a minister? He sounds more like someone who thinks of call waiting rather than the 'call.' "

"I've been wondering the same thing myself—it has to be the idea of a captive audience every week. Maybe I should try to steer him into politics—or TV evangelism."

"Anywhere but your church."

"Exactly."

Tom stretched his long legs out. Winnie-the-Pooh had gone back to the Hundred Acre Wood, and they tucked Ben into bed before sitting down to eat. As they ate, Faith told Tom about her visit to Hubbard House, eliminating Sylvia Vale's mistake but mentioning the tight spot they were in and how she could help.

"I don't see why not," he said. "I'll be able to pick Ben up occasionally."

"And I know Pix will help."

"Have you uncovered any skulduggery yet?"

"Not yet. Everything looks like it's on the very up and up."

"Which is what I've thought all along. Chat's friend may have been imagining things." That reminded Faith of Farley's ghost, and she gave Tom a hilarious account of the thoughtful wraith.

They cleaned up the kitchen and soon after climbed into bed.

"Feeling better, sweetheart?" Faith asked softly.

"Almost," Tom answered, reaching for her under the blankets.

Sylvia Vale greeted Faith at the door the next morning with exuberant relief.

"You've come back! That's marvelous. Mrs. Pendergast said you would, yet one never knows." She sighed. "It used to be so easy to get help in the old days. I've been here since Hubbard House opened, you know."

"I'll be able to come weekdays until everyone is back. Please don't worry."

"I won't," she said brightly, but Faith wasn't sure. Sylvia Vale seemed like someone who enjoyed her worries.

"I'll get to work, then," Faith said, moving toward the corridor that led to the annex.

"Just a minute." Sylvia darted into the office and returned with a thick cream-colored envelope. "All the Pink Ladies are invited, of course."

Faith took the envelope and thanked her, moving more quickly to avoid both the appellation and the possibility of a new, unwelcome, addition to her wardrobe. She ripped open the envelope on her way downstairs. It was a heavily embossed invitation to a dinner dance on December fourteenth at the Copley Plaza in Boston for the benefit of Hubbard House. Two tickets were enclosed. That was next Wednesday. She didn't think they had plans, and it would be a way to see the cast of characters. She hadn't even met Dr. Hubbard yet—father or son. They were sure to be there. She wondered if Denise would be going.

.It was raining, and there were more people in for lunch. The kitchen was so busy that Faith barely had time to say hello, much less ask Mrs. P. for the inside dope on Hubbard House. They had started to set out the trays when Mrs. Pendergast said, "Can you do these? I've got some marrow bones and a piece of beef set aside to make soup for tomorrow, and I want to put it on."

"Oh," said Faith, with all the ardor of an ingénue who's just heard the star may have twisted an ankle, "let me. I can make a lovely, rich bouillon. It's very nourishing."

"If you like," Mrs. Pendergast agreed. "There's some greens and carrots in the fridge you might want."

Faith did and merrily set about assembling a good strong stock. She'd clarify it in the morning and bring some leeks and Madeira or port to add.

There was enough time for a visit with Farley before she left, and he regaled her with stories of various inhabitants of Aleford—mostly long gone. She tried to steer him toward the Hubbard family, but there didn't seem to be anything of interest there to Farley, except sympathy for Dr. Hubbard—"Poor Roland. Losing Mary so young." Faith did learn, however, that Millicent Revere McKinley's father had had a lucrative bathtub gin business, and she filed the information away for possible future use.

That night Faith told Tom she definitely had to get back to work. Making such a large amount of stock was a poignant reminder of Have Faith's past glories when she had had any number of pots going at once.

"It's exhilarating—of course I love to cook for you and Ben, but there's not quite the scope for imagination a banquet offers."

Tom was amused. "Maybe Mrs. Pendergast will let you do the main course soon if she likes your bouillon—and then who knows what next."

Mrs. Pendergast *did* like Faith's bouillon. Faith offered her a steaming cup after she had added the egg whites, Madeira, leeks, parsley, and other seasonings before straining it.

"Very tasty—and you're right. It does look nourishing. Are you going to bring up Mr. Bowditch's tray today?"

"Yes, I have time, if you don't need me here." Faith felt as proud of her bouillon as of her first *galantine de lapereau.*

Muriel Hubbard was in Farley's room when Faith entered. She was about to take his blood pressure and had his medication in a small paper cup.

"Hello, Mrs. Fairchild, how nice to see you," she said.

"It's always nice to see Faith," Farley added gallantly. "What have you brought today besides your charming self, my dear?"

"Vegetable quiche, salad, rolls, fruit compote, and some bouillon I made."

"That will be a treat. Muriel has one or two necessary things to do with my poor old self; then I will consume it with relish. Can you stay a while?"

"I'm afraid not today, but I will see you on Monday, and you know when you feel up to it, someone will come and get you for church. I'm sure it will be soon."

Muriel agreed. "Mr. Bowditch will be up and dancing at our annual Hubbard House Christmas party, just like last year, I'm sure."

"Save me a waltz," Faith said, and left.

The afternoon was filled with errands, and she was tired by the time she and Ben got home. She was a little surprised to see Tom in his study. He got up and put his arms around her.

"What is it? Tell me quick! My parents . . ."

"No, darling. It's Farley. He died this afternoon."

"Oh no! And he seemed so well when I left."

"I'm afraid they found him face down in your bouillon, Faith dear."

3

"My bouillon!" Faith cried. "That's impossible. There couldn't possibly have been anything wrong with it. I tasted it myself. So did Mrs. Pendergast. And what about the rest of Hubbard House? Oh, Tom, don't tell me there's more!"

"Honey, I'm sure it was simply a horrible coincidence. No one else is the least bit sick. Farley had a very weak heart. In fact, it's amazing he'd gone on this long."

They walked over to the couch and sat down. Ben wriggled between them and, whether from fatigue or the first stirrings of tact, kept quiet and nuzzled Faith's arm.

Meanwhile Faith was reviewing every ingredient in the bouillon and every step in making it. Too much Madeira for a man with a serious heart condition? Mrs. Pendergast hadn't said anything, and she had the part-time dietician's list of instructions by her side at all times. Besides, there wouldn't have been any alcohol left after the soup was heated.

A sudden thought struck her.

"Tom,"—she could barely get the words out—"do you think he *drowned* in the soup?"

The idea had also occurred to Tom, but he had deemed it more prudent not to mention it.

"I suppose it's possible, darling. But I'm sure it will turn out to be his heart. Dr. Hubbard said he would call back to talk about funeral arrangements, and I'll ask him to let us know the exact cause of death."

Tom brought his arm around to encircle his little family more closely and looked down at the two heads by his side. Every once in a while he thought he could detect a hint of red in Ben's mop—a little like Tom's own reddish brown hair—but today it shone as golden blond as Faith's, and they could have posed for a Breck shampoo ad.

"They'll never want me back at Hubbard House again," Faith said soberly.

"Come on now. You're being ridiculous."

"Well, wouldn't you be if someone had just died in your bouillon?" Faith retorted.

"Of course it's terribly upsetting, but if you're going to volunteer in an old age home, you'll have to get used to the fact of death." Tom spoke slightly sternly. He didn't want Faith going off the deep end about something that was not in the slightest her fault. Poor Farley could just have well fallen into his mashed potatoes. It was a question of balance—or aim.

"Yes, I know that. I thought of it the first day I was there, but Hubbard House is such an undeathlike place. It's hard to believe all those sturdy people out playing golf and taking courses at Harvard Extension aren't going to keep on living forever."

"True, it is hard in this case. The residents of Hubbard House represent an admirable—and I might add very privileged—sector of the elderly population. They have goals and don't consider that they're through so long as there's a breath left in their bodies."

"Exactly. And Farley was one of them until only a few hours ago. It still doesn't seem possible that he's dead. He was fine—a little short of breath, as usual, and that was all. We were talking about dancing together at the Christmas party."

"Think of it as a good death then. Mercifully sudden."

Faith felt tears pricking at her eyes. Maybe it would be too difficult to remain at Hubbard House much longer. Assuming that they wanted her back, that is. She wondered how the people who worked there all the time were able to cope with the deaths of those they had grown close to. Her upbringing and continued sojourn in a parish had provided her with strong, difficult-to-define beliefs—Tom referred to her as a combination of pantheism, early Christianity, and anthropotheism, with special emphasis on the "anthro" part—but whatever she was, she thought she should certainly have become used to death by now. She'd been to enough funerals. Yet she wasn't. No matter what she believed lay ahead, it was still the end of this life.

"Farley never married, but he has a number of nieces and nephews and their children, all of whom were devoted to him, I understand. He spoke to me about his wishes regarding a funeral a year or so ago. He wanted to be cremated and buried in Aleford in the Bowditch plot with a simple graveside service. One of his nieces lives in Beverly Farms, so I'll probably have to go up there this evening or tomorrow morning to talk with her."

"Not tonight, Tom. Go in the morning if you can. Let's have a quiet night here."

Tom realized he hadn't been home for the entire evening all week. He also realized there was a Celtics game on. But that had nothing to do with it.

"Good idea. There's no rush, since they have been expecting this for years, and I don't feel as pressed as I might to comfort the bereaved or whatever it is I do. Besides, it's been an incredibly busy week."

"Besides," Faith added, "there's a game on. I'll dig out the chips and you drive to the packy for some brew."

Tom laughed. "I won't watch if there's something you'd rather do or watch yourself," he offered nobly.

"No, darling. After Cyle, you deserve it." She stood up and pulled Ben to his feet. "I'll be in the kitchen making soup."

On Sunday Faith sat in church waiting for the lector to find her place and start the lesson. Cyle had lighted the second Advent candle, and that appeared to be the extent to which Tom was willing to allow him to assist in the service. Eventually he'd have to increase his duties—even, God forfend, let him preach—but Tom had told her he didn't want to traumatize the congregation more than was absolutely necessary. It appeared Cyle was a singer, and Tom had immediately thrust him into the choir. Faith looked over her shoulder to the organ loft. She recognized him immediately from Tom's description. He stood gazing down on the congregation with the suggestion of a saintly smile lurking at the corners of his mouth. He was quite pretty. Brown, artfully tousled curls. Big, blue eyes and a pink-and-white complexion. A perfect choirboy. She turned back hastily as Mr. Thompson, the organist and choirmaster, shot her a look with "Why me, oh Lord?" written all over it. Cyle must have been making musical suggestions.

It was a lovely, sunny morning and the church was, as usual in winter, freezing cold. Faith had tried to snare one of the pews with the hot-air registers when she had arrived as a new bride; the usher had gently but firmly steered her to a pew below the pulpit and told her it had always been the minister's family's spot—and always would be, Faith had mentally finished for him. It might not be the most comfortable, but it did have a good view. She could keep an eye on Tom, her fellow parishioners during the hymns, and the altar. Today the Alliance had decorated it with spruce boughs, holly, pinecones, and a few crimson Christmas roses. They were keeping the poinsettias for the grand finale.

She realized the lesson had started and dutifully turned her attention to Saint Luke: "And there shall be signs in the sun, and in the moon, and in the stars; and upon the earth distress of nations, with perplexity; the sea and the waves roaring." She stopped listening after "perplexity." These *were* perplexing times. Forget about the world at large. It was too much to consider, except as a dull throb constantly at the back of one's mind. But what about the perplexity at Hubbard House? What about Farley? Was it possible that something was put into his soup? Bizarre as it might seem, could Howard Perkins have stumbled onto a plot to do away with Farley? Was Howard's own death natural? They had both had heart conditions. Very convenient. But then much of the rest of Hubbard House did too.

No, it didn't make sense. She had learned from Charley MacIsaac and her own painfully direct experience that people get killed because they have something somebody else wants—*cui bono?*—and the somebody else is usually somebody he or she knows. Like the warm body lying next to you at night, plotting while you slumber away. No, this wasn't a murder case. It just didn't feel like one.

She realized she didn't want to leave Hubbard House until she'd learned what Howard had found out. He had had the advantage of living there, but she had the advantage of knowing she was looking for something and not being afraid to pry. If Mrs. P. would let her, she'd be back in the kitchen on Monday morning watching for signs—maybe not in the sun and the moon, but everywhere else.

Tom's family had always had a large Sunday dinner after church. Faith's mother had always served something light and quick—her perennially favorite "nice piece of fish and salad"—before whisking the family off to the Metropolitan Museum or Carnegie Hall for the second worship service of the day. The Fairchilds played touch football on Sunday afternoons, weather permitting, and sometimes even when it didn't. Faith had scratched the football, but served up a joint-and-Yorkshire-pud type menu to Tom and whatever guests were present every Sunday. These meals were often slightly hilarious—the more serious tasks of the day over and only a hearty dinner and postprandial nap to worry about. Faith couldn't remember Tom indulging in the nap part, but Charley MacIsaac had fallen sound asleep in the big wing chair in the living room on more than one occasion. Today they had invited the church school director, Ms. Albright—Faith wanted to feed her up and keep her healthy—and an old college friend of Tom's, Allen Corcoran, who was in town on business. Faith was more than surprised to see Cyle walk in the door chummily with Tom. She was furious.

"This is Cyle Brennan. Cyle, my wife, Faith." Tom had the grace to look deeply chagrined.

"An apt choice of name, Mrs. Fairchild." Cyle smirked.

"I wouldn't know. I didn't choose it," Faith snapped back. She didn't doubt that whatever his future wife's name was, it would be changed to "Faith" or something else appropriate. Then he would tell people about the coincidence. In fact, Faith's name was preordained. Generations of Sibley women were named Faith, Hope, and Charity after a trio of pious ancestresses, and Faith's father had not chosen to break the tradition. Jane Sibley had averted the possibility of a Charity by stopping at two children—Faith and her sister, Hope.

Tom was making piteously grotesque faces over Cyle's head, and Faith quickly shoved a small glass of sherry into Cyle's hand and parked him in the living room. As the door back into the kitchen swung shut, she turned to Tom, who answered her question before she had a chance to ask it. "Don't blame me, darling. There are strong and powerful forces at work here. I'm going to have to pray harder. I swear I didn't invite him, but a voice that sounded much like mine was pulled from my throat and issued an invitation. He followed me into the vestry while I was taking my robe off. Maybe I would have been better able to resist if I had kept it on. I'll remember that in the future."

"And well you should. This is the one and only time he's coming. Bad enough to have the incubus bothering you all week without having him disturb your Sunday dinner too."

Tom looked gratefully at her. "Now, how can I help?"

"Ben went down for his nap nicely. They must run around a lot in Sunday school, so he's taken care of for the moment. All you have to do is pour some sherry for the others when they arrive and pass these." She'd made some tiny choux pastry puffs filled with Roquefort cheese and walnuts. "But don't let Cyle start eating them yet or there won't be any for the rest of us." She left in a huff to lay another place at the table before returning to the kitchen to finish the strong mustardy vinaigrette she would pour over the steamed Brussels sprouts moments before serving. She checked on the crown roast of lamb and gratin Dauphinoise—cheesy potatoes, Tom and Ben called them—and put the butternut squash soufflé in to bake. Every fall she felt a brief regret for all the summer food that wouldn't appear for another year except in some colorized form; then fall food started and there was nothing wrong with squash, apples, sprouts, and the rest of the things one took over the river and through the woods to grandmother's house. The apples were appearing as pie, but with a mille-feuille crust instead of the more traditional one. If anyone asked for cheese, she'd give him a squeeze.

Just as Tom started to carve, the phone rang. This was such an ordinary occurrence in their lives that Faith didn't even get annoyed anymore. It was like ants at a picnic. You lived with it.

"I'll get that, honey. Please start."

It was Dr. Hubbard. Faith wasn't sure what to say or

47

ask, but he solved the problem for her by dominating the entire conversation.

"Sorry to bother you, but your husband was anxious for the results of the autopsy. Had to do it because of the soup, you know." He gave a brief laugh, although Faith failed to find anything funny about it. Perhaps if it hadn't been her particular bouillon . . .

"Anyway, tell Reverend Fairchild it was cardiac failure—Farley's ticker—just as we thought, and we wouldn't have had any bother if he'd fallen backward, but Farley always did like to do things his way." Another laugh.

"You can have the funeral anytime you want now. Well, I'll let you go. Drop by and introduce yourself when you come tomorrow. We're enormously grateful for your help, and I hope we'll see both you and your husband at our little shindig on Wednesday."

Faith thanked him and walked back to the table filled with relief and intense curiosity to meet the man behind the voice.

They were all tucking into their lamb and listening to Cyle expound on transubstantiation with varying degrees of lack of interest. Faith hastened to interrupt him with the news. Cyle took a bite of potato, carefully finished chewing, then commented, "It's so sad to see that generation going. We'll not see their like again, I fear."

What did this boy read? Faith wondered. Frances Hodgson Burnett?

"I was especially fond of old Farley. He seemed to be in perfect health last week when I saw him." Cyle fixed Faith with a mildly accusatory eye. Had he heard about the bouillon?

"I didn't know you were acquainted with Mr. Bowditch," Tom said, his back up at "old Farley."

"I wasn't until he went to Hubbard House. The mater is one of their Pink Ladies—that's what they call the volunteers—and I've always made it a point to visit and help in any way I can."

Tom had trouble hiding a grin. Faith had neglected to tell him about the Pink Ladies, and she knew he couldn't wait to tease her about her new moniker.

Cyle continued to address the air. "Yes, men like Farley are a vanishing breed."

Which considering their ages is no surprise, Faith almost replied.

"Men who know the true meaning of service. Who are devoted to their brothers."

"And sisters?" Faith murmured. Pamela Albright's lips twitched.

"I happen to know we're in for a little windfall, Tom. Farley mentioned it to me—in confidence, but sadly that no longer applies," Cyle said fatuously. "And Hubbard House too, of course. Farley was devoted to Hubbard House."

The Reverend Fairchild had had enough.

"Catch the Celtics Friday night, Allen?"

It was a pleasant lunch despite Cyle's presence, but they all breathed a collective sigh of relief when he announced he had to leave before coffee as he had an appointment.

"So sorry," Faith said crisply, and suggested to the others that they take their cups into the living room. If he had such an important appointment, why had he wheedled his way into dinner in the first place? Nowhere else to go? With a passing thought that quickly evaporated in the winter air as to what this appointment might be, Faith led the way through the door into the living room. Tom hastened to see Cyle out.

Allen sprawled comfortably on the couch. "Talkative young bastard, excuse the language," he commented as the front door closed. They all exploded in laughter.

"I have half a mind to put him in charge of the pageant. He has so many ideas about how it should be done correctly," Pamela said.

"At least get him sewing on the angels' robes," Faith advised. "So long as he's here, let him be useful."

Allen stood up. "Come on, Tom, the classy hotel they're putting me up in gives me guest privileges at some health club. Let's go knock a few squash balls around. You can give yours whatever name you want and I have a few for mine. Then we can hit the steam room and our troubles will melt away." Allen was a lawyer, and according to Tom, he wasn't particularly pleased with the way the case he was working on in Boston was going.

"Sounds like heaven," Tom said. "Give me a minute to help Faith and I'm your man."

"I'll help too—it's the least I can do for such a delicious repast," Allen offered.

"No, go on—it sounds like exactly what the doctor ordered, or would have, and I'm going to clean up in a leisurely way—there isn't that much to do."

"Are you sure, Faith? Otherwise I have to be going too," Pamela said.

"Oh, stay—not to clean up, but have another cup of coffee."

"I really can't. I shouldn't even have taken the time for lunch, but I can never resist one of your invitations."

They left, and Faith reveled in the solitude of the house for almost fifteen minutes before Ben awoke and she took him to the playground. Life at two and a half was an endless round of pleasure.

She wanted to get out of the house too, she realized. She'd been spending every spare moment finishing the Christmas cards, and last night she and Tom had wrestled with the tree lights for an hour before even starting to trim the balsam fir Faith preferred for the smell that filled the room. A service that untangled the lines, replaced missing bulbs, and strung the lights on the tree so the wires didn't show would make a fortune. She was sure something like it must exist in New York: S.O.S. Tree Lite, or Baby Let Us Light Your Tree.

When Tom got home, he called Farley's niece, whom he had seen the day before, to talk about funeral arrangements. After a brief conversation, he told Faith, "The funeral is set for Tuesday. I suppose you'll be too busy at Hubbard House to come, but of course the Bowditches will understand."

"Come on, Tom. It's not like you to be devious. What did she say?"

"She didn't say anything, but you're right. I was being less than direct. Falling into one's soup as a last mortal act is slightly ludicrous, and it might be better if people were not reminded of it by your presence. Not that anyone in town thinks you had anything to do with it."

"Balderdash, with an emphasis on the first syllable. It's the bell all over again. When tales are told hundreds of years hence, the one about the minister's wife who desecrated a landmark and was a suspected poisoner is going to be a favorite to pass the time while traveling from planet to planet. I'm surprised Millicent hasn't called. But don't worry, darling. I hadn't planned on attending the funeral and I'm not mad at you for not wanting me there and not saying so, although I probably should be."

"No, you shouldn't, and if trying not to hurt your wife's feelings . . ." Faith closed his mouth with a kiss. The conversation was going nowhere, and with Ben fast asleep, they were wasting precious time.

Millicent called as they were going upstairs—ostensibly to find out when the service would be. Tom answered the phone and decided not to give Faith a report of the conversation, which was all Faith had predicted and more. There was no question in Millicent's mind. If Farley had had a decent Yankee lunch of Welsh rarebit on toast, her own personal favorite, he'd be alive today.

The next morning Faith was back at Hubbard House. As she drove into the parking lot, she felt increasingly apprehensive about what Mrs. Pendergast would say. She pushed open the kitchen door slowly and peeked in. Mrs. P. turned around. There was no preamble.

"Now it wasn't your fault. What you need to do is forget about the whole thing and get busy with this fruit cup here."

Faith walked across the room toward her.

"Of course," she continued, "can't say anybody ever dropped dead in *my* food."

She could kiss any idea of further food preparation good-bye, Faith realized, and reluctantly let go of her lofty plans for a culinary revolution at Hubbard House.

Denise arrived by the time Faith and Mrs. Pendergast had started to set out the breads and again offered to help. She put her hand on Faith's shoulder.

"I heard about the soup mishap. I hope you're not feeling upset about it. Farley had some good innings."

"I know, but I do feel a little guilty, although I realize it had nothing to do with what he was eating."

"It's always so difficult when someone here dies. I don't say 'passes on' or 'goes to his maker.' It's death, and I'd like to say I don't plan on going, but unfortunately I know better. One of the ways I have gotten to know better is by being here. So many of the residents have made their peace with life—or death, depending on your point of view. They're not eager to go, yet accepting. Quite a few of them work for Hospice and help see each other out. I'd like to have a good friend by my side when I'm near the end."

"And you will," Faith assured her. They worked for a while in companionable silence; then Faith thought the time had come to ask some questions about the Hubbards.

"I met Muriel Hubbard the other day, but none of the rest of the family. Do you know them well?"

"I know them, but I wouldn't say well. We're all so busy doing our own individual things here that we don't get to know each other unless we see one another outside. And that lets Muriel out right away. I don't think she ever leaves the place except for an occasional shopping trip and church. In fact, she may even do her shopping by mail, so it's just church. I'll be surprised if she's at the Holly Ball Wednesday night. She usually stays here to keep an eye on things. You're going though, I hope."

Faith had forgotten the benefit was called the Holly Ball. She'd talked it over with Tom and they were going. She wanted to get a look at the attendees, and he thought they should show their support for Hubbard House—and he always liked to dance with Faith.

Denise continued to talk about the Hubbards. "I see Dr. Hubbard quite a bit coming and going. He's a sweetie, and I don't see how this place could exist without him. It's not just that he knows everyone by name, but he really knows them—their aches and pains, sorrows and joys. Donald is a good doctor, but he doesn't have the same charisma."

"What's Donald's wife like? Does she work here too?"

"Charmaine? No, she doesn't work here. She'll be at the ball and you can judge her for yourself. She got back from her latest cruise or spa last week, so she's in town."

"Is she French—'Charmaine'?"

Denise laughed. "She might like to be taken for French, but she actually sounds more like a Georgia peach, although I have it on good authority that the Molloys, that's her maiden—and I use the term loosely—name, were never south of Providence."

They finished the baskets and Denise left. She promised to put Faith and Tom at her table. "If Leandra lets me," she added.

"Who's Leandra?" Faith asked.

"You'll find out Wednesday night," Denise answered, and vanished out the door.

The kitchen was oddly still after she left, and Faith felt a heaviness in the air, which the pungent smell of overdone veal did nothing to lighten.

"Why are you so interested in the Hubbards?" Mrs. Pendergast didn't beat around any bushes.

Faith was momentarily taken aback.

"I'm interested in Hubbard House. That's all. You remember I told you my aunt was considering moving here, and of course I want to tell her everything I can."

"Indeed." Mrs. Pendergast looked skeptical. "Well, tell your aunt"—her inflection suggested strong doubts as to the existence of said aunt—"that she won't find a better-run, better-staffed retirement home in the country, and the Hubbards, all of them, are what make it that way."

So there.

Faith felt her hand smarting, though an actual ruler had not been produced. She didn't have Farley's tray to take up, so she mumbled "Good-bye" and headed for the door.

"See you tomorrow," Mrs. P. boomed at her retreating back.

Upstairs, her backbone was instantly restored, and she thought she would take Dr. Hubbard up on his offer to meet him. Sylvia Vale was outside her office putting a fresh sprig of freesia in the vase. It was white again, and it appeared that much about Hubbard House was unvarying. Sylvia, however, had changed her navy suit and was resplendent in a purple, gold, and green print silk shirtwaist dress.

In response to Faith's request, she answered, "Of course. I should have taken you to meet Dr. Hubbard when you came, but Mrs. Pendergast was *so* insistent on having you report to the kitchen *immediately* that I never did get a chance. We'll do it right now." She tripped off on high heels that were dyed to match the green of her dress, and Faith followed.

Dr. Hubbard's office was in the front corner of one of the original Aldrich houses.

"This was the library of Deborah's house—that was the name of the daughter Nathaniel Aldrich, the original owner, built the house for. We still call the houses Nathaniel's and Deborah's, as the Aldrichs always did. Dr. Hubbard has kept this house very much as it was. His son's office is across the hall, and there's an apartment where Dr. Hubbard lives now at the rear of the house. Upstairs we have several residents' rooms, a room for guests who may be visiting relatives or friends here, and Muriel's apartment."

Faith realized she should have come to Sylvia Vale in the first place. If she could keep her talking, she'd tell Faith about every nook and cranny and every occupant at HH.

"I have a small nest in Byford center," Sylvia prattled on, and Faith was struck by an image of Sylvia in her colorful plumage perched in a nest like Big Bird in the middle of Byford Common.

Sylvia knocked at the door, and a voice Faith instantly recognized from both her conversation and Tom's earlier description as belonging to Roland Hubbard answered, "Come in." They did.

"Dr. Hubbard, this is Mrs. Fairchild, who has been so kind about helping us out."

Roland Hubbard rose from behind his mahogany Duncan Phyfe desk and walked around it toward Faith, his hand already extended. He was a tall, powerful-looking man with a thick shock of white hair and deep blue eyes. A patrician. He took her hand and covered it with his other in a lingering grasp. She had never decided whether she liked this kind of handshake or not. It was difficult to terminate, but then wasn't it also more personal than the other—an American equivalent to being kissed on both cheeks? Dr. Hubbard dropped her hand.

"I'm happy I can help you, and I hope I can do so occasionally in the future. I'll be starting my business after the new year—I'm a caterer—but I'm sure there will be time to come here also." She was not sure when, yet it seemed like the right thing to say. After all, you couldn't very well tell the head of Hubbard House that you were here only to investigate, and when you had discovered whatever the matter was, you'd be history.

"Anything you can do, my dear. We old folks appreciate seeing a young thing around the place. Of course, I say that facetiously. Even though the average age here is seventy-nine, I don't think many of us would describe ourselves as 'old', rather 'seasoned.' And we are the fastest-growing segment of the population, which suggests a certain liveliness. Now if you'll excuse me, I'm afraid much of my job is paperwork and I'm trying to clear my desk of this Everest before Wednesday's frolic."

"Of course, Dr. Hubbard." Sylvia looked up at him, her eyes slightly dilated with pure devotion. "It was good of you to take the time."

So it was like that, Faith thought. Sylvia bustled her out the door and back into the annex. "A truly selfless man," she told Faith. "He lives completely for others."

"How nice," Faith commented. There didn't seem to be any other appropriate comment to make. She could understand the fascination, if not the devotion. Roland Hubbard was extremely well preserved, and while his voice did not have tones of liquid gold, its sharp Yankee clip was softened by the warmth he injected into it. The way he had of looking straight into one's eyes, the "I'm talking to only you" manner, was indeed seductive.

"Incidentally, have you seen the dining room?" Sylvia laughed preparatory to making a joke. "It would be a bare cupboard without you!"

"No, I haven't seen it," Faith replied, and hoped Sylvia had time to give her a tour.

Sylvia did seem to have time, and showed Faith the elegant dining room with curved windows overlooking a garden and large deck. "During the summer months, we eat out on the deck that Doctor Hubbard added. It's almost like a resort!" Sylvia told her. There was also a small dining room off to the side for the residents to use for private parties and a good-sized library on the other side. They walked back through the living room.

"This was one of the few changes the Hubbards made. Originally part of it was the entrance hall." She gestured to the left and pointed back at the grand spiral staircase toward the rear of the room. "The wall between the hall and the Aldrich living room was removed to make a larger space." Faith commented that it was a beautiful room, and Sylvia agreed.

"You know the basement, and I understand you've also seen our nursing wing." Sylvia tactfully omitted any further comment. "This corridor connects the annex with the other house. Upstairs in this house is devoted to residents' apartments and rooms. So important to have one's own space and possessions, I think. I'd hate to end up with nothing except a locker and a bed. But Dr. Hubbard has assured me that there will always be a place for me here."

"And certainly you don't need to think about that for a long time," Faith assured her. Sylvia looked to be in her mid-fifties. She brightened at Faith's remark. "Thank you, my dear. But I'm not as young as all that."

Maybe sixty, Faith amended to herself.

She went home after retrieving Ben from school and spent the rest of the afternoon cooking and cleaning. Tom was leading a study group on the Apocrypha and trudged in wearily at nine o'clock. He was ready for bed. The Holly Ball was beginning to look like not only an investigative outing but a welcome break in Faith's domestic routine. It was definitely time to get out of the house.

Wednesday Faith rushed through her chores at Hubbard House. She was trying a new hairdresser, not Denise's but one she had gotten from a perfect stranger whose cut she'd admired in the checkout line at the Star Market.

Just as Faith was leaving, a woman burst through the door and ran over to Mrs. Pendergast. "Mrs. P., you absolutely saved my life! Here, I brought you these." She thrust a slightly wilted centerpiece of roses and orchids into Mrs. Pendergast's hands. "It was from the table, and I thought you might be able to use these for lunch." She put a brown paper bag on the counter. "They're the leftover caviar canapés. It's my way of saying thanks."

Mrs. Pendergast wasn't rushing to make any introductions, so Faith did the honors herself.

"Hello, I'm Faith Fairchild, a volunteer here."

"How sweet of you, I'm Charmaine Hubbard. I'd love to stay and chat, but I have a million things to do to get ready for tonight. Hope to see you there." And she was gone with one final wave from the door before exiting.

So this was Charmaine. Charmaine—a woman fighting an all-out battle against advancing years armed with turquoise Spandex and plenty of mousse. So far she hadn't been doing too badly. Very svelte, and a mane of glistening streaked hair. If there had been tucks, they were out of sight. She looked a little like Charo, or Farrah Fawcett when she had a mane of hair, and the faint southern accent, real or assumed, gave her a perennially youthful allure.

Faith knew better than to ask Mrs. Pendergast a direct question. But even Mrs. Pendergast, faithful unto death, couldn't stifle her annoyance. She was emptying the contents of the bag into the garbage disposal and muttering aloud, very aloud, "As if I'd serve leftover soggy fish egg canapés nobody wanted to eat in the first place to my ladies and gentlemen!" She looked over her shoulder at Faith with a slight grin. "Called me up in tears last night about seven o'clock. The fancy chef she'd hired to do her dinner party couldn't figure out how to turn on her oven, and she'd never done it either. I had to drop everything and go over. They were both in a tizzy. He was carrying on about his cream brewlays or some such thing and she was wailing that the guests were arriving. I guess they never heard of a match."

Where was Donald while all this was going on? Faith wondered in passing, but this thought was quickly overshadowed by one of greater interest.

What would Charmaine wear to the ball?

4

The Copley's rococo Oval Room, complete with cloud ceiling, had been partly transformed into a winter wonderland. The rosy-pink walls were decked with holly, and each round table sported a seasonal centerpiece. A nearsighted person taking off his or her glasses would have seen a warm blur of green, gold, silver, and white with flashes of red. Alberta balsams in large tubs were decorated with small twinkling white lights and scattered throughout the room. The balsams mixed pleasantly with the other scents emanating from the hors d'oeuvres buffet and the napes of female necks.

Faith had no trouble spotting Charmaine. She had obviously decided to combine the time of the year with the spirit of the place and looked like a Watteau shepherdess who had come across a bolt of cloth of gold and tinsel trim while keeping watch over her flock by night. Her gown started as a sparkling *bustier* and ended as layers of filmy white net. She wore a pair of enormous white satin leg-o'-mutton sleeves halfway down her arms and unaccountably carried a small silver basket containing one red rose. Long earrings of tiny silver bells dangled almost to her shoulders, and she was tinkling her way merrily across the dance floor greeting one and all. She had probably wanted to appear in the enormous scallop shell the Copley kept on hand for brides, Faith thought, but even tan, tawny Charmaine couldn't justify that at the Holly Ball.

"Are we going to try to find our table—it's number twenty-four—or do you want to stand here and check out what everybody's wearing a little longer?" Tom asked her.

"Let's find our table, then dance and check out what everybody's wearing."

Faith herself had opted for a deceptively simple Isaac Mizrahi silk gabardine sheath. It was short, demurely covered her collarbones with a ruffle, then plunged almost to the waist in back. It was red, and she'd bought it for the holidays. She hadn't expected to get an opportunity to wear it around Aleford much, and it was another reason she was pleased about the ball.

They found their seats, and Faith could see from the place cards that they were indeed at Denise's table, but Denise herself was nowhere in sight. It would have been difficult to spot anyone other than Charmaine in the crowd. There were about four hundred people—volunteers, Hubbard House residents, and benefactors eating, drinking, chatting, and/or kicking up their pumps. The din was uproarious, and the proper Bostonians (and those from outlying suburbs) were having a grand old time. Sylvia Vale floated by swathed in scarlet tulle with an elaborate matching turban that might have led some observers to believe she either had read the invitation incorrectly and thought it was a costume ball or was part of the entertainment—

Madame Glenda and her Magic Doves. Sylvia waved to Faith and mouthed "See you later" with her Cupid's-bow lips.

"And I thought I might not have fun," Tom commented. "First lead me to the goodies, then lead me to the band."

They inched their way across the dance floor to the food. Faith cast a professional eye on the buffet. There was a nice assortment of hot and cold hors d'oeuvres, and waiters were constantly bringing more, so none of the trays had either a ravaged look or the forlorn lack of appeal a full tray presents when others are empty—leading to the inevitable question of why no one wanted to eat whatever was on it. (This tended to happen with the fish-paste cocktail sandwiches at certain local functions Faith had reluctantly attended.) They filled their plates, got some champagne, and sat down to watch the action from the pretty little gold bamboo chairs the Copley had thoughtfully placed along the sidelines.

Dr. Hubbard galloped by, and presently Faith spotted Denise.

"There's my friend Denise," she told Tom. "The woman in the black crepe Armani dress over there."

"Pretty, but not my type. Too fashionable," Tom commented.

"And I'm not?"

"That doesn't deserve an answer. Let's just say I like to run my fingers through some hair, not an inch of stubble. If I want that, I can stop shaving for a couple of days."

What was it with men and long hair? If Tom and his ilk had their way, we'd all be Rapunzels, Faith reflected.

"I wonder who that is she's dancing with. I haven't seen him at Hubbard House. Maybe someone she's seeing."

Denise's partner was handsome in a Richard Gere sort of way, and his tuxedo was a bit more current—and snuggly fitting—than those of the men who were waltzing around him. They mostly sported the timeless boxy numbers from Brooks dug out from the backs of their closets year after year for occasions like this.

Faith looked over at Tom. He looked good in black—fortunately for his calling—but she had to admit she preferred the well-cut tux from Barney's she had given him their first Christmas together to his robes.

He caught her stare. "Want to dance, honey? It is a ball, remember."

"Love to," she replied, and jumped up. "I don't think my card is filled."

"Lucky, lucky me," Tom whispered in her ear as he pulled her close.

"Dance me over to Denise—I want to say hello," Faith instructed him, and veered toward the other couple.

"I was under the impression that the dance floor was the one place where I got to lead, darling, but it looks like I'm wrong there too. Just shove me wherever you want."

"Martyr," Faith said, and steered toward Denise.

As they got closer, Faith became aware that Denise was involved in a heated conversation with her partner. Her cheeks were red and she seemed close to tears. When they drew up next to them, Faith heard her say, "Please, *please*. You know I wouldn't ask you unless—" She broke off abruptly at the sight of Faith and composed her face in a welcoming smile.

"How lovely to see you, Faith. And you must be the Reverend Fairchild. I'm so glad you could come and I was able to get you at my table."

"Yes, we saw. You can tell us everyone's names." Faith hoped the hint wasn't too blatant, and to cover up asked hastily, "Is Mrs. P. here?"

Surprisingly, Denise's partner answered.

"Mrs. Pendergast! In this crowd! Do you think she got an invite, Denny?" he asked mockingly.

"Of course she did," Denise answered in a slightly angry tone. "She told me she'd rather put her feet up. I think her sister-in-law was coming over and they were going to watch their tapes of 'The Golden Girls' and have a glass or two of Kahlùa. A big night," she finished on a lighter note.

The music stopped and Dr. Hubbard walked up to the band leader and took the microphone.

"Would you take your seats now, friends? They're going to be serving dinner and you're also going to have to hear from me."

The crowd moved immediately to the round tables, neither prospect being an unpleasant one, it appeared.

Faith and Tom followed Denise. She still had not introduced them to the man with whom she was dancing, nor did he seem to be seated at her table.

Someone who obviously knew Hubbard House, Faith noted. Could it be Donald Hubbard? But Donald was in his mid to late thirties, and this man was much younger. Besides, there was something about him that suggested a profession other than medicine. She realized what it was. He was tan—and this was the wrong time of year for those doctors who frequented the course or courts to have one. Then she remembered Charmaine had recently come back from a cruise. Perhaps her husband had gone with her.

Faith sat down, and a waiter brought a steaming bowl of what she saw from the menu card was crawfish bisque with Armagnac. She liked eating someone else's cooking as much as and sometimes more than her own—if it was good. She took a sip. This was. The rest of the menu was appropriately festive: Boston Bibb lettuce with pomegranate-seed dressing, beef Wellington, wild rice, and plum pudding for dessert. They were going to have to do a great deal of dancing to burn it all off, she told Tom.

"Don't worry, I'm ready."

"Neither of you looks like you've ever had to worry about a calorie in your lives, whereas I've been on a diet continuously since I was thirteen." Denise sighed. She reached into her pocketbook and took out a pack of cigarettes. "Oh, I almost forgot. No smoking. Roland is quite a crusader."

Faith had noticed all the signs at Hubbard House with a picture of the bird and "No Puffin' " on them, but assumed it was because of a state requirement. She was thankful for Dr. Hubbard's convictions. She hated to eat with the smell of smoke surrounding her. As to what people wanted to do to themselves elsewhere, that was their own business.

Dr. Hubbard was starting to speak, and the microphone didn't make any untoward noises for him, nor did he find it necessary to test it. He started in with no ado at all.

"Residents of Hubbard House, my charming Pink Ladies, spouses, friends—friends all, I'd like to welcome you to yet another Holly Ball. Although we have already passed the time of year when we give collective thanks, I have always felt that this gathering is my personal thanksgiving. It is the time when we gather together in joy, and as I look out at all of you, I feel enormously thankful—for what you contribute to Hubbard House with your time and other resources, but most of all for the opportunity you grant me to continue doing what I have loved best in my life. As many of you are no doubt aware, Hubbard House came into existence a little over twenty-four years ago. Before that I was a doctor—a country doctor in those long-ago days. It was a wonderful experience—all those night calls." He paused for the laughter. "But when my dear wife Mary's illness prompted me to look for something that would keep me closer to her side, I knew immediately what I wanted to do. With her invaluable advice, I set about to create a place where one could live as an elderly person with both dignity and security. Where the individual would be cherished from the time he or she entered until leaving. I hope and pray we have accomplished this and will continue to do so for a long time to come."

He stopped at the thunderous applause, then continued.

"So many others came on board to help us, and many of them are still here raising the sails"—another pause for appreciative laughter. "I'd like to introduce a few of them, though of course they are well known to you. First my esteemed colleague and son, Dr. Donald Hubbard, and his lovely wife, Charmaine."

They stood to more applause, and Faith got a look at Donald. Roland's wife must have been short, she instantly thought. Otherwise Donald looked quite a bit like the old block. Charmaine had taken his arm and waved.

"Next my daughter, Muriel, without whom . . . as they say." Muriel stood up. She was wearing a black taffeta dress with a white collar and small jet buttons down the front. Faith saw her instantly at age eleven, still wearing smocked dresses with sashes. The braces had probably gone on about then too. Poor Muriel—one of those girls who got the lead in *Our Town* in high school and kept playing Emily earnestly ever after.

"And of course Sylvia Vale, my administrative assistant, who was there when we opened our doors." Sylvia rose and bowed regally.

"John McGuire, the chairman of our board of trustees, who keeps me honest." A genial, portly man with a fringe of silver hair stood amidst the laughter.

"And finally, two ladies—the pillars of the temple, so to speak—Leandra Rhodes, current president of our Residents' Council, and Bootsie Brennan, the head of our Ladies' Auxiliary—the Pinkest Lady of them all."

So this was the noxious Cyle's mother—a diminutive creature in rose velvet. Either it was Nice 'n Easy or Cyle hadn't produced any gray hairs in her shining gold locks, which Faith sincerely doubted. Small women like Bootsie, probably weighing all of a hundred pounds, were often heavyweights in other arenas, Faith had learned, and she didn't doubt that Bootsie—and what was that a nickname for?—could take anybody in the room.

Leandra Rhodes—she remembered Denise had mentioned her. She was tall and stately, with a braided crown of gray tresses. No touching up for her. She wore an ancient, slightly rusty looking turquoise taffeta-and-velvet gown that had seen a great deal of service—most likely first purchased for Waltz Evenings at this very hotel. Her white kid gloves—so difficult to get cleaned nowadays and looking pearly gray even from a distance—came up over her elbows. Faith was not fooled for an instant by the genteel shabbiness. Leandra was a classic Boston lady, a low heeler, with plenty of Adamses, Higginsons, and Shaws gracing the family boughs, just as there were also the fruits of her ancestors' labors stored away in the State Street Bank. She looked like a woman who knew exactly what she—and everyone else—should do.

"And now, please eat, drink, and enjoy yourselves, though as your doctor I am bound to warn you—not too much."

He sat down and the applause continued. Donald stood up and raised his glass. "To my father, the memory of my mother, and to Hubbard House," he said.

Someone cried, "Hear, hear," and everyone drank a toast.

Dr. Hubbard rose again and held his glass up. "The evening would not be complete without a toast to absent friends. Let us stand and remember."

The man was a consummate artist. Faith felt a lump in her throat. If Dr. Hubbard was as good at medicine as he was at public speaking, she thought they ought to beg him to take them on as patients.

Tom echoed her thoughts. "Quite a guy. Think what a different life most elderly people would have if there were more dedicated people like Roland Hubbard."

Two people whom the Fairchilds had not yet met smiled across the table. "He isn't a plaster saint; he's as genuinely caring as he seems," the woman said.

Denise came out of the reverie she'd been in since they'd sat down, and evidently recalled her duties as hostess. "Please let me introduce all of you. This is Julia Cabot"—she motioned toward the woman who had just spoken—"and her husband, Ellery, Hubbard House residents. Then my dear neighbors, Joan and Bill Winter, and the Reverend Thomas Fairchild and my new best friend, Faith Fairchild. Joel was supposed to escort me, but tickets to some revolting rock concert proved more interesting. I can't imagine why."

Everyone laughed and began to tell stories about their children. Faith felt a cold sweat starting as it did every time she contemplated the thought of Benjamin the teenager. It didn't matter that the Miller teenagers next door had always seemed at least somewhat reasonable and Pix averred it was not just in public. But hormones run amok could produce any number of catastrophes. Though even if they were disagreeing, at least they'd be able to have a conversation, something rather difficult at present. It was a vaguely comforting thought.

Tom and Faith danced some more and the evening meandered along pleasantly. Faith told Tom he ought to dance with Bootsie and tell her what he thought of her son. He replied that one cross to bear was enough, and in any case he made it a rule never to dance with women named Bootsie.

Denise's table proved to be an agreeable mix of people. Those who were dancing switched partners easily. Julia Cabot, in particular, was a superb dancer and thanked Tom so heartily at the end of her spin that he immediately engaged her for another. Her husband looked up at her affectionately. "Poor Julia doesn't get much dancing out of me anymore, I'm afraid. A problem with these May/December romances." Julia kissed him and told him to stop talking nonsense, then waltzed gracefully away. She was an attractive woman with light-brown hair piled up on her head and dressed in a long, full-skirted emerald-green satin gown. Ellery addressed the rest of the table—quite proudly, Faith noted. "I'm eighty-two and I'm not supposed to say how old Julia is, but let's just say I was doing my darndest to make the freshman crew team at Harvard when she was born."

With Tom busy dancing and the others chatting away, Faith thought she would take the opportunity to work the room a little in the hopes of picking up some information. Now that she knew who they all were, she'd go directly to the Hubbard table and see how they were doing. She wandered over to where the family was sitting. Dr. Hubbard was dancing with Sylvia Vale, and they swept energetically by in a near imitation of Arthur and Katherine Murray. As Faith approached, she was greeted warmly by Muriel, who was sitting with her brother and Charmaine.

"Mrs. Fairchild! How splendid that you could come. Do sit down and meet my brother and his wife." Was it Faith's imagination or were the words "and his wife" in a lower register?

"Mrs. Fairchild and I have already met, thank you Muriel. She's working in the kitchen," Charmaine told her husband, making Faith feel not unlike Cinderella at the ball.

Donald took Faith's hand in both of his. It must be a family trademark, she thought. He was actually quite attractive, with a slight cleft in his chin that his father didn't have. It made his face very much his own. He dropped her hand gently. "My father mentioned that you were so kind as to pitch in during our flu epidemic, and we're very grateful. I'm sure this is a busy time for you and the Reverend."

"I'm glad I could do it," Faith said, then wondered what to say next—something like "We're all friends here. How about telling me what's really going on at Hubbard House?"

Charmaine reached under the table and pulled out a purse that would have proved ample for a polar expedition and prepared to redo her face. She caught Muriel's disapproving glance and said, "If you'll excuse me," and left.

A few yards from the table she stopped to talk to

Denise's earlier dancing partner. She was tossing her hair around and he had one arm casually flung around her waist. Faith looked back at Donald and Muriel. She was not surprised to see a look of deep disgust on Muriel's face, but she was stunned by the look of intense anger that had transformed Donald's kindly expression. He looked as though he wanted to kill someone.

Charmaine and whoever it was broke apart, and the man continued on toward the table.

"Good evening, Muriel, Donald, and I don't believe I know this beautiful lady," he said.

It was clear Donald wasn't going to make any introductions, although a mask of indifference had replaced the one of hatred. Muriel, ever mindful of her manners, did.

"Faith Fairchild, Edsel Russell. Mr. Russell is in charge of the buildings and grounds at Hubbard House." Then she added, "Mrs."—and this time there was no doubt about the emphasis on the word—"Mrs. Fairchild is a volunteer."

Edsel Russell gave something between a nod and small bow toward Faith. "Please call me Eddie. Everybody does. My mother, God rest her soul, thought Edsel was classy, but then she had never seen the car."

Faith laughed. "Well, I hear they are becoming highly collectible. I suppose it's another example of if you wait long enough, whatever you're holding on to will come back in fashion." This was not one of her maxims but Tom's, and in his case it was more like continual use, rather than stockpiling, say, one's old Diors until hems went up or down again.

"Could I 'collect' you for the next dance, Mrs. Fairchild?"

It wasn't that he was unattractive, and he was probably a good dancer. Men like Eddie usually were. But Faith didn't feel like giving him the satisfaction of an acceptance. It was clearly why he had come to the table. Besides, the line was too corny.

"Perhaps later, thank you. I'm a bit tired now," she told him.

"Time to go to the bench then. How about you, Muriel?"

The man was either a cad or an oaf or both. Donald was drinking a glass of champagne and his hand trembled. Faith half expected him to fling the contents at Eddie and declare, "That is my sister, suh, whom you impugn!" She also expected Muriel to decline—politely of course but, Faith hoped, with some frostiness.

None of these things happened. Donald put the glass down and Muriel rose with alacrity and danced off in Eddie's arms.

That left Faith and Donald, and just as she was about to ask about Eddie Russell's duties—he being clearly the first real fly in the ointment she'd found at Hubbard House—Donald excused himself. Faith got up quickly, since there is nothing so pathetic as one person sitting alone at a table with a lot of partially consumed food and drinks, and made her way back to her own table. She passed Eddie and Muriel. His eyes were half closed and he was humming along to the music; hers were wide open.

She sat down next to Tom.

"Where have you been? They played 'Windmills of My Mind.' "

Tom could be very sentimental. He still thought *A Man and a Woman* was one of the greatest movies of all time and got choked up when Kermit sang "The Rainbow Connection."

"I was talking to the Hubbards and met the guy who's in charge of buildings and grounds at Hubbard House—"

Whatever Faith was going to say about Eddie was lost as the Oval Room plunged into sudden darkness. A woman screamed, and almost as quickly as they had gone off, the lights went on again. It was as if a reel of film had broken in the middle and, when the projector started again, it started in a freeze frame. Everyone stood poised in position. Most were facing the direction of the scream. Since her mouth was opened for another, Charmaine was the obvious source. Perhaps she saw Muriel's palm ready to slap her sillier, or perhaps she decided Camille was a more touching act. Whatever the reason, she snapped her lips closed and swooned into a chair. Donald bent anxiously over her. Faith's first impulse was to dash over to the Hubbard table, lift the cloth, and search for a body beneath. Instead she looked around to see who was where. There was general movement now, and Dr. Hubbard was striding over to the microphone. Donald was attending to Charmaine. Muriel was watching her father. Eddie was nowhere in sight. No one was missing from Faith's table with the exception of Denise.

Dr. Hubbard had the microphone and his voice was bracingly reassuring. "One of the staff has been a little overzealous in turning down the lights for our pudding procession," he told the crowd. "I think we're ready to begin now."

The lights dimmed appropriately and waiters suitably liveried marched out bearing silver salvers of flaming plum pudding surrounded by holly wreaths. The pale-blue flames reflected in the mirrored doors that encircled the room, and the effect was lovely. An appreciative murmur echoed throughout until someone started clapping, and the applause spread. One pudding was placed on Dr. Hubbard's table and the others were lined up on the buffet. The last flame wavered and faded, and the lights went on again. The orchestra struck up "We Wish You a Merry Christmas," and the crowd moved toward the figgy puddings for a taste.

Everything was apparently fine.

Faith was not a big fan of plum pudding, although she liked looking at it. Too rich and cloying. Only the English—and she was excepting those English like Elizabeth David in this case—could have thought to pair it with hard sauce, that dense mass of white sugar spiked with too little brandy.

While Tom went to join the queue, Faith thought back

over the evening and watched the scene in front of her. Muriel was dancing with her father, stretching her arms up high to reach. In earlier days she would have stood on his shoes. Maybe she still wanted to—Daddy's little girl?

She had learned more about the Hubbard family, Faith realized, but nothing earthshaking. Sure, Muriel did not seem to be a fan of Charmaine's, but then what sensible person would be? Donald was apparently besotted with her, but maybe they had great sex. Who knew? Eddie Russell presented some possibilities, and he seemed to be very friendly with Charmaine. It was possible that Howard Perkins had stumbled on this hanky-panky, but Howard was a New Yorker, and a little nooky in the linen closet or wherever was not going to cause him serious concern. It might be something with Eddie, though. That felt right.

Tom came back with a wedge of pudding large enough for the whole Round Table and some *friandises* for her.

"What are you thinking about so earnestly? I could see your beetling brows all the way across the room. Have you solved Chat's case? Does Dr. Hubbard have his hand in the till? Although from what I understand about the finances of places like Hubbard House and how difficult it is to keep them going, there can't be much to spare. Farley told me Roland Hubbard has never asked anyone to leave—even when the money ran out."

"I think that's why we're here tonight. It's kind of a scholarship fundraiser. As to what I have been thinking about, you're right. I'm still looking for the skeleton in the closet."

Tom took a last colossal bite of pudding and said, "Let's tread a few measures, then go home. I know Samantha is spending the night and we don't have to rush, but I'd like to get to bed myself."

"Me too," Faith answered demurely.

It was handy—no, more than handy, definitely a gift from the gods—to have a baby-sitter next door, and Faith prayed unabashedly that Samantha's devotion to Ben would continue for years to come. After all, there were lots of excellent colleges in the area. Since tonight was a school night, she was sleeping over. Faith shuddered as she remembered what Lizzie's mother, Arlene, had told her last week—that she had called twelve people and still not been able to find a sitter. Faith couldn't in good conscience wish zits or perpetual bad breath on Samantha, but she did wish that the fifteen-year-old would continue her pattern of infrequent dating or find someone steady and settle down immediately—preferably in front of the Fairchild fireplace watching Ben.

Tom and Faith danced their last dance and prepared to take their leave. Tom was exchanging phone numbers with Bill Winter. They had both gone to the same high school on the South Shore, although a few years apart. New England was often like that, Faith had discovered. If it wasn't someone Tom had grown up with, then it was someone from college or a cousin of someone who knew his brother. A village.

Faith turned and realized that Eddie Russell had slithered up to her side. "Ready for our dance? You promised, remember?" He smiled, and he did have a captivating smile. Tom was still wrapped up replaying the Norwell-Hanover Thanksgiving game of 1976, so she decided to dance with Eddie. Purely for research; the man was such a sleaze.

"I do remember. I didn't promise, but let's dance anyway."

They walked to the dance floor and started to dance. The orchestra provided a plaintive rendition of "Memories" and Eddie went into his dancing mode, closing his eyes slightly and humming tunefully along with the music. He began to pull her closer in gradually increasing increments, and at the same time his hand began to ascend from her silk-covered waist to her bare back. At the first touch of vertebrae, Faith said, "Get your hand off my back, Edsel dear, and don't do it again."

"Come on, Faith, you didn't wear a dress like this for no reason."

Faith stopped dancing and stepped back, still in his arms.

"Why don't you go do to yourself what you have in mind to do to me?" she told him succinctly.

It took him a moment to get it, and he flushed angrily. She was walking away by then.

"Is that any way for a minister's wife to talk?" he called after her.

"Probably not," she answered, and went to find Tom. Definitely time to go home.

They said good night to Denise, who had gotten a strong second wind somewhere and slowed her hectic re-creation of the twist to beg them to stay. "You can't go yet! The party's just starting and the band is playing all these oldies. I've requested a hustle next. It's such a hoot!" She seemed genuinely excited about the prospect, but the Fairchilds, less enthusiastic, said good night again and threaded their way through the writhing dancers.

Out on the sidewalk, while they waited for their car to be brought around, they were joined by Donald and Charmaine. Charmaine was leaning on Donald's arm ever so slightly and had a determinedly gallant look on her face. What exactly was it she had survived? Faith wondered. Their car arrived first and Donald tenderly helped her in. "She's very tired," he told them, and drove off quickly.

Tom and Faith laughed. "After your description of her with the moldly leftovers, I didn't think Charmaine could provide much more amusement, but I should have known better. Women like that are a never-ending source."

They got into the car to drive home, first detouring to drive past the lights on Boston Common. Garlands of red, blue, green, and gold were strung in the bare tree branches like jeweled necklaces, gaudy but beautiful trimmings against the sedate brick townhouses lining Beacon Street behind them. A parking space appeared—too good to waste—and Tom and Faith walked up to the state house totally surrounded by the ancient trees and their unaccustomed diadems. They strolled back to the car reluctantly, and as they turned west on Storrow Drive away from the distraction of the lights, Faith realized that Charmaine hadn't been carrying her enormous purse. Nor had Donald. She didn't seem the type to forget her essentials. Nor mislay them. It was puzzling.

The next morning—or actually the same morning—arrived too soon, but they managed to get themselves up and even dressed and fed. Ben was revoltingly cheerful.

"I must be getting old," Tom said. "I used to get by on a lot less sleep than this and be loaded for bear the following morning."

"What a curious expression that is," Faith commented. "But it's true—I really feel it the next morning when I've been out late. I blame Benjamin and all the sleep deprivation we suffered when he was a baby. We just haven't caught up. One good thing though: when we're in our eighties, we won't need so much sleep and we can stay out as late as we want."

"Great. By the way, were you also thinking of waiting until then for Ben the Sequel?" Tom had been subtly and not so subtly hinting for some months that it was sibling time for Ben.

"You never know." Faith smiled and got into her car. She was not opposed to having another baby. It was just hard to cross that bridge from nice idea to fact. And it wasn't as if they were not trying. They just weren't *trying*—and all the unspontaneous counting of days that involved.

Mrs. Pendergast was already up to the salads when Faith arrived and, contrary to all Faith's expectation, was full of curiosity about the ball. She wanted to know what everyone had been wearing, what they had eaten, what Dr.

Hubbard had said in his speech, and so forth. Faith was happy to oblige and was rewarded by an unguarded comment or two from Mrs. P.

After Faith had described the gowns of Leandra Rhodes and Bootsie Brennan, Mrs. Pendergast chuckled. "Those two! They hate each other like poison. Each thinks the other is purposely working against her. You should have seen the fur fly when Mrs. Rhodes started a fund drive sponsored by the Residents' Council to buy books for the library. Well, according to Mrs. Brennan, that was taking over the job of the Auxiliary. They were the only ones who were supposed to raise money for Hubbard House. Mrs. Rhodes said if so why weren't they doing a better job of stocking the library, and Mrs. Brennan said it was her impression that most residents had their own books, and finally the whole thing ended up in Dr. Hubbard's lap, as usual, and he just put them both in charge of the thing, as usual. So Mrs. Rhodes gets all the residents to donate what they can and Mrs. Brennan goes outside. It's pretty even. Then Mrs. Brennan's son comes up with some huge secret donation and it looked like she'd won. But Mrs. Rhodes turned around and got a secret one herself. Of course everybody figured out soon enough it was their own money."

Faith laughed. "It sounds like it must be some library. I'll have to take a closer look."

"It is, but they raised so much money that in the end they decided to put most of it in the general fund, because you know—though I hate to say it—the people here do have their own books or go over to the town library, and they never really needed so many books in the first place."

"Why do you hate to say it?" Faith asked.

Mrs. Pendergast looked over her shoulder and muttered under her breath, "Never cared much for Mrs. Brennan—Bootsie, what kind of name is that for a woman anyway? Even for a cat it's going some. Always wanting to know 'What are we giving them today, Mrs. P.?' She's never scraped a carrot in her life, that one."

Faith sympathized. It looked like Cyle and the mater were cut from the same cloth. "What does Mr. Brennan do?" she asked Mrs. Pendergast, although Tom would know.

"It's what he did. Died and left a rich widow a year after they were married. Right after his son was born."

Faith stifled the remark that was called for—something along the lines of "took one look," or "how did he stand it a year?"—and got busy with the bread.

Mrs. Pendergast had had enough of true confessions. "There's snow in the air. Smelled like it when I went to start my car this morning."

Two years ago Faith would have scoffed at the quaintness of this archetypal New England prophecy, but she thought it smelled like snow herself this morning. There was a kind of smell, or lack of smell. The air was dry, odorless, and empty—waiting to be filled with flakes.

"Anyhow," Mrs. P. continued in the same folksy vein, "it's time for some more snow. You know what they say: 'A green Christmas means a full graveyard come spring.' "

Faith wondered what cheerful soul had first made this observation and decided to ignore the homily in favor of the here and now. "Should we make up some stew and a few soups in case the weather gets bad and the weekend help can't get here?" she asked.

"I've already done a beef stew and it's in the freezer. If you want to help with some soup, that would be getting it done. But"—she looked over her ridiculous diamanté glasses at Faith—"no bouillon."

5

It was three o'clock. Ben had awakened from his nap, and Faith was restless. Too early to start dinner, and she didn't feel like doing any of the things she had to do. Like iron. She knew not what worldly goods she might bequeath to her children, yet of one thing she was sure. There would be a basket of ironing sitting in the closet.

"Want to go see Pix and play with the dogs?" she asked Ben, confident of his response. There was nothing Benjamin liked better than rolling around on the Millers' kitchen floor with their golden retrievers. It wasn't necessary to bundle him up too much for the quick dash across the driveway, and soon she was knocking at Pix's kitchen door.

"Are you busy? Or would you like some company?" Faith asked.

"I'd love an excuse to stop. Every time I add these up, I get a different number." She pointed to a pile of papers on the kitchen table. "It's the final tally for the cookie sales. We have to make sure the number of boxes sold equals the number delivered and paid for."

Pix was the town coordinator for the Girl Scout cookie drive again, even though Samantha hadn't been a scout for some time. It was one of those jobs that, once having fallen to Pix, stuck. She was active in everything from the preschool PTA to Meals on Wheels. All the organizations in town knew a good thing when they saw it, and she was the original girl who couldn't say no.

"Don't you ever think of shedding a few of these responsibilities?" Faith wondered.

"Believe me I try, but they say 'just one more year' and I agree. But this really *is* the last year for the cookies. Sam was very annoyed at having his precious Porsche outside while the Tagalongs and Trefoils were in the garage."

Sam Miller, a Boston lawyer, had purchased the sports car as a defiant gesture toward the depredations of middle age when he had turned forty several years earlier. The other less benign gesture—the prerequisite affair with a younger woman—made at the same time had fortunately not been repeated, nor did it seem likely that it would.

"Give me your calculator and let me help you with this. If there's one thing I'm good at, it's settling accounts," Faith offered.

Pix put a cookie in each of Ben's hands and placed him high up on a stool so the dogs wouldn't eat the cookies before he could, then put a plate of them on the table. She poured two mugs of coffee and they settled down to work. Faith had become used to drinking bottomless mugs of coffee in Aleford's suburban kitchens. Her espresso days were definitely over, she thought with a slight inward sigh.

The job was soon done.

"You're a wizard, Faith. It would have taken me hours to do it."

"It's good practice for February, when I start the business again. My profit depends on calculations like this."

"I can't wait. I'll never have to cook for another dinner party again." Pix, who had shot the rapids whitewater canoeing coast to coast, regularly skied the bowl at Tuckerman Ravine, and had taught her teenage son to drive, went completely to pieces at the prospect of entertaining in Aleford.

"I've told you. I'd be happy to get everything ready for you anytime. You don't have to hire me," Faith protested.

"No, you're a professional. It's your bread and butter, so I'll wait my turn."

Ben was opening Pix's cupboards and soon became engrossed in her museum-quality and -quantity Tupperware collection. There was a shape and size for every food yet discovered. Faith knew Pix didn't mind the mess.

Pix was the only person, apart from Tom and Charley MacIsaac, whom Faith had told about Howard Perkins' letter and Chat's call. Pix had lived in Aleford all her life, but her ear had always been kept to a different kind of ground than Millicent's or even the chief's. A camping ground. Still, she might know something about some of the people Faith had met the night before, and she started off by asking about the younger Hubbards.

"Of course I know Charmaine and Donald. They've lived in town since they got married, which must have been about ten years ago," Pix responded. "But our paths don't cross very often. Besides, Charmaine is away a lot. They don't have any children, so I guess she gets bored around here. She's always off to Florida or on a cruise somewhere."

"Boring stuff like that," said Faith.

"Well, boring to me. Muriel was a couple of years behind me in school. I always felt sorry for her. It wasn't that she was unattractive, but she was so serious no one ever dated her much, and she didn't even have many girlfriends, except for a few who were in Future Nurses. I remember her mostly rushing to class with a big stack of books—all by herself."

"What about someone named Edsel Russell? Ever run into him?"

"His older brother was in Sam's and my graduating class, but I don't know Eddie. There's a big age difference."

"You mean Eddie Russell is from Aleford! I should have guessed," Faith exclaimed.

"He's from Aleford, though he hasn't been here much. He left when he was a teenager. I don't know if he ever finished school. His father, Stanley, ran off when the kids were young, and his mother died about ten years ago, so there was nothing back here for him. His brother, Stanley Junior, is a career Army man. He's at some base in Texas."

"I wonder why Eddie came back to Aleford," Faith mused.

"I can't tell you that, but I can tell you how. It was pretty hot gossip at the time—about two years ago. Charmaine met him down in Boca Raton. He was the golf pro or something like that at the resort where she was staying. Hubbard House had an opening, and he must have needed a job."

"And maybe Charmaine decided he could be of service in other ways?"

"It *has* been hinted. She's not known for her devotion to Donald, and a lot of people wonder why he ever puts up with her."

"Love, my dear, blind infatuation. It sticks out all over him."

"Last night must have been very interesting then. Tell me, what did Charmaine wear? Anybody who wears a chartreuse body suit and a lace T-shirt to do her marketing in was bound to look pretty spectacular at the ball."

Faith filled her in, and they spent some more time talking about the Hubbards and Eddie Russell, in particular, but it was speculation that didn't take them anywhere.

Faith stood up. "I've got to go and get supper ready. Let me know if you remember anything more about the Hubbards or Eddie. I have a hunch that whatever Howard found out has to do with Charmaine and Eddie. Maybe they're operating some sort of scam using Hubbard House as a front—kickbacks from the hospital suppliers, that's a possibility, or doctoring the books. From the giant Rolex Eddie was sporting, it's my guess he likes a healthy cash flow."

"But Dr. Hubbard or Muriel would know if something like that was going on. Besides, it isn't likely they'd let Charmaine anywhere near the books, and Eddie would only have access to transactions dealing with maintenance. Of course, that could be pretty lucrative."

Faith made a face. "Don't be so logical. Charmaine and Eddie are the only leads I've been able to come up with so far, slim though they be. Well, there's still plenty of time before Christmas to find out. Although I would have liked to have more to report to Chat. She's calling tonight. I got a letter from her yesterday announcing the fact so that she'll be sure to find me home, I suppose."

"Anyway, you're having fun, aren't you?"

"Yes, I suppose I am. I like the people at Hubbard House, even though some of them are a bit like characters from that game Clue. The cook, Charmaine, Sylvia Vale, Leandra Rhodes—her name may not be Mustard, but I heard at the ball her husband *is* a colonel, retired, and he *does* have a mustache."

"Just so you don't find a body in the conservatory with a candlestick next to it."

"Don't worry. Whatever this is, it isn't murder."

She slipped Ben back into his polar-fleece jacket and headed for the door. The dogs began to bark in disappointment. Ben started to join them.

"He has got to stop identifying with your dogs so totally," Faith said. "When Lizzie was over the other day, they were running from bush to bush lifting their legs and falling down convulsed with laughter."

Pix was convulsed herself, and they left her surrounded by her canine children, Dusty, Arty, and Hanky.

Chat did call that night and seemed satisfied by Faith's description of her activities to date. After Faith told her about Eddie and Charmaine, she commented, "They sound like the types who go around selling shares in nonexistent diamond mines—not literally, because the residents of Hubbard House seem too savvy for that, but its equivalent. Perhaps this delightful duo approached Howard, or someone else told him about a scheme. Try to see if you can get close to them and maybe they'll try to rope you in. Act dumb and naive. I know that's a stretch, dear."

"The idea of getting any closer to Eddie than the next county is pretty loathsome, but for the moment it's all I have to go on."

"In any case, it doesn't appear that anything at Hubbard House is going to place your pretty little head in peril, and you're leaving Benjamin at home, so he's safe—as opposed to your last escapade. I may have a large number of nieces, but you know you're my favorite and I wouldn't want to be the cause, though indirect, of any harm."

"Hope told me you told her *she* was your favorite niece," Faith chided.

"And so she is. You all are. Now, this is costing me a fortune and I'm saving all my pennies for Christmas gifts."

"I hope you haven't changed your mind about coming to Aleford for Christmas, instead of going to Darien with Mom and Dad—especially if you are doing all that shopping."

"No, I'll be with you. But I simply can't understand why your sister and Quentin are dragging poor Jane and Theodore all the way to Connecticut on Christmas Day to be with Quentin's parents when it is Theodore's busiest time of the year."

"Because Hope thought it would be nice for the two

families to be together. Remember, come January we'll all be related by marriage."

"Well, much as I love her, I think it's a bit selfish, and besides, I was used to going to them for Christmas Day."

Faith thought it was a bit selfish of Hope herself. After Christmas Eve and Christmas Day services, Theodore Sibley was always exhausted and had been known to doze off while carving. But she also knew how delighted her parents were with the upcoming nuptials, and they had met Quentin Lewis' parents only once before.

"You were invited, Chat," Faith reminded her.

"I'm just beginning to get used to Quentin. I certainly don't want to meet any more of them before the wedding."

Hope's fiancé's Filofax was filled in up to and beyond the year 2000, and fortunately Hope fitted into the general scheme of things. Since Hope herself had been reading *The Wall Street Journal* and *Forbes* since early adolescence, they had everything in common. The one thing that made it all palatable so far as Faith was concerned was that the two of them were crazy about each other.

"We're just happy you're going to be here, Chat."

"That's kind of you, dear. I'll get you something especially nice, and don't worry, I'll stop at Dean & DeLuca before I get on the plane and bring as much as my poor old arms can carry. Now good-bye."

She hung up before Faith had a chance to express her delight and thanks. She was very happy that Chat was coming. With a husband and father in the business, holidays could not be spent en famille, and even though Tom's family would be with them, she liked having a member of her own tribe around.

"It's already beginning to snow," Tom commented the next morning as he looked out the kitchen window. "Are you sure you ought to go over to Byford today? Those back roads could get pretty treacherous before noon."

"Don't worry, sweetheart. Besides, I promised Mrs.

Pendergast I would help finish cooking enough for the weekend in case the storm is as big as they're predicting."

"All right, but go slow and leave early if things start to look bad."

Faith was in a cheerful mood as she drove to Hubbard House. The snow was beginning to stick, and it looked like Christmas was just around the corner, which it was. She was planning her Christmas Day menu in her mind and hadn't gotten past duck versus goose when she realized she was at the Hubbard House driveway. A small truck was spreading sand on the hill, and she followed it up to the parking lot. Eddie jumped out and came over to open her door. His cheeks resembled ripe McIntosh apples, and he looked excited.

"I bet we're in for at least ten or eleven inches. Reminds me of the storms when I was a kid around here and we'd go plowing. We'd be out all night. It was great."

He looked like a kid again for a moment, and Faith felt she might have liked him then—before all the layers of crap had built up.

"There is something exciting about the prospect of a storm," she agreed. "I'd better get in and start helping Mrs. P. fill the larder."

"I think I'll go grab a cup of coffee, and if she's in a good mood, she might give me a doughnut."

She wasn't.

"We don't have time to waste today, Eddie," she told him abruptly. "Now get your coffee and skedaddle."

Faith had never heard anyone in real life use that word, nor seen anyone actually skedaddle, which Eddie very quickly did.

"Talk your ear off, that one—and worse," she told Faith. "Never so much as an 'Anything I can do to help, Mrs. P.?' Oh no, just born with his hand out. Now let's get going."

Mrs. Pendergast obviously thought all of Hubbard House might be snowed in for the rest of the winter, and the next few hours were spent baking breads and cooking enormous pans of such Yankee staples as Indian pudding, baked beans, and brown bread. In between, they got lunch together. Faith went upstairs to the office at eleven thirty to hear a weather report and call Tom. There was still a great deal to do, and she wanted him to pick up Ben if he could. The snow was falling in thick sheets, but according to WEEI the roads were clear. She told Tom she wanted to stay a few more hours, and he agreed with such alacrity to get Ben that she knew Cyle must have trapped him in his office.

"Cyle is there, right?"

"Absolutely. Yes, indeedy. No trouble at all, honey. You do what you need to do."

"Poor baby. There's lentil stew in the fridge and some of that Virginia ham. Fry it up and heat the stew for lunch. That should get the bad taste out of your mouth."

"Okay, thanks, and drive carefully."

"No, Tom, I want to spend the night in a snowbank. Stop worrying!"

She went downstairs, and after refusing as tactfully as she could some of the finnan haddie Mrs. Pendergast and her paprika can had prepared for the residents' lunch, she set to work.

"We may have some of the day crew stuck here this weekend, so let's do extra of this chicken casserole," Mrs. Pendergast advised. The casserole bore a distinct resemblance to chicken à la king—exactly which monarch was to blame Faith had never heard. She managed to keep Mrs. Pendergast from going crazy with the canned pimientos and substituted some tarragon instead. She also convinced her that the biscuit on the side would be a novel change from the soggy-biscuit-underneath-and-on-top approach. She looked down at her watch and realized with a start that it was past three o'clock. "Oh! I didn't know it was so late. I'm sorry, but I do have to go now."

"Thank you so much, Mrs. Fairchild. I'm going to stay on myself and spend the night here, but everything is in fine shape."

"Who knows? Maybe the storm won't be that bad. And please, call me Faith."

"Thank you, Faith—and you can call me Violet if you like."

It would be hard, Faith thought, but she would try—for Violet's sake.

She ran up the stairs and through the living room. Several of the residents were standing by the windows looking at the mounting drifts of snow and making predictions.

"It might be another 1978," Ellery Cabot observed.

Faith could never figure out if local residents made this remark (which they tended to do when more than a few flakes of snow fell) fearfully or nostalgically. It was usually followed by reminiscences of exactly how many days they were without power and confined to their respective dwellings by the over-three-foot snowfall.

Ellery's wife, Julia, turned and saw Faith. "Are you sure you should drive home in this? It's really coming down now."

"I'll be all right," Faith replied. "Aleford isn't far, and once I get on Route 2, the rest will be easy."

"If you change your mind, there's plenty of room here," Julia offered.

"Thank you," Faith said, pulled open the front door, and stepped outside. A blast of snow and cold air hit her full in the face as the door slammed shut behind her. It was worse than she thought, but she had no desire to spend the night away from home.

The car started at once, and she inched down the long driveway. It had been sanded again, and she pulled onto the main road with a sigh of relief that was immediately drawn back into her lungs less than half a mile later as the car slid completely out of control. She steered in the direction of the skid, stayed calm, and came to a halt hood down in a pile of snow the size of the state of Alaska.

"Damn, damn, damn," she muttered aloud and

smacked the steering wheel. She didn't even have her Leon Leonwood Bean boots on, the ones for which she had reluctantly traded her Joan and Davids her first winter in Aleford. She was wearing her down parka and warm gloves, though. She got out of the car and tied her red muffler to the antenna, where it waved cheerily in the wind.

"Damn this weather. Damn this climate. Damn this place." She'd never gone off the road in Manhattan. She didn't even have to drive in Manhattan.

She crossed the road and started back the way she'd come. Soon her feet had lost all feeling and the snow was choking her. Her cheeks stung painfully. She kept her head down and tried to keep the flakes from gluing her eyelashes shut so she could see where she was going. She felt like Little Eva on the ice floes. After what seemed like twenty-four hours, she saw the almost obliterated sign for Hubbard House and started trudging up the steep driveway. When she got around the bend, the sight of the lighted houses looming up ahead was so welcome that she started to sprint and immediately slipped and fell headlong, but un-hurt, on top of one of the frozen rhododendrons.

The Cabots were still gazing out the window and had the door open before she reached the top step.

"Oh, Faith, what happened? Are you all right?" Julia cried.

"Come over here by the fire, dear," Ellery said. "Julia, get some brandy, would you?"

"I'm fine," Faith whispered. "But my car went off the road. I've got to call my husband."

"Of course, but warm up a moment first," Ellery advised, and guided her over to the hearth, where she took off her things. The snow fell in large clumps on the deep-red oriental rug. Ellery gathered up the sodden garments and Faith collapsed in an enormous wing chair. Her toes and fingers immediately began to throb painfully.

Julia returned with a large snifter of brandy, some slippers, and a towel. She also had a lap rug, which she threw over Faith. After a few minutes, pleasant feelings of warmth and safety began to creep over her. Various parts of her body stopped hurting. She almost nodded off, then sat up with a jerk. "I've got to call Tom. He'll be frantic."

He was. After she had reassured him, she told him how admirable it was that he wasn't saying "I told you so."

"I know and I did," he said. "I was afraid you'd get stuck, and I hate to spend the night without you."

"Me too," agreed Faith. The brandy and warm surroundings had restored her. "Well, since I'm here I'd better go down to the kitchen and help Mrs. Pendergast get dinner."

"I think you've done enough, honey, but if you feel like it. It's up to you."

"It's that or learn to play cribbage."

"You could sit and read a book. In any case, it hasn't been my impression that Hubbard House was filled with sedentary cribbage players."

"You're right. They're probably out shoveling snow, filling bird feeders, or looking for other hapless maidens, like myself, with kegs of clam chowder tied around their necks."

Faith hung up and went back to the living room to thank the Cabots. They were waiting in front of the fire, and when she told them she was going down to the kitchen, they were adamant she remain with them and sit at their table for dinner.

"Mrs. Pendergast has all the help she needs and then some," Julia told her. "I was down there a little while ago, and Leandra has organized crews from now to the end of the emergency, which could be months from the look of her forces."

Faith gave in and tucked herself back before the fire. She picked up a newspaper and pretended to read. She missed Ben. She missed Tom.

Ellery left to get something from their apartment, and Faith asked Julia, "Have you lived here long?"

"For about five years. The house was getting to be more than we wanted to manage, and although Ellery is in excellent health, we thought it best to be in a facility where he could get more extensive care if he needed it and I could be near him. He's over eighty, you know." Faith had been surprised to hear Ellery's age at the Holly Ball and expressed it aloud now.

"He certainly doesn't look his age," she commented, swiftly changing "that old" to "his age" in the interests of politeness.

Julia nodded, "I'm somewhat younger, and a few of my friends warned me about moving here. In some places the less elderly residents become a bit like pets—infantilized. Even though at times a woman in her sixties might like to be thought of as a young thing, as a steady diet it wouldn't have been too pleasant."

"Then it hasn't happened."

"No, partly because I'm still working, so I'm only around in the evenings and on weekends. And Ellery and I are out a great deal. It's also because so many of the people here are fiercely independent. They don't need or want someone to wind their wool or fetch their slippers."

Faith stretched her feet out in front of her. "It was very nice of you to fetch them for me, though." She decided she liked the Cabots. On closer inspection, Julia was even prettier than she had seemed at the ball. Her hair was down now and framed her face in soft waves. Ellery looked like the generic New England Yankee gentleman of advancing years he was—ruddy complexion from sailing out of Marblehead, tall, wiry, white-haired, with clear blue eyes that didn't miss much. She guessed he did something downtown. It was immediately confirmed.

"Ellery's first wife died early in their marriage. We met when I came to practice in his law office. He likes it that I'm there to report back to him, and he still goes in occasionally. He's painstakingly working on a book of memoirs—

wanted to call it *My First Hundred Years,* but Eddie Bernays beat him to it."

Faith spent what was left of the afternoon in front of the fire chatting with Julia and meeting some of the other residents. She was confirmed in her first impression—that the group at Hubbard House was a resilient, vigorous one, involved in both the small world around them and the larger one outside. One man spent a half hour describing his work organizing a local recycling station. Another woman stopped by to remind Julia that the committee that met to invite local authors to come and speak would be meeting on Monday night. Faith didn't doubt that the inhabitants of Hubbard House suffered the aches, pains, and various discomforts old age brought—some of them serious—yet they dealt with them and kept on going. Business as usual, if possible.

Ellery reappeared and they went in to dinner. The dining room was full and everyone was enjoying the novelty of the first big storm. There was an air of excitement in the room and a noise level, though subdued, that Faith guessed was higher than usual. She was hungry and dug into the chicken casserole. It wasn't Lutèce, but the tarragon had perked it up a bit.

There was no sign of the Hubbards, and Faith asked if they took meals with the rest of the residents.

"Muriel is usually too busy upstairs and has a tray, but Roland eats with us most nights. I imagine he's had things to do because of the storm, and Donald lives in Aleford."

They were eating their apple crisp when Leandra Rhodes appeared in the doorway and sailed over to their table. Hair wisped out from her braid and she was flushed. She had somehow managed to get a smudge of flour on her face, which she wore as a badge of honor.

"Goodness." She plopped down in one of the empty chairs at the table. "We've been busy in the kitchen. I see you got stuck, Mrs. Fairchild, and as soon as I finish downstairs, I'll get you settled. Mrs. Pendergast says you're a

91

caterer and that you made the dinner tonight. It certainly was delicious."

Faith hastened to enlighten them that her sole contribution had been a bit of seasoning, but she had a sinking feeling that she was destined to go down in the culinary annals of Hubbard House as the Pink Lady who made the good chicken à la king.

"If you're busy, I can show Mrs. Fairchild where she can stay," Julia offered.

"That's all right, dear, I have time. I'll just pop back downstairs, and why don't you meet me in the living room in half an hour?"

"Thank you, it's very kind of you," Faith said, wondering if she was expected to go to bed at eight o'clock.

After dinner there was general movement toward the living room and library. Some residents were starting bridge games and one group spread out a Scrabble board with evident familiarity and gusto. Faith made it a point to avoid any and all such activities, much to the disappointment of her husband, who had been raised on Monopoly tournaments and every form of cards known to man. Faith when pressed would play poker, but the line was drawn on anything else.

She looked over the shelves of the library to find something that would help her pass the time yet not keep her awake. She quickly eliminated *Remembrance of Things Past* and *Buddenbrooks*, books she really would read someday, and took down an Agatha Christie she'd already read instead. She could never remember them very well, but there would be enough familiarity so the suspense wouldn't keep her awake.

Leandra was not in the living room yet and Julia Cabot appeared with a small satchel.

"I thought you might like to borrow a nightgown and other sundries," she said.

"Thank you," said Faith delightedly. "I was wondering if I would have to sleep in my skivvies. This is so thoughtful of you." The two sat down on one of the window seats overlooking the garden. It was impossible to see anything except the whirling snow.

It occurred to Faith that Julia was a good source of information, and if Chat was right—that Eddie or someone else was bilking the residents in some sort of plausible scam—it might be that the Cabots had been approached. How to phrase it?

"Julia, have you ever noticed anything around here, well, that struck you as not quite right? That someone might be on the take, so to speak?" Faith was about to elaborate when Julia turned to her wide-eyed.

"How did you find out? Don't tell me she's stolen something from you too!"

This was a new wrinkle. "Stolen" and "she"? Faith quickly revised her previous scenario and switched from suspicions of Eddie, Charmaine, or who knew who else trying to pluck the sophisticated chickens at Hubbard House to a soon-to-be-revealed (she hoped) pilferer. All those trinkets from Firestone and Parson's carelessly strewn on the tops of all those mahogany dressers. She should have thought of theft in the first place.

"I haven't lost anything, but someone I know may have." That was a fair assumption to make. Howard might have been a victim.

They were virtually alone in the secluded window seat, but Julia lowered her soft voice ever further. "Ellery and I have discussed it many times. It is a sickness, of course, and I believe both Dr. Hubbard and Muriel are aware of it. At least that's what Mrs. Davidson—she's over there in the blue dress playing bridge—told me."

So the Hubbards knew and they weren't doing anything about it! This seemed to be a bit excessive shielding of one's own, as well as an exceedingly broadminded view of crime.

"It's been very well established that kleptomania is a psychological disorder," Julia continued.

"Kleptomania!" Faith exclaimed. "Oh dear, I don't think we're talking about the same thing." It wasn't going to be so neatly solved after all.

Julia looked at her straight in the eye. "I'm talking about Leandra." She obviously expected Faith to follow suit when the appearance of the lady in question put an abrupt stop to the conversation.

"Oh, there you are, Mrs. Fairchild. I did say the living room, I believe, but you may not know your way around here very well yet."

Julia Cabot gave Faith an unmistakably piercing look. "Oh, I'd say Mrs. Fairchild is learning quite a lot about Hubbard House, Leandra."

"Thank you again," Faith said hurriedly, and followed Leandra obediently out of the room. As they left the library and went down the hall, she noticed that Leandra carried a handbag the size of a steamer trunk. She fervently hoped it had only rolls in it tonight.

Leandra's problem must be a well-kept secret. If Bootsie Brennan ever found out that Leandra was lifting the teaspoons, she'd be on the phone to Norma Nathan and every other gossip columnist of her ilk in an instant. One of Dr. Hubbard's pillars would be turned to salt in no time flat. Faith shuddered. Poor Leandra.

Poor Leandra was happily leading the way into one of the original houses, Deborah's—the one with Doctor Hubbard's office and the family living quarters. They walked up the imposing double staircase with the Palladian window at the landing. A large antique brass chandelier, suspended from the ceiling, reflected softly in the dark glass. At the top of the stairs, Leandra turned right and opened a door at the end of the hall.

"This is our guest suite." She forged ahead and switched on the lights. It was a spacious room in the front of the house with the kind of four-poster bed that's so high off the floor, you need a little flight of stairs to get into it. The bed was hung with heavy chintz draperies that matched the ones at the window. A quilt appliquéd with birds and flowers in the same colors served as a bedspread. The rest of the furniture was determinedly Victorian and also giant sized—a marble-topped bureau, a dressing table, an armoire big enough to conceal a dozen lovers, and a night table with the room's one and only lamp. The ceiling fixture cast an uncertain glow into the shadowy corners.

"The bathroom's in there." Leandra flung her arm toward a closed door. "Now I'm sure you must be tired, so I'll leave you. See you at breakfast."

Faith managed to say an appropriate thank you before the door closed firmly. She sat down in a low-slung velvet-covered chair by the window, but got right up again and pressed her face against the window. The glass was freezing, and the sensation was pleasant for a moment. If anything, the snow was coming down harder. She felt like Jane Eyre. It had been a day abounding with tragic heroines. She missed Tom. She missed Ben.

She looked at her watch. Eight thirty. It was going to be a long night.

Julia had put a nightgown, robe, soap, new toothbrush, toothpaste, flashlight, and comb into the bag. Faith was still wearing the slippers and gave a belated thought to the whereabouts of her shoes. It was too early to get ready for bed, though. She opened the bathroom door. The room was tiny—it might have been a closet in another life—but it had all the essentials. She climbed up on the bed and stretched out on top of the spread. The mattress was lumpy. The princess and the pea. She turned on the bedside light and grabbed *The Mysterious Affair at Styles*. Enough pathos and time for some good old-fashioned foul play.

By page six she was asleep, and when she woke up it was past eleven o'clock. She felt curiously relieved. Now she could get up, change, go back to sleep, and head for home by the dawn's early light. Even if she had to snowshoe.

Faith put on the gown and the robe—Vanity Fair, and while not screaming sultry seduction, it did indicate an interest in nightwear other than flannel. She brushed her teeth and went over to the door to the hall, opening it a crack. The only light was coming from the large window. There wasn't a sound anywhere, and all Hubbard House seemed to have settled down for a long winter's nap. She looked back at the bedroom windows. The storm had stopped and the wind died down. The unsullied snow glistened in the moonlight. It looked like the inside of one of those glass snow domes before a child turns it upside down. She closed the door and walked toward the bed.

She could climb in and go to sleep—or she could take the flashlight Julia had thoughtfully provided in case of a power failure and take a look around. She picked up the flashlight and sat down to wait until one o'clock. It was what she had intended ever since Leandra had led her up the stairs.

She almost fell asleep again, but kept herself awake by wondering what she was looking for. Of course Howard could have seen Leandra take something, yet Faith suspected this was one of those in-house secrets. All the residents probably knew about it and simply dropped in on Leandra for a cup of tea and to retrieve whatever knick-knack they were missing. The big thing would be to keep it from the Auxiliary. It seemed even Hubbard House had its internecine feuds—just like the parish.

The grandfather clock outside Dr. Hubbard's office struck a single chime and Faith turned off all the lights in her room and crept out the door and down the stairs. Everyone was sure to be asleep by now. The moon was so bright, she didn't need the flashlight and slipped it in the pocket of the bathrobe.

If she remembered correctly from Sylvia's tour, the family apartments and residents' rooms were at the rear. She had already decided that she should start by having a closer look at the offices of both Dr. Hubbards.

Donald's was locked. If she was going to stay in this line of work, she'd have to get some rudimentary instruction in lock picking. You were supposed to be able to open anything with a credit card these days, but it might not be true for older locks. The problem was finding someone to show her how. Aleford adult education tended to run to courses in patchwork and chair caning.

She crossed back to the other side of the foyer. There didn't seem to be any light coming from under Dr. Hubbard's door, but just in case he was in there catching up on his paperwork, she'd have to have a plausible excuse for barging in. Sleepwalking? A bit farfetched. And she knew where the kitchen was, so she couldn't say she was feeling peckish. It would have to be the old headache routine. Desperately seeking aspirin.

Dr. Hubbard was not at his desk or anywhere else in his office. It too was lit by the moonlight streaming through the long windows. She closed the door, stepped in, and turned on the flashlight. A glance at his desktop offered nothing more interesting than a stack of thank-you letters to contributors at the Holly Ball. The drawers were similarly unrevealing, except for the fact that the good doctor had a sweet tooth and keep a cache of Good & Plentys in the lower left side.

There were several wooden file cabinets against one wall, and Faith turned her attention to those. Two were locked and a third was filled with old medical journals. The fourth contained folders, and a glance at the first few indicated that they were resident records. If the cabinet wasn't locked, they couldn't be confidential, Faith reasoned with more than a twinge of guilt. She picked one at random. It belonged to a couple named Ross and contained nothing except a sheet with names to call in an emergency, the length of time they had been at Hubbard House, and a fee schedule. The others all seemed to be the same. The rest of the file drawers were empty. She was beginning to consider going back to bed.

Dr. Hubbard's diplomas hung in a line on one wall. There was a portrait—of his wife, Faith presumed—over the fireplace, and next to the door was a large photo of Hubbard House. She went over to take a closer look. A much younger Dr. Hubbard stood on the porch in front of the main entrance with his arm around his wife. She was tiny and looked quite frail. Several children were sitting on the top stair with urns of geraniums flanking them. Everyone was smiling. She took it down and brought it over to the window for a closer look. It was easy to recognize Muriel. She had the same hairdo and seemed not to have changed at all. It was harder to recognize Donald. He was pudgy and must have moved slightly when the camera clicked, so his face was out of focus. There was a third child, a boy, between them. She turned the picture over. Someone had inscribed it in a neat copperplate: "Hubbard House Opening Day May 15, 1964," then underneath, "Standing: Dr. Roland Whittemore Hubbard and wife, Mary Howell Hubbard. Sitting, L to R: Muriel Elizabeth Hubbard, age fifteen, James Howell Hubbard, age five, Donald Whittemore Hubbard, age eleven."

James Howell Hubbard? Another child? Why hadn't anyone mentioned him, Faith wondered. Where was he now? He'd be around thirty, around her age in fact. Surely if he was a member of the family in good standing, he would either have been at the Holly Ball or have been mentioned. My beloved son. Unless he wasn't so beloved or unless he was dead. But if he had died, someone along the line would have mentioned it. Aleford was big on tragedy. Charley would have told her that first day in the Minuteman Café, speaking in hushed tones and talking about what a damned shame it was. No, Faith was convinced. James was someone people didn't talk about, and finding out why was the first solid lead she'd had since meeting Eddie Russell. Eddie Russell, who was about the same age as James.

She carefully put the picture back on the wall and

looked around to see if there were any more revealing family portraits. She opened the one closet in the room. It was filled with folding chairs, stacks of books, and several musty old jackets and coats. Things seemed to have been shoved in with little regard for order. She was beginning to realize that much of New England was like that—tidy on the surface, but when the closet door opened and the contents came tumbling out, watch out.

But Faith was happy with her discovery. It almost made having to spend the night worthwhile. She turned out the flashlight and prepared to go to her well-deserved rest. As she opened the door, she heard a sound from the direction of the stairs and darted back. Someone else was up.

She ducked into the closet in case it was Dr. Hubbard and waited. Nothing happened. After what she judged to have been ten minutes—she'd left her watch next to the sink upstairs—she tried again. No noises this time, and she crept quietly to the bottom of the stairs. She had her headache story in case she ran into anybody there. It would have been harder to explain why she was coming out of Dr. Hubbard's office.

She heard more noises at the end of the hall upstairs and slipped into her room in relief. It looked like a busy night at Hubbard House. She took off her robe and decided not to turn on the light in case it shone beneath the door. She didn't want any insomniac visitors asking her why she was up too. She crawled up the stepladder, slid beneath the icy sheets, and reached over to the other side of the bed to pull the covers closer.

But instead of the quilted spread, her hand touched flesh. Wet flesh.

She screamed and turned on the light. Her hand was covered with blood, and lying beside her where he had no doubt dreamed of being was Eddie Russell.

Only Eddie wasn't going to get any action tonight or ever.

Eddie was dead.

6

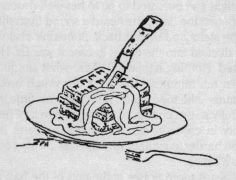

Faith screamed again. Eddie's wrists were bound to the bedpost behind his head with a black silk cord, and his ankles were tied together with more of the same. In between, his body was bare except for two knives sticking straight up—one from his throat and one from his chest. The brass trim on the handles picked up the light and glittered menacingly. Blood had seeped out around each wound and dripped onto the spread.

She jumped out of the bed, nearly breaking an ankle in the precipitous descent, and raced for the door. She was down the stairs before she paused to think what to do first.

Eddie had been murdered—and recently. Whoever had done it was still under Hubbard House's roof someplace, unless he or she had left by dogsled. No one had responded to her screams, which meant either she hadn't been heard or someone didn't want to be noticed. Faith shook her head to drive away the feeling of faintness and disbelief that threatened suddenly to overwhelm her.

This couldn't be happening.

She went back into Dr. Hubbard's office and called Charley MacIsaac, trying to keep her eyes from the blood on her right hand. She let the phone ring, and finally he answered in the tone of someone who had planned to sleep until spring. As soon as she explained what had happened, he was fully awake.

"Now, Faith, you go get Roland and don't move from his side. The two of you sit outside that door until you see me or someone else from the police. I'll be there as soon as I can. No nosing around. When you hang up, just go straight to Roland. You'll be safe with him."

Faith hung up. What did Charley think? She had had no desire to join Eddie while he was alive and considerably less now that he was dead. She wanted to scream again at the thought of the dead body lying next to her in bed.

She went to the rear of the house and, by opening several doors, came across what was obviously a living room. There was a closed door to one side, and she guessed this must be Dr. Hubbard's bedroom. She walked across the room and knocked loudly. She was shivering without the bathrobe, and the cold winter light coming through the windows was like a shower of ice. She knocked again and heard someone stir.

"Dr. Hubbard," she called, opening the door a crack, "Dr. Hubbard, it's Faith Fairchild, and I'm afraid there's been an accident."

Roland Hubbard appeared at the door. He was wearing a flannel nightshirt and struggling into a voluminous navy-blue bathrobe.

"What's happened?" he asked briskly, not at all drowsy. Faith imagined doctors must be used to waking up in a state of complete alertness. Like mothers.

"Eddie Russell is dead. He's been murdered. I've called the police and they'll be here soon."

"What!"

Faith could understand his expression of total bewilderment. She felt that way herself.

She repeated herself. "Eddie Russell is dead. He's been murdered. I called the chief of police in Aleford and someone will be here as soon as possible. Chief MacIsaac said we were to sit outside the door and wait."

"What door?" he asked.

Faith felt foolish. Of course, "What door?"

"The door to the guest room in the front of the house upstairs." This was getting trickier. She was going to have to use the aspirin ploy after all. "Actually, I was sleeping there—my car went into a snowbank and I had to spend the night here. I woke up with a headache and left the room to try to find some aspirin."

"You mean the body is in your bed?"

"Well, yes. But I wasn't." Faith took Dr. Hubbard's arm and steered him toward the door. "I think we'd better get upstairs. I can explain while we wait." Although there really wasn't anything more to explain—at least not to Dr. Hubbard.

As they were about to enter the corridor, Faith glanced at her hand.

"I've got to wash this off—and maybe you could find me a blanket. I'm freezing."

"Of course, of course." Roland was all business and soon the damnéd spot was washed away—though not the memory of the location—and Faith was bundled up in a heavy Hudson's Bay blanket.

They reached the door of the guest room and Roland stretched his hand out toward the ornate brass knob.

"Chief MacIsaac said we weren't to go back in the room, just sit outside." He hadn't exactly said so, but after two other murder investigations Faith knew what they liked you to do. Stay put and don't touch.

They sat side by side companionably on the floor with their backs against the thick door. Faith hoped whoever was coming wouldn't be long. It wasn't that the position was so uncomfortable. She had no wish to get back into bed, but it was a challenge to all her social skills to come up with adequate small talk. The one question she wanted to ask besides the obvious "Who killed Eddie?" was "So, Dr. Hubbard, what's the story with your son James?" and that hardly seemed appropriate. In the end, it was Roland who broke the silence.

"I've known Edsel Russell since he was a boy. He's always had his problems, but I can't believe he's come to the end of his life in this manner. He had a decent, hard-working mother who married the wrong man. Oh, Stanley was good-looking—like Eddie—and had a lot of flash." Dr. Hubbard sounded so bitter that Faith wondered if he had been one of Mrs. Russell's rejected suitors. "Those two boys never really had a father. Even before he abandoned the family, he was always off someplace on various dubious get-rich-quick schemes." The bitter tone in Dr. Hubbard's voice had distilled into acid. "Stanley Junior, the older one, went into the service. He's been all right, but Eddie never found his feet, and the tragedy is he had so much influence on other, weaker people he came into contact with." His voice changed and now he sounded tired. He paused a moment. "I like to think his work here had changed all that, and we had no complaints. I don't suppose it could have been suicide? Although he wasn't despondent to my knowledge."

Evidently wishful thinking, and Faith was sorry to disappoint him. It wasn't going to be pleasant, or good for public relations, to have a full-scale murder investigation at Hubbard House. She pictured the knives sticking straight up like soldiers at attention from Eddie's body.

"It wasn't suicide, Dr. Hubbard."

He was silent after that. They heard the clock strike

two. Was it only an hour since she had crept down the stairs to conduct her investigation?

"Well, Mrs. Fairchild, with this storm, we could be here a fair amount of time. You start with your life story and I'll tell you mine."

Faith would have preferred that he go first, but he was right. They were going to be waiting a while, and she obediently sketched in the salient details of her life to date. He was very interested in all the clergy in her family. It led to a lengthy digression on his part concerning his maternal grandfather, who was a Congregationalist minister in western Massachusetts, and Roland's boyhood days in the Berkshires. Faith was trying to move him along when they heard someone pounding vigorously at the front door.

"It must be the police, and the door is locked," Dr. Hubbard said.

"I'll be all right here. You go and let them in." Faith wasn't altogether sure that he wouldn't take advantage of her absence to nip into the room for a quick look.

It didn't take long, and a few minutes later she heard him say, "Up here" and then there were footsteps on the stairs. One pair was reverberating throughout the house. Faith closed her eyes. When she opened them, an enormous figure—dwarfing Dr. Hubbard, who stood respectfully to one side—loomed over her. She was right. It was him again.

"Aren't we getting a little long in the tooth to be a candy striper, Mrs. Fairchild?" It was Detective Lieutenant John Dunne of the state police.

John Dunne hated being called out at night—especially winter nights—and Faith Fairchild was the last thing he needed in an investigation that had already gotten him ticked off before he'd even started.

"Why, Detective Dunne. This is a surprise. I didn't know Charley was calling you."

"He did. Now, if you'll kindly step aside. I presume the victim is in here."

He entered the room followed by a younger—and smaller—man also in plain clothes carrying a camera and a large briefcase. Dunne came out soon after.

"I understand the name of the deceased is Edsel Russell and that he was in your employ, Dr. Hubbard?"

"Yes, he was the head of buildings and grounds. He's been working here for two years."

They were interrupted by the arrival of several more police officers—two in uniform hovering over a frail man wearing a badge pinned crookedly onto his down parka. He looked to be in his late eighties and had a woolen watch cap pulled over his ears. Erratic tufts of white hair on his cheeks and chin indicated he had missed the same spots while shaving for several months. He was walking slowly and careened first toward one wall, then the other. He stopped in front of them, took off his gold wire-rimmed glasses, which had fogged over, wiped them carefully on a large white handkerchief pulled from a pocket, replaced them, and put out his hand to Dr. Hubbard.

"Bad business, Roland. They tell me young Russell is dead. Very bad business. Probably a vagrant driven in by the storm. Seen anybody like that about?"

Who could this possibly be? Faith wondered. It had to be a mistake.

It wasn't. It was Francis Coffin, Byford's venerable chief of police.

"No, no strangers around." Dr. Hubbard looked at Faith. "Mrs. Fairchild here is not a resident but a volunteer stranded by the storm. She was sleeping in the room."

"And didn't notice anything? Young woman, you must be a sound sleeper indeed."

"I wasn't in the room when the murder took place." Faith hastened to correct any possible impression that she might be the most likely to perpetrate.

John Dunne was getting impatient. Francis Coffin was the reason Charley MacIsaac had called him. Francis Coffin was the reason he wasn't home lying next to his wife under an emperor-sized down comforter.

Dunne was from the Bronx and had moved to this alien territory to please his wife. She was from Maine—up near the Canadian border—but she knew she could push him only so far from his native turf. When Charley had called to tell him there was a problem in Byford, a murder no less, Dunne had moved heaven and earth to get there before the locals. Quaint, picturesque, whatever, but Francis should be in a rocker at Hubbard House, not investigating a murder there. Dunne found it typical of New England that the residents of Byford insisted Coffin keep his post, never thinking about what this might mean for their own health and well-being, just because he'd been there for fifty years. Francis Coffin was a living legend, with an increasing likelihood of the legend part overtaking the living.

Dunne took charge. No one objected.

"Dr. Hubbard, the state police are cooperating with the Byford police in this matter, and a crime prevention and control unit from the district attorney's office will be joining us soon. I'd like to wake the residents in turn, starting with this section. Is there a room we can use for questioning?"

"Certainly. You may use my office downstairs if you like."

"I'll start with Mrs. Fairchild, and perhaps one of the officers here could drive her home afterward." He looked at her sternly. Sure, thought Faith, find out what I know, then pack me off. She was used to Dunne's ways. It hadn't stopped her before.

"I'll show you my office, then. Francis?" Dr. Hubbard stepped forward, but Chief Coffin didn't follow.

"I haven't seen the body yet, man. Can't start asking questions until I've seen what happened." He rubbed his hands together. Francis enjoyed being a cop. Retirement wouldn't have been any fun. Not that much ever happened in Byford, but whatever did came his way.

Dunne had been afraid of this. If he let the old codger in, they'd have his prints—along with Faith's—to eliminate from everything.

"Detective Sullivan is going over the room now, and the CPAC guys will be here soon with the medical examiner, Frank. I'd appreciate it if you would come with me and assist, since your knowledge of the local scene is so much more extensive than mine." It might work.

Faith caught his eye. Dunne couldn't help a slight grimace, which on his very much less than handsome face contorted the expression into death throes. She took it for what it was and did her part.

"If there is some way of getting me home, I would appreciate it very much." And she would. She was struck with a longing for the parsonage, Tom, Ben, and her own safe, warm bed, for which she didn't need a ladder.

Her words got them moving. Dunne took the hall in two strides and was quickly out of sight while the rest straggled on behind Chief Coffin. Roland sprinted ahead to lead the detective to the office.

The clock struck three as they descended the stairs. Time was creeping by.

Faith felt a bit odd upon entering the room she had so recently been casing. All the lights were turned on and it was full of people now.

"Would you like to question Mrs. Pendergast, our cook, after Mrs. Fairchild? She too was forced to spend the night here and is in another room upstairs. When you are finished, she could provide us with some coffee."

Dunne looked at Dr. Hubbard gratefully. This must be why everybody thought he walked on water.

"Great idea. Perhaps one of your guys would like to go with him, Frank."

"I'm sure the good doctor knows the way, Johnny," Chief Coffin said, and smiled at Roland.

Detective Dunne gritted his teeth, whether at being

called Johnny or Coffin's ineptitude Faith couldn't be sure. Probably both.

One of the Byford officers stepped into the breach. "I'll go, Chief. No problem." He ambled out with the doctor. They were used to scenes like this.

Dunne sat down at the desk and Faith took one of the chairs in front. But this was no doctor-patient consultation.

"Now, Mrs. Fairchild. Faith," he said wearily. "What are you doing here?"

"There's a flu epidemic and most of the kitchen staff is out sick. I'm helping for a few weeks. When I left today, my car went off the road and I had to come back and spend the night." She looked him straight in the eye. Had Charley told him about Howard Perkins' letter?

Charley hadn't taken the time, but had said that Faith was over at Hubbard House snooping around like usual. Dunne looked straight back at Faith.

"I'm sure you are anxious to get home after the shock you've been through. I'll be by in the morning to talk to you further."

So he did know, Faith guessed, but didn't want the others to know. Francis looked like a babbler.

"However, I do need a few more facts. What time was it when you left your room and how long were you gone? And"—it seemed to have occurred to him suddenly—"where were you going?"

"I woke up with a headache"—Faith was almost beginning to believe this herself—"and went to find some aspirin. I heard the clock strike one just before I left my room. I came downstairs to see if by chance Dr. Hubbard or someone else was still up, but there was no one around. I was probably gone no longer than thirty minutes."

She saw Dunne lift an eyebrow. It was one of his endearing gestures.

"Thirty minutes to find an aspirin?"

"Well, I'm not sure of my way around yet," she demurred.

"I'll bet." He jotted something down. "Then you came back to your room, and tell us please exactly what you saw."

"I couldn't see anything. The room was dark."

"You didn't turn on the light?" he interrupted.

Faith flushed slightly, "No, I didn't want to disturb anyone."

"I see."

"Besides, there was so much light from the windows, I didn't need a light. I got into bed and reached over to pull the blanket closer."

She shuddered. "Only I touched Eddie's neck instead. My hand was wet. Then I did turn the light on and I saw the blood and the knives and I think I screamed. I jumped out of bed and I know I screamed. Then I ran downstairs, called Charley, and went to get Dr. Hubbard."

"Was the door open or closed when you went back upstairs the first time?"

"It was closed. And I had closed it when I left."

Dunne wrote some more. "Was there anything else you noticed? Take your time."

Faith thought. "I did think I heard someone in the hall when I was downstairs shortly before I went back to my room, and again upstairs in the rear of the house when I got to my door," she reported.

Dunne started to ask something, paused, and seemed to reconsider. He stood up without asking anything further.

"I will need you to have another look at the room." He meant the body and Faith knew it. "We have to be sure nothing was apparently moved during the time you were away from the door."

They went up the stairs. Faith felt like a small rowboat being guided down the Hudson by Big Toot. Dunne knocked at the door and Detective Sullivan answered.

"Just about finished here, John. And the others should be here any moment. No forced entry at the window and nothing odd. Some women's clothes in the closet. His are on the floor next to the bed."

"The clothes in the closet are mine," Faith said, glad she had been tidy. Old admonitions about clean underwear and not using safety pins to hold up your hem came floating back incongruously into her head.

Dunne ushered her into the room. "We'll go over this later, Ted. For now, I want Mrs. Fairchild to tell us if she notices whether anything has been disturbed."

"I didn't really see much," she said.

"I know. Take a quick look at Eddie and tell me if somebody's been here."

Faith did. He looked garishly white in the dim light in the room. The two knives were still standing stiffly erect. The black bondage cords looked tight enough to cut off his circulation—if he'd had any. His eyes were closed and his lips parted. His face looked exactly the same as it had when they had danced together briefly at the Holly Ball.

"Nothing's been changed that I can see," she told them.

"Okay, take a look in the bathroom."

Faith walked across the room and looked in.

"One of the towels is gone," she said immediately. "There were two on the rack. But I didn't go in here when I came back, so it could have been taken by the murderer either the first time or while I was getting Dr. Hubbard. Probably the first time. He must have needed to wash his hands." She rubbed at the spot on her own hand so recently despoiled. "Which reminds me. I used the towel from Dr. Hubbard's bathroom to dry my hands after washing the blood off there, so you can eliminate that one."

"Good girl. Now let's get you out of here and you can tell me what's really going on tomorrow. By the way, Charley was going to call Tom."

Faith was relieved. She'd been rehearsing various ways to tell him—and they all stank.

Mrs. Pendergast and Dr. Hubbard were waiting inside

his office with the Byford police. Faith remembered Mrs. P. had come prepared to spend the night. No one at Hubbard House could have had a bathrobe of such proportions, or such style—turquoise, orange, and yellow parrots perched in a quilted jungle. She looked like an exotic tea cozy. She greeted Faith with some confusion and possibly an attempt at humor in a grim situation: "Another body? Didn't give him any of your bouillon, did you?"

"Bouillon? Another body? What's this all about?"

Before Faith had a chance to reply to John Dunne's query, Roland Hubbard spoke. "Mrs. Pendergast is a little upset—as are we all. She's referring to the unfortunate death of one of our residents of heart failure a week ago. He had been eating some of Mrs. Fairchild's delicious soup at the time he was stricken."

Dunne looked incredulous. He had half a mind to take Faith into the office and find out what she knew, but he wanted to see her alone.

"Tomorrow," he muttered, then remembered all his dear mother's chidings and held out his hand. "Thank you for your help, Mrs. Fairchild. We will be in touch."

Faith left with one of the officers, and as the door closed behind them, Francis Coffin jumped up excitedly.

"Piece of cake, eh, boys? 'Shersay the femme.' It's obvious they had a lovers' quarrel and she did him in. And what about the story about being asleep when it happened!" He began to laugh helplessly. "Did you have that soup of hers tested, Roland? Maybe we've got a typhoon Mary on our hands. Well, no need to look further. We've got the killer."

Dunne nodded his head toward Mrs. Pendergast, whose mouth had dropped open to the carpet. "Shut up, Frank. I know Mrs. Fairchild. Her husband's the minister over in Aleford and she's not a suspect at the moment. Why don't we get on with this and perhaps—Mrs. Pendergast, is it?—could make a pot of coffee?" He'd had it with the niceties, and he knew Chief Coffin wouldn't even notice the difference.

"Don't see what a minister husband has to do with it. Their wives are just like anybody's else's. Put their pants on one leg at a time."

Dunne was trying very hard not to listen. It crossed his mind that he might have a difficult time conducting the investigation with Coffin in the same room, since at the moment he was ready to throw the chief up against the wall and listen happily to the sound of all his brittle bones breaking. One of the officers from Byford picked up on the mood. It wasn't hard.

"Chief, maybe the lieutenant could spare us for a minute and we could get a few winks out in the living room. I know I could use them, and we're going to have a lot to do in the morning."

Dunne made a mental note of the man's name. He definitely deserved a promotion.

Faith felt like a schoolgirl as she drove home through the chill winter night in the Byford squad car. And tomorrow's detention was one she wasn't going to get out of no matter how many apples she brought the teacher.

They passed the spot where she had gone off the road and she pointed her car out to the officer, who told her he would get someone to take care of it the next day. She continued to think about what she would tell and not tell John Dunne in the morning. She knew it would be morning and as early as he could get there. She'd gotten to know him very well during what she chose to remember as the time she'd solved the case of Cindy Shepherd's murder with some help from the police. It was unlikely that this was how Dunne characterized the events.

Faith walked through the snow up the front path, or where she knew the path to be. The snow was piled high against the storm door and she tugged valiantly trying to get it open. Just as she was considering going around to the back, where the door was sheltered by a small porch, the tiny opening she'd achieved was widened by a mighty shove from inside. The Maine balsam wreath her friends from Sanpere, the Fraziers, had sent went flying off into the snow-covered bushes.

Tom. He was up. Granted, it was a rare husband who could sleep after learning that his wife had been about to spend the night with a corpse.

She was a little apprehensive. He might be annoyed, but she also knew he'd be so glad to see her that the annoyance would melt at contact.

"Faith! Are you all right! What in hell is going on!"

She was right—it was all mixed up together and she was in his arms for a long minute before he remembered to be upset again.

"Faith . . ."

"I know what you're going to say and I'm as shocked and upset as you are. Let's go to bed and I'll tell you all about it, if I can keep awake. Besides, I've never been so cold in my life."

Faith had been able to supplement Julia Cabot's nightgown and the blanket with her own parka, which she had found in the coat closet off the living room together with her shoes, but it was not enough. Something like what Admiral Byrd and his men had worn would have been a closer approximation.

At last nestled snuggly in their not-so-wee little bed, she found the more she talked, the wider awake she got. It was Tom who began to nod off.

"So you see, I'm not in any danger. Nobody except the Cabots and Leandra Rhodes knew I was sleeping in that room. Perhaps some of the people I saw at dinner assumed so, since it was the guest room, but they wouldn't have known for sure. Which means that I wasn't the intended victim, unless Leandra's kleptomania transforms itself into other aberrations."

"Leandra's what?" Light was beginning to streak in the

113

window, and Tom realized he wasn't going to get any sleep. Maybe Faith would make waffles.

Faith told him about her conversation with Julia Cabot and moved on.

"Let's assume Eddie was the right person in the wrong spot—I'm sure the murderer would have preferred the body not be found so soon—what was Eddie doing there and why two knives?"

"The what he was doing there is pretty obvious, don't you think? A tryst or whatever scumbags like Eddie call it. A quickie?"

"Yes. It must have been a quickie, because he was on top of the spread. He didn't want to mess up the bedding so someone would notice later. He probably used that room a lot. I hadn't gotten into the bed yet, so nothing was disturbed, and my clothes were out of sight in the closet."

She remembered her purse was in the closet too and gave a thought to the contents, realizing that it was being gone over carefully and labeled exhibit something. She didn't think there was anything more incriminating than a Mass Millions ticket and a few cosmetics, which might suggest her natural look wasn't entirely due to the amount of time she seemed to be spending outdoors lately. She carried a knife, but it was the Swiss Army variety and not the kind sticking out of Eddie's chest and larynx.

"To be more precise, the question is why was he doing his kinky number there in the Hubbard House guest room and not in his own place or a motel in Danvers? The storm would have kept him off the roads, but his apartment was right there."

Tom mumbled something in reply. He was dozing off.

Faith sat up abruptly. "I can't sleep after all, Tom. Besides, Ben will be up soon." They had been trying to put Benjamin on a more humane schedule, but no matter what time he went to sleep, he was still up with the chickens. Faith had given a passing thought to leaving out a bowl of cereal or some yogurt in his room next to his toys, but quickly abandoned it as she pictured the havoc a two-and-a-half-year-old could wreak on a house whilst his parents slumbered blissfully unaware.

Tom sighed. "I'll get up with you. In any case, our friend John should be dropping by soon too."

Faith had told Tom about Detective Lieutenant Dunne, and Tom was pleased the detective was assigned to the case. Francis Coffin's reputation was not unknown in Aleford.

"I'll make some waffles. Put Dunne in a good mood."

"It will put me in a good mood," Tom said. Then, as he watched Faith pull her nightgown up over her head, added, "And speaking of moods . . ."

There was the patter of little feet in the hall.

"Damn. I swear that child is psychic."

"Really, Reverend Fairchild, I didn't know you believed in the supernatural. Anyway, I'll give you a raincheck. Ben does sleep sometimes."

The Fairchilds were sitting down to waffles with blueberry syrup when the front doorbell rang.

"I'll go, Faith, and this isn't like the other time. We tell Dunne everything. Not that we know much."

Not that you know much, Faith said to herself, but she had no intention of holding out on John Dunne. There wasn't any point, except for the fun of it, and that seemed a bit immoral.

Dunne walked into the kitchen, rubbing his hands together. Faith expected to see sparks. His dark curly hair had a few more strands of gray than the last time she'd seen him—he was in his early forties now—but otherwise he appeared much the same. He'd bowed to the season and traded his Burberry for an elegant, three-quarter-length dark-brown shearling—much like the one Faith was giving Tom for Christmas. He was wearing a well-cut Harris tweed jacket underneath and an old school tie far from De Witt Clinton in the Bronx, where Faith happened to know he'd prepped. She'd often wondered where he got his taste for elegant attire and decided it must be due to his size. If one was going to cut such a large figure, let it be in style. Besides, looking at his clothes kept people from looking at his face.

The Fairchilds had become close to Dunne during the investigation of Cindy Shepherd's murder. Faith felt an odd sense of kinship with this fellow New Yorker who also admitted to being still homesick after all these years, although it was corned beef, egg creams, and Orchard Beach he longed for. Faith liked a good egg cream herself and headed straight for the Carnegie Deli and corned beef sandwiches whenever she was in town, but she had a few more items—all located on the isle of Manhattan—on her list. She liked to think they were things such as the Metropolitan Museum, Lincoln Center, and MOMA. In reality she often skipped a visit to these venerable institutions in favor of a quick trip to Bloomie's, Balducci's, and friends' galleries in SoHo or NoHo, or a few on Madison.

"Just what I had in mind. Breakfast." Dunne sat down at the table and had the grace to grin. "You can tell me everything while I eat. And you do make the best coffee I've ever had."

"Is that a hint?"

"Yes, even though I've consumed several gallons of Mrs. Pendergast's brew in the last couple of hours."

Faith put a gigantic stack of waffles on a plate and poured him a cup of coffee. She settled down across from him. Ben had finished his waffles and was trying unsuccessfully to engage the detective's attention by waving his syrup-covered hands at him. Tom took a last mouthful, scooped his son up, and took him out of the room.

"All right," Faith said. "But if I tell you everything I know, will you tell me everything you know?"

"Probably not."

"Oh."

"Do I have to remind you that this is a murder investigation, not a game, Mrs. Fairchild?" Dunne assumed Faith had had enough of semiprofessional sleuthing after coming perilously close to being a victim the last time. Apparently not.

"Don't worry, even if you won't share, I will."

Faith started with Chat's call and Howard Perkins' letter, then described how she had started working at Hubbard House and Farley Bowditch's death. She finished up with her impressions of various family members, Hubbard House residents, and Eddie Russell from the Holly Ball.

"Do you think there's any possibility that he knew you were sleeping in the guest room and was waiting for you?"

This had not occurred to Faith and she swiftly considered it.

"Somehow I don't think so. I hadn't gotten into bed, so unless he opened the closet and saw my clothes, he would not have known I was there. The room would have appeared unoccupied. And I didn't see him again after he came into the kitchen for coffee at around ten o'clock in the morning. No, I think he *was* waiting for someone, but not me. Besides, he couldn't have tied himself up."

"True, it would have been quite a trick, yet we can't rule any of this out completely." John paused and polished off the stack of waffles in a few bites. His teeth looked sharp and his mouth cavernous. "You still haven't told me where you went."

"I thought I might as well look around a bit so long as I was stuck there," Faith admitted. "I thought there might be something in Dr. Hubbard's or Donald's office that might help me figure out what was bothering Howard."

"So what did you turn up?"

"Not much. Donald's office was locked and Dr. Hubbard's mostly ran to vintage copies of the *New England Journal of Medicine*. I did find out there is another child, though, a son—James. He was in one of the pictures on the wall."

"Dr. Hubbard mentioned him. He's the youngest. Works in Arizona. Okay, what else?"

Faith sipped her coffee. There really wasn't anything else, except James. And Leandra Rhodes, but she didn't think the poor woman's kleptomania was relevant.

"Nothing I can think of. Now it's your turn. What do you make of it?"

"Not much, yet. The guy had a reputation with the ladies—that's clear—and he may have been involved in some other enterprises. We're running a check on him in Florida. There's nothing on his sheet here. But screwing around doesn't usually get you killed, especially with two knives."

"Maybe whoever it was wanted to make sure he was well and truly dead."

"Oh, he would have been truly dead with one at least—the one in his throat—right through the trachea to the spine, according to the M.E.'s quick and dirty first look. I haven't heard about the other one in the chest yet. Two knives may have been insurance or—"

"It could have been two people!" Faith exclaimed excitedly. "Like what was it, *Murder on the Orient Express?*"

"As I was saying, it could have been insurance, maybe two people, which is getting pretty exotic, or some kind of message—like that damn rose you found the last time."

"Was there anything special about the knives? They looked like the kind hunters use to skin their prey."

"Among other uses, yes. Puma knives—available in every Army-Navy store from here to California. Don't suppose you have any more waffles?"

"No, but I can make some more, or I have some walnut bread."

"Jam?"

Faith brought the whole loaf to the table with butter and a full jar of Have Faith damson preserves. It was easier.

John sliced off a piece and slathered it with jam and butter.

"They were all there, you know."

"Who?"

"The family. Donald came over to check on things after he'd finished at the hospital. Had a patient in bad shape. Charmaine didn't want to be alone. In case the lights went out, she said. Once they were there, they decided to spend the night. Stayed in what used to be Donald's old room on the third floor and is always kept available for him."

"Did they know I was in the guest room?"

"Muriel said she had heard something about it, but the rest said no. Mrs. Pendergast thought you were staying on the other side of the house near the Cabots." He ate his bread in a ruminative manner. Faith was reminded of a cow. A whole herd of cows. "You know, what makes it tough is that there were so many people around. Usually someone gets killed in less crowded circumstances."

It was true. There was an embarrassment of suspects.

"What about the towel? Did you find it? Was there blood on it?"

"Yeah, we found a bloody towel—five of them to be exact, mixed in with a couple of hundred others in the basement the laundry didn't pick up because of the weather. The lab will go over them, but I doubt they'll come up with much since they were with all the others and any hairs or whatever could have come from others on top of them. Not the kind of evidence the DA shouts hallelujah about. Anyway, if one matches Russell's blood type, we'll have something."

Faith was disappointed. She'd considered the towel one of her contributions to the case and pictured it hanging on somebody's towel rack or stuffed at the bottom of a closet.

"Still, those might not be the right towels," she reminded him.

"Don't worry, we haven't stopped looking."

Tom came in.

"Ben's watching 'Shining Time Station.' I get a shock every time I see Ringo Starr in that train conductor's uniform and about five inches tall, but then Ben didn't know him when. What about it—have you two solved this thing?" He sat down and sliced himself some bread.

"Not yet," John replied.

"And not 'you two.' I shouldn't have said that. As you know, my wife seems to have developed an unaccountable affinity for murder—investigations, that is—since we've been married. I like to think it's chance and not boredom."

"Probably both," Faith retorted, a bit put out at being discussed *in absentia* while sitting there.

John Dunne was looking slightly embarrassed. "Actually, Tom, one of the things I came to discuss with you and Faith was 'us two.' You see, Faith is in a position to hear a great deal. I am absolutely convinced she is in no danger, otherwise I would never suggest this. You know that. And we'll give her a wire if she likes. Everything to keep her safe and sound. But we'd like her to go back on Monday and keep her ears and eyes open. Nothing else." He looked pointedly at Faith. "We don't have much of a handle on this one, and though I hate to admit it, we need her help." The last words were dragged from him.

Tom looked incredulous—at the proposal, Dunne's admission, or both.

Faith looked thrilled.

She was going undercover.

7

Faith sat staring into the flame of the third Advent candle on the altar. Next Sunday would be Christmas. She turned to look at the rear of the church as the choir started to sing "O Come, O Come, Emmanuel." Cyle was absent, and she didn't think it was her imagination that the faces in the loft were a bit more beatific than usual. Tom's was. He'd been in a good mood ever since Cyle had called early that morning to announce a slight cold, nothing serious. She looked back at the candles. The Alliance had embroidered a special Christmas altar cloth many years ago, and the gold threads glowed against the scarlet silk in the soft light. Ropes of pine twined around large pots of white cyclamen on either side of the altar. Christmas was indeed coming.

But first there was work to do. And she didn't mean last-minute shopping. After Dunne's invitation, she'd been delighted. They'd be a team. Then his next words had quickly dispelled any thoughts of Tommy and Tuppence or Nick and Nora. Watson was what he had in mind.

"Only for a day or two and only what comes your way. We'll handle the rest. We don't want you going around asking questions or opening up people's private file cabinets in the middle of the night."

They'd talked some more. Tom was resigned and Faith felt like a woman with a misson. She'd dug out a notebook, sharpened a pencil, and gone over to Pix's, but learned nothing more than she had on Thursday. Pix was full of questions, though, not having heard about the murder. It was while talking to Pix that Faith first felt sorry for Eddie. She'd been so busy speculating, she hadn't given much thought to the victim. He'd been a lecherous creep, maybe worse, but he'd been young, full of life. She pictured him stretched out on the bed, waiting. She knew what it was he anticipated and it certainly wasn't death.

As though in answer to her inward musings, Robert Moore, today's lector, began to read the epistle from I Corinthians. Faith listened carefully and, when he got to the section about judgment, took special notice. It was a lesson she had been trying to learn for most of her life.

Therefore judge nothing before the time, until the Lord come, who both will bring to light the hidden things of darkness, and will make manifest the counsels of the hearts: and then shall every man have praise of God.

One of the Sunday-school children read the second lesson from Mark remarkably well, and the service moved on to Tom's sermon. Faith gave him almost her full attention, wiping all thoughts of Hubbard House from her mind but occasionally straying to her gift and food shopping lists. Tom had wanted to give Ben trains—electric trains. Real trains. Faith had persuaded him to consider Brio wooden ones as more age-appropriate—for Ben, that is. She still had to pick them up. And order her goose from Savenor's market. She was startled as everyone stood for the final hymn and quickly joined the singing: "Veiled in darkness Judah lay, Waiting for the promised day. . . ."

Back at the parsonage they ate a hasty lunch and Tom left to pay some calls. He was concerned about some of the elderly parishioners who hadn't been able to get to church because of the weather. Faith draped Benjamin in an apron, and the two set about making gingerbread dough. They were soon covered with flour despite the precautions, and Faith was enjoining Ben to stop eating the dough— "immediately!" He laughed mischievously and prepared to dip his finger in again. The room smelled like cinnamon and ginger. Yuletide smells. They were making the cookies to hang on the tree with bright red ribbons. If Ben kept snatching at the bowl, the branches were going to look a little sparse.

"Oh no you don't. There won't be enough for the cookies, sweetie." She lifted him off the stool and went to the counter for an apple. She put it in his hand firmly, well aware that it was not the substitute he'd had in mind. He'd heard the magic word, and an apple was definitely not a cookie. But apple it was, and he was soon munching away at it and contentedly opening cupboard doors, dragging out the pots and pans.

Faith had started to roll the dough when there was a knock at the back door. It was Cyle. If you're sick, you're supposed to stay at home, she thought grumpily. He was the last person she wanted to see.

"Hello Cyle. How are you feeling?" She tried in vain to inject some genuine caring into her voice. "Tom's not home right now. May I take a message?" That should be clear enough.

It wasn't.

Cyle walked into the kitchen uninvited and sat down

at the table. He looked terrible, although he didn't seem to exhibit any of the traditional cold symptoms—red, drippy nose, watery eyes, balled-up Kleenex in the palm. No, he looked rather as if he hadn't slept in several weeks. His face was pale and pinched with deep circles under his eyes.

"I'll wait," he said morosely.

"He could be quite a while. I can have him call you the moment he returns." Was this apparition going to encamp in her kitchen all afternoon?

"Still, I'll wait. I really need to talk to him." He lifted his eyes pathetically. Faith wasn't affected. She had the feeling that even if Cyle was terminally ill, she'd have trouble wrenching some good old-fashioned charity from her soul. He was that bad. Or she was.

"Ben and I are making cookies. You're welcome to just sit there if you want." She returned to her dough. Oh all right, she said to herself, and the better Faith asked him if he'd like a cup of coffee or tea.

"Tea. Earl Grey if you have it."

He'd want lemon too.

She brewed him a cup of tea and went about her business. Ben tried to interest Cyle in some parallel play by dumping a bag of Duplos at his feet, but Cyle wasn't interested. Ben began to make a little car with the blocks by himself, and Faith was beginning to think they'd stay fixed in their various attitudes until Tom came when Cyle said bitterly, "Women. It's hard to believe someone you've loved so much could do this."

An unhappy love affair, which was no surprise. Even though her curiosity was piqued, Faith had no desire to act as Cyle's confidante, so she said in what she hoped was a noncommittal way, "Problems, Cyle?"

"Problems! That's putting it mildly," he said angrily, and sat up straighter.

Well, I haven't done anything, you fool, Faith thought. No need to take it out on me, though this was without question the norm for this young man. Whoever happened to be nearest would get it full blast.

"You found him, didn't you? You were there Friday night."

"Eddie Russell? You mean what happened at Hubbard House?" Faith was surprised.

"Yes, Eddie—Edsel." He sneered. "What have the police been saying about it? Who do they think did it?"

"I don't think they have any idea at this point," Faith replied. This was getting interesting. "Why do you ask? Was he a friend of yours?"

"Friend! Oh yes, my friendly neighborhood black-mailer." The words poured out before he had a chance to stop them, and he looked around the kitchen quickly. Seeing only Ben, he seemed to be reassured. "What I said is in absolute confidence, Mrs. Fairchild. It's why I came to see Tom."

Faith didn't think the confidentiality of the confessional extended to ministers' wives and Cyle knew that, but she agreed it would go no further. No further than Tom, since Cyle had been planning to tell him anyway.

"Why was Eddie blackmailing you?" she asked. One never knew. He might tell.

"It was mother."

"Your mother!" Bootsie, the iron-willed Madame Alexander doll!

"I'm afraid mother was, well, indiscreet with Eddie when he first arrived to work at Hubbard House. Oh, he was good, very good. Told her he was leaving soon and how much a moment with a beautiful older woman would mean. Anyway, she tumbled." Cyle was starting to talk like a real person, Faith realized. "Of course, he had no intention of leaving. He was probably humping his way through the entire membership of the Pink Ladies and any other females around. Nice little sideline."

"And then he told her that unless she paid up, he'd tell

everyone what the head of the Auxiliary was up to," Faith guessed.

"Exactly. Mother told me all about it last night. She's frantic. She thinks the police are going to think she did it."

Bootsie or one of the other victims. It was getting harder to think of Eddie as the victim, even though he was lying on a mortuary table somewhere.

"Was she paying a lot of money?"

"Fortunately, father left us amply provided for." Stuffy Cyle had returned. "Eddie was smart enough not to bleed her. It was just a nice steady hundred here and there. Mother was actually grateful to him, she told me! Can you believe it?"

Faith could.

"You do know what she has to do, and I'm sure Tom will tell you the same thing."

"Yes, we've got to go to the police. But it's so humiliating."

Light dawned. It wasn't that Cyle was worried his mother might be up for murder one, but that she had slept with the help.

"I'm sure she won't be a suspect. No one was traveling about much on Friday night. Besides, she has you for an alibi."

"I was in town Friday night. With a friend. Mother was alone, and of course she didn't go anywhere, but there's no one to prove it. And she has a four-wheel drive Bronco for bad weather."

Leaving the Mercedes in the garage, of course. Well, Bootsie could have driven over to Hubbard House. Must have a key, and blackmail was a possible motive, yet Faith doubted the whole thing. She was pretty certain Dunne would too. Why would Bootsie Brennan jeopardize her social position for a paltry few hundred dollars, give or take? Besides, from the sound of it, she was still more than a little attracted to Edsel.

Faith gave Cyle John Dunne's number and promised

that Tom would call him as soon as she had had a chance to fill him in on the perils of Bootsie. She bundled him out the door with what she hoped was not unseemly haste and then finished her cookies. She couldn't wait to tell Tom.

Tom was home in time for supper and, in between bites of the cassoulet, which had been filling the kitchen with fragrant aromas of duck, sausage, and beans since the day before, heard Faith's tale with astonishment and amusement.

"I know I shouldn't be laughing at all this, but when I think of that woman all dressed up in her buttons and bows at the Holly Ball parading around as the queen of Hubbard House being blackmailed for a roll in the hay with the handyman, I can't help it."

"Since when have you started using euphemisms like 'roll in the hay,' Tom?"

"Since people named Bootsie entered my life."

Faith conceded the logic of that.

"If Eddie was blackmailing Bootsie, it stands to reason he was doing it to others as well, don't you think?" Tom asked.

"Yes, and it gives me something to go on tomorrow. I'll be on the lookout for furrowed foreheads. John is also going to be happy to have this lead. He seemed convinced that the murderer was someone in Hubbard House at the time, and this gives him a line to follow."

"I think I'll give Cyle a call now," Tom said, soaking up the last trace of sauce from his plate with a piece of crusty French bread. "Although I have no idea what to say. 'Sorry your mother is such a foolish and wanton woman' somehow doesn't sound very compassionate."

"You'll think of something. Just make those sympathetic murmuring noises you ministers are so good at."

"Ah yes, the murmuring noises, soon to be available on tape from your local ecclesiastical mail-order supply house."

Tom returned shortly. "I didn't get to make many

noises of any kind. Cyle was on his way out and almost cut me off. He did say they'd been in touch with Dunne and he'd come down to talk to them, so if not exactly public knowledge, at least it's police knowledge at present."

"I don't care much for Bootsie and family, but I still hope they don't find out about it at Hubbard House. She is a dynamo, and the Pink Ladies are essential to keeping the place running."

They moved into the living room and sat before a fire reading Ben his favorite books of the moment, *In the Night Kitchen* and *Katy and the Big Snow,* until he dropped off to sleep and they carried him up into the hibernal regions of the bedrooms and put him in his bed. He had forsworn his crib at the beginning of the fall in favor of an old spool bed Aunt Chat had unearthed from her attic. They kissed him good night, slid the little bars into place that would keep him from falling out, and walked back downstairs arm in arm.

"At last," said Faith.

"At last," agreed Tom.

Monday morning was sunny and cold, but the roads were clear. The Byford police had had Faith's car towed to a garage in Byford center, and Tom was driving Faith over to get it. It was parked in front.

"I'll wait to make sure everything's okay," Tom said.

"Thank you, darling. I'll go ask in the office."

It was, and she stuck her head out to tell Tom, waved good-bye as he drove off, then quickly went back in.

Scott Phelan was sitting at a battered gray metal desk leaning precariously back in the chair behind it. He had on grease-stained coveralls, and no amount of Lava soap would ever get his hands clean. He looked gorgeous.

"Nice to see you again, Mrs. Fairchild. Hear you found another body. Getting pretty good at this, aren't you?" He smiled, and for more than a fleeting moment Faith wished she didn't take her vows so seriously. Scott looked like the handsome one in Tom Cruise's family. They'd met two years ago when Scott had agreed to give Faith some information that gave one of the suspects in Cindy Shepherd's murder an alibi. She'd seen Scott several times since then at the Willow Tree Kitchen, a New England equivalent to a roadhouse—seedy, but with ruffled Priscilla curtains at the windows. Scott ate there every night and the Fairchilds went occasionally for the chowder and chili, which were excellent (in contrast to the rest of the menu and a wine list limited to two screw-top offerings—red or white).

"Still hanging out at the Willow Tree?" Faith asked.

"Yeah, but not for much longer. Trishia and I are getting married next spring."

"That's great, congratulations. She's a terrific girl." Trishia was the one who had led Faith to Scott.

Scott smiled slowly. It lit up the room. "Yeah, we're spending all our time together and I figured if we could stand each other this long, we're a pretty safe bet. She'll be graduating from Middlesex Community College over in Bedford then, so we'll have one party. Hope you can come—and the Reverend," he added after a distinct pause.

"We'd be honored."

Scott stood up and sauntered around the desk.

"Your car is fine. Not a scratch on it. You were lucky. And it started right up. We didn't even have to tow it."

"That's great."

As they headed toward the lot, it occurred to Faith that Scott might have heard something about Eddie Russell. Habitués of the Willow Tree knew most of what was going on in the area before it happened.

"Did you ever run into a guy named Eddie Russell in your travels?"

"You mean the stiff?"

"Yes. Did he come around the Willow Tree?"

"Yeah, old Edsel used to come around a lot. But not to eat. At least not lately. Wasn't good enough for him. No mixed drinks. Liked to impress the ladies."

"Well, what did he come around for then?"

"Look, Faith, think about it for a moment and then forget the whole thing. Eddie Russell was not a nice boy and he was into some pretty heavy shit."

"Drugs." As Faith said it, she mentally kicked herself for not thinking of it before. It fit so neatly into the rest of the picture. Dunne probably knew from the start. And it wasn't that she had led a particularly sheltered life.

"The man was a walking Rexall's. I asked him for Band-aids once. He didn't get it. Pretty stupid for a guy who thought he was smart—but he also got himself killed, which is about as stupid as you can get."

Faith had not regarded murder in this light, yet it made a certain amount of sense.

"So it was pretty well known that if you wanted drugs, you could get them from Eddie?"

"Everything from nose candy to weed. He wasn't a druggie himself, though. I heard him talking about some of his customers once. Thought they were complete losers. Trish and I laughed about it later. If anyone was a loser, it was Eddie."

"Why do you say that?"

"He was a type. Always wanted to be one of the big shots. But—what was he, thirty, thirty-one?—he wasn't anything but a handyman at an old people's home hustling on the side. I remember when he was first back from Florida. He was bragging about all the rich women he'd had down there. How he could have married any number of them—but you notice he didn't. A loser."

"Who do you think killed him?"

"Maybe he owed a lot of money to the wrong people and they wanted to make an example out of him. Maybe somebody's husband. Maybe somebody had just had enough of his face."

Or his blackmail, Faith speculated to herself.

"Knifed, right?" Scott said with more than a touch of relish. "You have to be pretty strong to drive a blade in—and get it in the right place."

Faith thought of the knives in Eddie's throat and chest.

"Oh, whoever it was got them in the correct places, all right."

"You mean there was more than one? Jeez, I hadn't heard that."

Something to regale the bar with after work at the Willow Tree.

"Yes, two knives. Ordinary ones, like hunting knives."

Scott reached into his pocket, produced a knife for her inspection, and flicked it open. The blade looked sharp enough to shave a peach.

"Like this?"

"Exactly."

As she drove away from the gas station, she realized how difficult it was going to be for Dunne to trace the murder weapons if virtually every male—and no doubt a fair number of females—of a particular age and background carried the same knife. She turned her attention instead to what Scott had just told her about Eddie. It provided another possible motive, but what drug dealer was going to pick the first heavy snowstorm of the year and Hubbard House, filled with people, to kill Eddie when the task could be accomplished so much more easily on a long car ride to a deserted beach, for instance? And why the whips-and-chains accoutrements? Faith hadn't thought it wise to reveal too much to Scott. The number of knives had been in one of the papers, but so far nothing had been said about the cords.

She pulled into the Hubbard House parking lot, got out, and went into the kitchen. The only alteration in her routine was that she was going to stay for lunch. Tom had grudgingly agreed to get Ben at school and take him to Lizzie's house.

"This hasn't been the merriest of Christmas seasons," he had said sadly earlier that morning.

"It will be, darling. Don't worry. I'm only going to help

for a day or so more, then we'll turn our full attention to the blazing hearth before us and sing Noël," she'd promised.

Mrs. Pendergast didn't hear Faith come in. She was running the enormous electric mixer. Faith walked over and tapped her on the elbow. She jumped a mile—or the equivalent for a woman her size.

"What are you doing creeping up like that! Most scared me to death!"

"I'm sorry, but you didn't hear me with that thing going."

Mrs. P. turned that thing off.

"I'm making a nice Lady Baltimore cake. People around here need something to lift their spirits." She looked at Faith darkly.

Faith had to protest. "Mrs. Pendergast, it wasn't my fault Eddie Russell was murdered. I just happened to be spending the night in that room. It could easily have been somebody else sleeping there. You, for example."

"Well, I stayed in my bed all night. That's all I know. And I never sleep in the guest room. It's too cold." She unbent a little. "Why don't you make up some frosting for the cake while I put this batter in to bake?"

Faith wondered if others at Hubbard House were blaming her indirectly. She supposed if she had stayed in her bed, Eddie and whoever would have seen she was there and the murderer would have canceled his plans—or pinioned Faith to the bed too for some knife-throwing practice.

It was a busy morning, and they were interrupted several times—first by Donald Hubbard, who was looking for his wife. She had been due to meet him in his office at ten o'clock.

"She's usually late," he said indulgently, "but not this late. I've already asked Muriel and some of the people Charmaine knows here. So far no one has seen her. Her car is in the parking lot, so she's around someplace."

"Did you try the Porters? She likes to go see Naomi's orchids, you know," Mrs. Pendergast offered.

"Good idea. I'll do that. Thanks, Mrs. P." Donald was in a good mood. The murder of Eddie Russell hadn't cast a pall on him. But his mood did have a thin overlay of concern, and Faith wondered whether it was totally due to the question of Charmaine's whereabouts. His next comment increased her doubts.

"I haven't had a chance to speak to you before, Mrs. Fairchild. It must have been a terrible shock for you to find poor Edsel. And then all the police interrogation."

"Of course it *was* horrible, but the police have been very kind."

"I don't suppose they've told you anything about a suspect," he said casually—too casually.

"No, I don't think there is one at the moment." She was about to ask him his opinion when Bootsie Brennan came flying through the swinging door, and he wisely beat a hasty retreat.

She left as quickly as she had come after asking what "we" were giving them for lunch today. Faith and Mrs. Pendergast looked at each other when she left and exploded in a fit of laughter.

"Someday I'm going to tell her 'we' are giving them bread and water today. Bet she says, 'That sounds yummy.' "

The next visitor was Denise. Faith hadn't seen her since the night of the Holly Ball, and the change was startling. Denise looked dreadful. She was wearing sweatpants and a worn Champion sweater under her fur coat. She didn't have any makeup on, and if her hair had been longer, it would have been unkempt. There were deep circles under her eyes, and the moment she entered the kitchen she reached into her bag and took out a cigarette. "I don't care what Roland says, I've got to have a smoke." They didn't stop her. She walked shakily over to the counter and sat down on one of the kitchen stools.

"Have you been ill? The flu?" Faith asked.

"Something like that," Denise said shortly. When she

lit her cigarette, Faith noticed her hands were unsteady and several of her nails had been bitten to the quick.

"Where's Charmaine? She was supposed to meet me here. We're having lunch. Have you seen her?"

Faith was surprised. She wouldn't have expected the two ladies to be friends.

"Donald was just here looking for her too. He went out to the Porters' cottage to see if she was there."

"Then I'll go up to his office." She stood up and swayed slightly.

"Are you sure you're all right?" Faith asked.

"I'm fine. Don't worry about me," Denise said with a flicker of her old grin.

The trays were done and Faith took her leave of Mrs. P.—Violet—and went upstairs to the dining room. Sunshine streamed in through the windows and there were yellow lilies in several large vases around the room. Sylvia Vale took care of the flowers, and Faith wondered where she'd found these gorgeous lilies in the midst of winter. The lady herself stepped through the doorway and Faith asked her.

"I really can't take any credit at all, my dear. Winston's sends me an assortment of cut flowers twice a week, and I simply put them in the containers."

People began to take their places at the tables, and Faith stood and considered which group would provide the most fodder. She settled on the Cabots. There was another couple she didn't know at the table. Two places were left. She turned to Sylvia, "Would you like to sit with me? I'm staying for lunch today. We could join the Cabots over there."

"Oh yes, how lovely—and the Porters."

So she'd be able to find out immediately if Charmaine had turned up, Faith realized.

The room was filling up rapidly. Dr. Hubbard sat at a table by the window, and Muriel joined him. She looked as imperturbable as ever and reached out to give her father's hand a reassuring pat as she sat down. Everything was proceding normally at Hubbard House—on the surface, anyway.

Mrs. P. was giving them beef pot pie today, which Faith had tried to bourguignonnize a bit by adding mushrooms, diced bacon, and wine. It wasn't too bad.

She didn't have to worry about drawing people out. Eddie Russell's death was the topic of the moment. Julia seemed particularly upset that Faith had been in the same room.

"We have a couch that makes up into a bed. I should have had you stay with us."

"Julia, please don't trouble yourself about it. Who could possibly have predicted something like this would ever happen?"

"I feel responsible too," Sylvia said. "There are any number of other places you could have slept. I don't know why Leandra took you to that old guest suite—it's so cold and drafty in the winter too. It *is* where we put our notables though," she gushed on, "and I suppose she meant it to be an honor."

Some honor, Faith thought, and stifled the urge she had to giggle or say something naughty that she had had ever since she sat down to eat with all these grown-ups.

"It is so sad," sighed Naomi Porter. "Danforth and I were very fond of Edsel. He was such a help to us in the greenhouse, carrying sacks of loam and really doing all the dirty work. It was lovely that he took such an interest in horticulture. He even had his own little section. Whenever I water his plants, I'll think of him."

Faith made a mental note to tell John Dunne to make a surreptitious raid on the Porters' greenhouse. She had a pretty good idea of what Eddie had been growing there, and it wasn't oregano.

"Be that as it may," Ellery Cabot was saying, "I hope the young man's death doesn't bring all sorts of negative publicity to Hubbard House. Let's hope the police clear it up quickly and we can go about our business."

Julia looked less sanguine. "I have a feeling finding out who killed Eddie Russell could be very complicated."

"Why do you say that?" Faith asked.

"Because he was—" The rest of Julia's words were interrupted by Denise's frenzied entrance into the dining room.

"Dr. Hubbard! Dr. Hubbard! Come quickly! Someone's attacked Charmaine and locked her up in the furnace room!"

Roland ran out of the room, closely followed by Muriel. Everyone looked at one another in stunned silence for a moment before a general hubbub broke out.

Faith got up.

"I have to make sure Detective Dunne has been notified."

She dashed down the corridor to the annex and took the elevator to the ground floor. She assumed the furnace was in one of the maze of rooms across from the kitchen, and as she drew closer, she heard voices. When she opened the door, she saw Donald and Roland Hubbard bent over Charmaine, who was stretched out on the floor. Her blouse was torn and there was a pillowcase lying next to her. She was moaning softly.

"Now, honey, the shot should take effect any minute. Be brave, my darling," Donald was saying.

"I'll call Emerson and we'll make arrangements to have her taken over there immediately," Dr. Hubbard said. He was leaning over her, prodding deftly at various parts of her body.

"No!" screamed Charmaine. "I hate hospitals! Don't make me go to a hospital!"

"Honey, it's just to make sure there are no internal injuries. We have to have some X rays." Donald talked in a soothing tone of voice.

Muriel stepped out of the shadows and spoke to Donald in a low voice. "Why don't we move her upstairs for now until she's less hysterical?"

Donald smiled at her gratefully.

Faith entered the room. She felt slightly awkward intruding on this domestic scene, but somebody had to.

"Has anyone notified the police?"

Donald looked up. "I asked Denise Samuelson to do that immediately, Mrs. Fairchild. We expect them at any moment."

"I know it's uncomfortable for her here, but I think they would probably not want her moved."

Nobody likes a know-it-all, and all four Hubbards looked at her with varying degrees of annoyance—Charmaine's deathly pallor displaying the least.

"Do you happen to know if Denise was going to call the state police or the Byford police?" Faith asked.

"I didn't give her a list of telephone numbers." There was no attempt to disguise the exasperation now. "My wife had just been attacked. I told her to call the police."

Faith was torn. She didn't know whether she ought to stay to make sure nothing was moved or go find Denise and make sure she had called Dunne. She decided to stay. If the Byford police arrived, she'd have to try to keep Chief Coffin from destroying whatever evidence there was. So far all she could see was the pillowcase and a piece of rope lying next to it. Presumably the attacker had pulled it over Charmaine's bouffant hairdo and tied it around her neck with the rope.

"Water, I need some water," Charmaine groaned, and tried to get up.

"Don't move, my dear. Mrs. Fairchild is unfortunately correct and we must let the police see exactly what happened," Dr. Hubbard advised. "I'll get you something to drink."

It was sweltering in the furnace room, and Faith half-heartedly hoped Roland would appear with a tray of frosty glasses for them all, but he returned with only one tumbler for Charmaine, which he lifted to her parched lips.

A few seconds later John Dunne appeared with Detective Sullivan and his paraphernalia. The room suddenly grew too small for the assemblage, and Faith found herself wedged next to Muriel. But leaving was out of the question.

Dunne took a stride over to where the victim lay. Faith could have sworn Charmaine's skirt had been hiked up several inches in the interim.

"Mrs. Hubbard, can you tell me what happened?"

Charmaine's accent moved south from the Carolinas to Georgia.

"I arrived here at about ten o'clock. I was meeting my husband, but first I went to find Mrs. Samuelson. We were supposed to have lunch today, and I wanted to tell her I couldn't make it. I thought I'd look in the kitchen when I didn't see her upstairs, and when I came out of the elevator, someone put a bag on my head and everything went black. When I came to, I was in here. I got the bag off, then I must have passed out again. I don't know how long it's been." She looked up at Dunne piteously. He didn't budge.

"Did you get any impression at all of your assailant? Did he or she say anything?"

"Not a word. Whoever it was was taller than I am, though. I think it was a man. I tried to grab at the bag and I believe I hit a shoulder. I was knocked out right after that." She touched her head gingerly. "This is where I was hit."

"She has a sizable contusion and there may be some concussion," Donald said. "There don't appear to be any other injuries, thank God," he added.

"No indication of . . ." Dunne glanced tactfully a little north of Charmaine's knees.

Donald choked slightly. "Absolutely not."

"Who found her?" He looked around the room.

"I did," Donald said. "Mrs. Samuelson and I were both beginning to get alarmed and were making a thorough search of the premises. My wife had made plans to meet each of us here, and her car was in the parking lot. And she's not a woman who breaks appointments."

Faith bit her lip.

Donald continued, "I was checking all the rooms—just opening the doors and looking in. Of course I didn't expect she would have any reason to be here, but there she was—unconscious on the floor."

Dunne looked tired. Faith was surprised. Obviously the attack on Charmaine had to be connected with Eddie Russell's murder, and Dunne should have been pleased that more clues were turning up. Although, she reflected, this meant more questioning and investigating, and the most obvious tie-in was the suggestion that some sort of maniac was on the loose. Not an appealing thought.

Dunne cleared the room and told the Hubbards Charmaine could be moved in a few moments. He motioned to Faith outside into the hallway.

"Go home."

She was indignant. "Well—"

"I'll see you later."

His left eye twitched. It might or might not have been a wink.

Faith went upstairs and got her coat. She still wanted to find out what Julia Cabot had to say about Eddie Russell, but she could see her tomorrow. Tom's "chestnuts roasting on an open fire" would have to wait a bit.

Chief Francis Coffin, supported on either side by trusty minions, was coming in the door as she was leaving. He stopped dead in his tracks. "Now don't tell me you were snuggled up with this one too!" He laughed so hard, he had to sit down to recover his breath.

"No," Faith replied frostily, "I did not find Mrs. Hubbard. Her husband did. I was merely here to help in the kitchen." He shook his head and his cap fell off. "Seems you have a knack for being in the wrong place at the wrong time. Better stay in your own kitchen. Bake some Christmas cookies." He heaved himself out of the chair and tottered out of the room. It was impossible to be angry at something so ludicrous.

She left quickly, got into her car, and was starting to

back out of the space when Denise knocked at the window. Her face was blue with the cold and her teeth were chattering. She looked even worse than she had that morning.

Faith braked quickly and leaned across to open the door.

"Get in quickly. You must be freezing!"

"I am."

Denise was immobile for a moment, staring ahead through the windshield. It was a beautiful winter landscape. The evergreens were frosted with snow, and in the distance the frozen Concord River slid like a silver ribbon under an old stone bridge. But Faith was certain Denise wasn't transfixed by the scene.

"Why don't you tell me about it?" she said gently.

Denise turned her head and considered.

"I suppose that's why I've been waiting. Is Charmaine badly injured?"

"I'm not a professional, but I'd say she was going to be fine." Surely Denise couldn't have been Charmaine's attacker, yet she was obviously relieved at Faith's words.

She shook her head slowly. "This whole thing is like a nightmare. And I didn't see how my life could possibly have gotten any worse."

The car was warm and the windows had steamed up, making a kind of cozy cocoon, but the parking lot at Hubbard House didn't seem the best place for true confessions. "Look," said Faith, "let's go to my house and we'll get something warm to drink and sort things out."

"If we only could—but I'll come to your house, Faith. I have to do something."

She slumped back in the seat and they drove to Aleford in silence. At one point Faith thought Denise might be asleep, but she opened her eyes again almost immediately.

Tom was in the kitchen. He started to say something jokingly to his wife when he saw Denise's face behind Faith and quickly pulled out a chair for her.

"Denise has come for some tea and sympathy," Faith told him.

"Then I'll leave you to it," he said tactfully.

"No, please stay, Reverend Fairchild. I'd like to have you here. I need—" She had trouble finishing her sentence. "I need some spiritual help."

Faith put the water on, and soon a steaming pot of tea was ready. Denise was too. She sat up and looked better than she had since her arrival at Hubbard House earlier in the day.

"I have a problem with drugs." It was a bald statement and seemed to exhaust her, but she kept going.

"When I was married, my husband was heavily involved with cocaine—the recreational drug, you know," she said caustically. "It was one of the reasons I divorced him. His son, Joel, knew, and it was mainly why he wanted to stay with me, I believe." She took a large sip of tea. "Joel doesn't know about me. But Eddie Russell did. He was my supplier. I'm addicted to diazepam—Valium. My husband used to take it with the coke and there was always plenty around. At first I just took one or two when I felt stressed, and believe me there was a lot to be stressed about in those days. Then my dependency increased, and even after he was gone I couldn't function without it. I'd try to keep myself from taking one; then I'd have terrible anxiety attacks. I couldn't leave the house without my precious vial of pills. I had kept my eyes open at Hubbard House, so I knew Eddie." She looked straight at Faith. "And no, it is not why I went there as a volunteer—to score drugs. I went because I was trying hard to find some meaning in my life—through the temple and through my volunteer work. But things were too out of control. Eddie actually approached me. Maybe I looked like a user. Anyway, he said we could have a good time together and he had ways to make it even better. I wasn't interested in him romantically, but we did have a brief affair. Then the relationship was strictly business."

Tom and Faith had been listening intently. The shadows were lengthening in the yard, but Faith didn't want to interrupt things by turning on the lights. Instead she reached across the table and put her hand on Denise's.

"Oh, Denise, I'm so sorry. I wish I had known you sooner. You've been in so much pain."

Denise seemed to falter again, then resumed speaking. "At first it was simple. I'd give him the money and he'd give me the drugs. Then he began to increase the price, and finally he began to really do a number on me by telling me he couldn't get any for a few days before coming through. I knew it was blackmail and I knew he was a liar and a sadist, but there was nothing I could do about it. When I heard he was dead, I went crazy. Fortunately Joel is away on a school ski trip. I haven't slept and I've torn the house apart looking for places I might have stashed some."

It was now so dark, Faith had to turn on the lights, and she took the teapot to add some hot water. Tom moved his chair closer to Denise.

"I was meeting Charmaine because I always assumed they were in it together. I'm pretty sure he got the stuff from her that night at the Holly Ball."

Faith remembered the mystery of the missing pocketbook—that big pocketbook, big enough to hold several CVS branches.

"So Eddie had something to do with the lights going off?"

"He liked to be dramatic. Told me to meet him by the main switch, and when he pulled it, he handed me some pills. He was like a kid that way."

Denise was talked out. She sat with her hands around the cup for warmth. Her face was lined and she looked about fifty years older than usual.

Tom spoke. "You know that Faith and I will do everything to help you. Which means talking to the police and then a treatment program, if that's what you want. The important thing for you to remember is you're not going to be alone."

Denise put her head down on the table and sobbed like a child. Faith stood behind her and stroked her head.

A few hours later Dunne had left and Tom was driving Denise to McLean's Hospital. Faith was back in the kitchen waiting for her husband's return. She was idly leafing through her recipe file looking for something new to do with squash—squash tortellini in brown butter?—but her mind strayed to Hubbard House, as usual. She'd started to phone Aunt Chat earlier with an update and decided it was too complicated to explain except in person. Instead she'd written on a postcard of the Aleford green:

Think I know some of what was troubling Howard. Tell you all about it at Christmas.
Love and kisses, Faith.

Denise's story had been deeply upsetting, but she seemed to sincerely want to end her dependency, and Faith sensed she had the strength to do so. It was impossible to avoid the thought that her relationship to Eddie gave her a strong motive for murdering him, but Faith pushed it from her mind. Denise had been at home on Friday night, no doubt in no condition to drive. Faith wondered when Joel had left for his trip. It would be nice if Denise could have a tidy little alibi.

Since she'd first heard that Eddie was a skilled practitioner in the art of blackmail, Faith had known other victims would surface. The question now was who next? She remembered the assurance with which Julia Cabot had spoken at lunch when she'd mentioned that it wouldn't be easy to solve the crime. What did she know? Faith closed her recipe file and decided to wait for Tom in bed. She was exhausted.

Upstairs she pulled the covers over her shoulders, leaving the light on so Tom could find his way. Just before she dozed off, she thought of what Dunne had said to her at the door away from the others as he was leaving. She'd looked at him quizzically. "So who's your favorite for the attack on Charmaine? Could be a pretty broad field."

He'd laughed. "You don't really think Charmaine would let someone else mess up her hair, do you? The question is, why does she want us to think so? Now, say good night, Faith."

And she had.

8

Leandra Rhodes was almost late for dinner. Her husband, Merwin, was in town meeting an old classmate at the Harvard Club, and she'd been struggling with the zipper on the back of her dress for ten minutes. She refused to give in and finally pulled it up triumphantly with the aid of a safety pin and a long piece of string. She hurried out of her room and stopped for a moment at the top of the stairs to catch her breath. She put her hand out and stroked the smooth banister. She doubted whether there were many craftspeople left, even in New England, who could carve such a spiral. But it wouldn't do to dilly-dally now, and she looped the pocketbook that never left her side securely over her arm and started down.

Down, down, down. Tumbling down until she came to a dead stop in a heap at the bottom.

"I don't like it. Sure it's possible that an old lady in a rush to get to dinner could trip over the pocketbook she's dropped, and fall down the stairs all by herself, but it's the timing. Too much going on at that place."

Faith agreed with Detective Dunne, who had just called to tell her about Leandra's accident the night before.

"Leandra was not the type of lady who trips. She would never put a foot wrong, literally or figuratively. Has she been able to say anything about what happened?"

"No, it's a miracle she's even alive. She's in the intensive care unit over at Mass General and hasn't regained consciousness."

"Of course, if it wasn't an accident, it means she was pushed, which is a horrible thought. And why would anyone want to hurt her?"

Faith imagined Bootsie Brennan might have entertained less than charitable thoughts about Leandra from time to time, but as a sparring partner Leandra was without equal, and on some level Bootsie must have recognized that. Besides, noxious as she was, Bootsie didn't seem like the type of woman who attempts murder—unless it was for a very good reason, like someone maligning her son. All these types. It reminded Faith of those old Peck and Peck ads, "There's a certain kind of woman who . . ." She and her friends at Dalton had had fun making up all sorts of lewd, and to eleven-year-olds hysterical, endings contrary to the image presented of the woman who chairs a meeting of the SEC but also bakes the best angel food cake in the neighborhood.

"All these types." Faith realized she was saying it out loud.

"What's that?" Dunne asked.

"I was just thinking about the cast of characters we're assembling."

"Look, why don't you go up again today and see

what's in the wind? I'll try to come by your house later this afternoon."

Faith had been planning to go to Hubbard House anyway and was happy to have the official blessing.

"Fine," she replied. "I'll see you later."

She broke the news to Tom and set off on her familiar route. The snow hadn't melted much, and it was getting dirty only by the side of the road. If you looked beyond, it was still like a scene from the top of a fruitcake tin.

Faith walked into the kitchen and headed for the closet to get an apron. Mrs. Pendergast was stirring a huge pot of milk on the stove.

"Cup custard. That's the kind of thing they'll want today."

"Comfort food?" Faith remarked.

Mrs. P. patted her waist. "To me most food could be called that, but that's right. Nice, soothing food. Nothing complicated. Now say hello to Mrs. Fairchild, Gladys." She called over her shoulder.

Faith hadn't noticed that there was another person in the kitchen. A cheerful-looking, middle-aged woman, her hair imprisoned in a hairnet guarded by several dozen bobby pins, came bustling over with her hand out-stretched.

"Glad to meet you. I hear you really held down the fort while I was sick. Feel fine now, but was I bad. I think I had all those flus at once—Hong Kong, Taiwan, whatever. Sick as a dog. Couldn't keep a mouthful down for over a week. I tell you—"

Faith wasn't sure she wanted to be told. "It's very nice to meet you. I was happy I could help." She looked at Mrs. Pendergast a bit wistfully. "I suppose you won't be needing me anymore, Violet." The name came easily.

Violet put an arm around Faith's shoulder while she continued to stir her custard. "Now, Faith, Gladys and I will manage. It's been a real pleasure to get to know you, and you come up whenever you want. I expect you need some time now to do all the things you should have been doing while you were here. Now, scoot and we'll see you Friday night."

"Friday night?"

"The Christmas party. It's lots of fun. And I'd say we could all use a little about now."

"I'll try to come. It depends on what my husband's commitments are. This is a busy time for him."

"Of course, but just come for a moment. I'm making all my specialties."

Faith wasn't sure how much of an incentive Violet's specialties were—probably confections from the trusty cookbook like peanut penuche, marshmallow tea cookies, and mosaic finger sandwiches, besides all the regular Christmas favorites like nut balls—these last unknown to Faith until a parishioner had offered her one last Christmas saying ingenuously, "Have a nut ball? They're my husband's and they're delicious."

She wandered upstairs in search of Julia Cabot. She'd talk to her, then get home before lunch. Tom would be pleased. What was in the wind was boiled dinner, and she didn't think she'd add to her knowledge of what was going on at Hubbard House by eating there. It would be more productive to sit down with John later and go over everything they knew so far—and she was pretty sure there was a lot he hadn't shared. Plus she had something to tell him too. She'd figured out a motive for the attack on Leandra.

It was possible that Leandra had dropped her pocketbook as she hastened to dinner, then lost her balance as she reached down to pick it up from the stair. But it was more likely that someone had grabbed the purse from her arm and pushed her. It would have been the only way to get it and its contents. Faith realized the unfortunate relevance of Leandra's kleptomania now. She had taken something that incriminated someone, and that person was prepared to murder again to get it back. Leandra never let the old black calfskin satchel—circa 1952, a testament to the importance of buying quality merchandise—out of her sight. It would have been too risky to try to get it at night with her husband in bed by her side, nor could the killer do what everyone else did, which was to ask Merwin for whatever they were missing. "Have you happened to see my fountain pen lying around?"

So the murderer had to be someone who was at Hubbard House both nights. It was slim, but it was the only thing that made sense so far.

Faith decided to call Tom and tell him she would pick Ben up. Humming a few bars of "Deck Us All with Boston Charlie," her *Pogo*-loving father's favorite carol, she pushed open the door of Sylvia Vale's office. Muriel was on the phone.

"Now, James, you've got to go—" She looked up, startled. "I'll have to get back to you on that, I'm afraid. Why don't you give me a number where you can be reached?" She jotted the number on a pad. "Thank you very much. I'll call you as soon as I can. Good-bye." She hung up. Her cheeks were flushed. She tore the paper from the pad and pushed it into her pocket.

"I'm sorry to be interrupting," Faith said. "I wanted to use the phone, but I can find another one."

"Oh no, you're not interrupting at all. Just one of those hospital supply salesmen. They're so persistent. How are you, Mrs. Fairchild?"

"I'm fine, but I'm sorry to say this is my last day at Hubbard House. The kitchen staff is back in full force."

"Oh, yes, I heard Gladys was better. We're terribly grateful to you for pitching in, and I hope you'll join us on Friday for the Christmas party here."

"I'm going to try to come for at least a little while. I remember the last time I saw Farley, you were talking about it."

"Yes." Muriel's face darkened. "I miss Farley. It's always a problem with this job. You get so fond of people and then they go. But, of course, *you* will be back to see us often, I hope."

"Of course."

"I'll leave you to your call, then. See you Friday."

"Oh," Faith remembered as she was leaving, "I was sorry to hear about Leandra Rhodes' fall. Have you heard how she is getting on? And Mrs. Hubbard too?"

"It has been a dreadful week," Muriel said, obviously not a woman prone to exaggeration even when life around her was. "Charmaine is fine. Donald took her for X rays, but we don't have good news about Leandra. She's still in danger."

"Oh dear," Faith said.

"Perhaps we'll have better news by Friday." Little Muriel Sunshine brightened and left, closing the door behind her.

Left to go call James back, Faith thought. She took a pencil from the desk and drew lightly across the impression made on the rest of the pad when Muriel had written the telephone number on the top sheet. Faith had seen Cary Grant do it in *North by Northwest* about sixty times, and she was pleased to find it worked just as well for her as it did for him. She'd have to hope James was not holed up in Mount Rushmore or its equivalent.

Then she called Tom and left a message with the parish secretary. She'd wait until she got home to try to find James. The Hubbard House office was all too public.

Julia Cabot was not one of the people whiling away the time before lunch reading in front of the fire in the living room. Faith remembered that she had said she was still working, but it might not be every day. There was a list of room and cottage numbers in the office by the phone, and Faith returned to see where the Cabots were. Number 20 in Nathaniel's house. She walked back to the staircase. It was hard to climb, knowing that Leandra had so recently made her descent here. Faith tried to block the picture from her mind of the old lady falling helplessly down the stairs, a well-groomed, well-bred rag doll.

Faith was glad to reach the corridor and soon found number 20, in the front of the house. She knocked on the door, which was immediately opened by Julia. "Why, Faith, how nice to see you. Please come in. Can you join us for lunch?"

"No, thank you, I have to pick Benjamin up soon. I just wanted to stop and say good-bye. The kitchen is up to full muster again."

Faith entered the room. It was large and partially divided by open shelves that were filled with Staffordshire figures. One side of the room was furnished as a living room with beautiful antiques. On the other side Faith glimpsed an IBM PC perched on top of an ornate Louis XIV desk. Julia followed her gaze.

"It is a little mismatched, obviously. But it means I can work at home when I want to. And the china is a passion we share, although I think Ellery mostly likes to use it as an excuse to go to England." She glanced fondly at her husband, who had been sitting in a comfortable-looking armchair by the window reading the paper. A pretty little tree decorated with small colored lights and blown-glass ornaments was at his side. He'd sprung to his feet as Faith came in.

"I'm sorry you're leaving," Julia continued, "but I'm sure we'll see each other again. You and your husband."

"We'd like that."

"But do sit down for a moment, can you?"

"Yes," urged Ellery, indicating a chair. "Come here by the window. The view is splendid."

Faith walked toward him. "I do have time to stay a few minutes."

The view was wonderful, and Faith had a sudden desire to see what the fields and woodlands in front of her looked like with each season. In her other life she had been more than content to chart the changing solstices and equinoxes by Bergdorf's window displays. If she wasn't careful, she'd soon be taking long walks and starting a life list of birds.

"I suppose you've heard the terrible news about our friend Leandra Rhodes," Ellery commented.

"Yes," said Faith. "It's hard to imagine how such a thing could have happened."

Ellery shook his head. "Fortunately she has a very strong constitution. Never known her to be ill a day in her life, and we have to pray it will carry her through."

"Darling," Julia said, "would you mind going to get the mail? I'm expecting a rather important letter."

There was no question. Julia wanted to get her husband out of the room. He looked at her curiously and went.

"Not too subtle, I'm afraid, but it upsets Ellery to hear about all this, and that is why you came to talk to me, isn't it?"

Julia was wearing a red cashmere sweater and well-cut charcoal-gray pants. She crossed one leg elegantly over the other and folded her hands loosely in her lap. She looked more likely to be about to discuss the latest play at the Loeb or Ozawa's last performance—or from the look of her trim figure, the best time to go to Canyon Ranch—than murder.

"Yes, it is. You said the other day that Eddie Russell's murder would be a complicated one to solve. I wondered if you were thinking of something specific."

"You're working for the police, aren't you?" Julia said.

Faith's mother, Jane Sibley, was a lawyer too, yet Julia's manner, though equally direct, didn't have the same effect on Faith. Tête-à-têtes like this with Mom usually resembled the talking-tos of Faith's childhood. She had often wondered if it was why Jane was so successful in court. The old "Can you look me straight in the eye and say that" approach. Nevertheless, Faith felt compelled to answer Julia truthfully.

"I'm not really working for them, but I do know Detective Lieutenant Dunne, who's in charge of the investigation, and I've told him some of my impressions of Hubbard House. That doesn't mean that I have to tell him everything you choose to tell me." Faith spoke reassuringly.

"Unless I confess I did it."

"You're one of the few people who have an unbreakable alibi. You and your husband. Both of you knew I was sleeping in the guest room."

"That's true. But I did want to kill Eddie. Many times. Fortunately—or unfortunately—I also believe in a few higher things that prevented me from acting on my impulses." Julia spoke very matter-of-factly. Faith didn't want to interrupt her train of thought and kept silent.

"Do you know that Eddie was a blackmailer?" Julia asked. Faith nodded.

Julia leaned back in her chair. "I don't know why it should seem so much worse to blackmail elderly people than another age group. It's the same crime. Yet somehow, preying on people who are at the ends of their lives does strike me as more reprehensible. They don't have time to recover. I know of three people Eddie was blackmailing here and I don't doubt there were others. You might be able to guess who one of them is—Merwin Rhodes. Eddie knew about Leandra's habit. When Eddie first approached him, Merwin confided in Ellery. Ellery has been his lawyer for years. Poor Merwin. He was afraid the knowledge would get beyond Hubbard House. People here have always been very understanding. Eddie was talking about telling the head of the Pink Ladies, Mrs. Brennan. Merwin feared she would insist that Leandra resign as head of the Residents' Council, and Leandra loves being in charge. He also thought the papers might pick it up and make sport with it—'Brahmin Deb Turns to Pilfering in Old Age'—that sort of thing. Ellery advised him not to pay, but he did. He said it wasn't much money."

"And the others?"

"One of the others got out of it by dying. It was a man

named Jim Keiller, a Scot, and very keen on golf. He and Eddie played together often and became friends. Eddie introduced him to a very nice, sympathetic young lady and then revealed she was a prostitute. Eddie had some naughty pictures and threatened to hang them on the bulletin board by the mailboxes downstairs."

"How did you find out about it?"

"After Jim died, a man who was here for only a short period of time told me."

"Not Howard Perkins!" Faith gasped.

"Why, yes, did you know him?" Julia was clearly puzzled.

"That's how all this started. He was a friend of my aunt's and wrote to her just before he died that he was uneasy about something that was going on here. She got in touch with me."

"And you turned up in the kitchen."

"Exactly."

"I knew Howard years ago when I was first practicing law in New York. The ad agency he worked for was one of our clients. We were very surprised to find each other here. He was a dear man."

"Yes," agreed Faith, "and a smart one. After Jim Keiller told him what Eddie was doing to him, he may have found out about some others."

"That's possible, yes."

"And who's the third?" Faith had a feeling she knew.

"Me. Or I should say Ellery."

Faith had been prepared for what Julia was going to say. The whole conversation had had confessional undertones. Now she waited to hear what Eddie could possibly have unearthed about this nice couple.

"Eddie had a kind of sixth sense for certain kinds of behavior. Perhaps because he was so weak himself, he knew how to ferret out others' weaknesses. It was as if he was tuned in to some sort of special world cable channel broadcasting signals that indicated who would want to have an affair, who wanted to use a particular drug, or who wanted to look at smut. Because he was scum, he only saw the same."

This was interesting and morally uplifting, Faith thought, but it wasn't telling.

"Ellery has always had a bad back. Disc trouble, and when the pain is too excruciating, he takes codeine. A year ago he developed a mild addiction to it, and I made the mistake of getting some from Eddie. I knew Dr. Hubbard was monitoring Ellery's drug intake carefully, and I couldn't get an increase from him. Ellery was begging me for more of the drug. It was incredibly stupid, but I was tired and strung out myself from taking care of Ellery. After it was all over, Eddie demanded payment. I had a choice." Julia's lip curled. "I could pay in cash or in kind. I suppose at my age he meant me to be flattered."

"What a creep!" The last vestiges of any sympathy she had entertained for Eddie slipped silently away.

"I didn't agree, though. Frankly, I told him to go fuck himself, because it was the only sex he was going to get— with me anyway. But I couldn't tell Roland without revealing Ellery's problem, and that was not my story to tell. He would not have been able to stay here if he'd thought Roland, who has been his close friend all these years, knew. He is very ashamed. Of course Eddie couldn't tell Roland either without revealing how he knew. If he told anyone else, I planned to deny the whole thing. I started watching him very carefully and told him if he didn't stop his activities, I'd go to Dr. Hubbard. This was last month."

"I don't see why the police have to know about Ellery, since he couldn't have killed Eddie. I would like to tell them the rest, though."

"Fine, if you think it will help. Anything to get this settled."

"And what about Leandra? Do you think it was an accident?"

"No. I wish I could. But I also can't think of any reason

why someone would want to kill her or how it connects to Eddie's death."

"And how about the attack on Charmaine?" Dunne had told Faith to go along with Charmaine's version of the event, despite his own skepticism. They might get more information that way.

"It's very puzzling. Possibly someone Eddie was blackmailing. Wanted to scare her, so she wouldn't keep the business going."

Faith looked slightly confused, and Julia said, "Oh yes, I'm fairly certain that Charmaine and Eddie were partners in many ways. She's not as silly as she looks. But I don't think she'd commit murder. Too worried about her position, or hoped-for position, in society."

Ellery walked into the room with a stack of letters. "I hope what you're waiting for is here, my dear."

"Thank you, I think I have already found part of what I've been waiting for." She looked at Faith gratefully. "Do you know I'm suddenly very hungry. Are you sure you won't change your mind and join us for lunch, or haven't you developed a taste for New England boiled dinner yet?"

Faith did not know how to answer. What leaped to mind was scarcely polite—something like "only when old shoe leather and boiled dishcloths are not available." She rose and thanked them instead, then quickly went down the hall around the rear to the elevator. There was no way she was taking the stairs.

She picked Ben up at school and settled him at the table with a dish of applesauce while she made sandwiches for their lunch. Ben liked food to appear immediately. He wasn't much for deferred gratification at this stage. She was having some trouble with it herself. She wanted to call James' number, but she'd have to wait. The demands of a two-and-a-half-year-old boy were too unpredictable, and the last thing she wanted was to be interrupted in the middle of the conversation by Ben's newest

156

activity—a manic imitation of a character he'd invented called "Super Dog." Super Dog could fly, leap tall dog-houses at a single bound, and crush any number of dog bones in one bare paw. The furniture was taking quite a beating, and Faith was trying to restrict Super Dog to the yard, but it didn't always work.

By two o'clock, Ben was asleep surrounded by the several dozen stuffed animals he insisted on keeping in his bed. Faith hoped someone would simply give him some Gund stock for Christmas rather than another bear, irresistible as they might be.

She went downstairs and got the number from her purse. There wasn't any area code, which meant Muriel knew it or it was nearby. She dialed and it started ringing. Her lucky day.

A man answered. "Winthrop Chambers."

"May I speak to James Hubbard, please?"

"Jimmy? He's not here right now."

"Do you know when I might be able to reach him?"

"It's kind of hard to say. He's usually here in the morning. Who should I tell him called?"

"That's all right. I'll call him back. Thank you."

Faith hung up quickly. She went to get the Boston phone book from the closet. The Winthrop Chambers was on Beacon Hill—the wrong side, away from the common. It was probably a rooming house or some sort of resident hotel. She'd find out in the morning when she went there. Now that she knew where he was, it would be better to go in person. A phone is too easy to hang up.

She hoped John Dunne would come before Ben woke up, but time passed and he still hadn't arrived. It was after three and a shrill cry, "Mommee! Mommee!" meant Ben was awake and ready for more action.

She had no sooner set Ben up with gold twine and the box of wooden spools he had painted to make necklaces for Christmas presents when the phone rang. It was Detective Dunne.

"I'm up to my ears here, Faith, and I won't be able to get over today. Maybe tomorrow. Find out anything?"

Faith gave him a quick report on her conversation with Julia.

"The guy was a real operator," Dunne commented. "I'm not surprised he got iced. Now I've got to go. By the way, I don't think there's any point in your going back there."

"I thought I'd go to the Christmas Party on Friday night. Maybe someone will drink too much eggnog, break down, and confess."

"That would make life easier, but I doubt it. Still, going to the party is a good idea. Get your husband to go with you. No wandering around those halls in the dark."

She remembered to tell him her theory about why Leandra might have been pushed, then they said good-bye and she hung up the phone with a slight feeling of annoyance. All these big—and in Dunne's six-foot-seven case very big—overprotective males. She knew their attitude was supposed to make her feel cared for and cherished, but they wouldn't talk to Murphy Brown that way.

Ben was singing the *Winnie-the-Pooh* theme song over and over to himself and threading the spools. The capacity for endless repetition that children this age had always amazed Faith. Ben only knew the words "Winnie-the-Pooh," and it was beginning to sound like a mantra. She sat down next to him with her notebook. So far it didn't have anything written in it. She gave Ben a kiss on the top of his head, and he interrupted his tune to smile radiantly up at her. Maybe another child wasn't such a bad idea.

Time to play What Do We Know? she told herself—the "we" being Dunne and Fairchild, which sounded like something that ought to go public and make a bundle on the stock market.

She wrote "Edsel Russell" on the top of the first page and listed the following notes: "Thirty years old. Born in

Aleford, left as teenager. Good-looking. Liked women. Liked kinky sex. Dealt drugs. Not a user. Blackmailer."

Then she wrote: "Motives, Means, and Opportunity." It looked serious. She paused. She knew for certain that he was blackmailing Merwin Rhodes and Bootsie Brennan. He might have been planning to blackmail Denise, as well as sell her drugs. He'd tried to blackmail Julia. He'd black-mailed Jim Keiller, but Jim was dead and in no position to commit murder. Julia was out because she knew Faith was in the guest room. Merwin Rhodes was probably out for the same reason, but Leandra might not have told him. Bootsie was unlikely because of the weather. The same for Denise. Anyway, John Dunne said they hadn't turned up any tire tracks or footprints outside in the snow. She started to jot this all down. Somehow she couldn't envision any of these people tying Eddie up and then decorating his chest with knives. There was also the strong possibility that someone else at Hubbard House was being blackmailed.

Dunne had let her see a list of who was there that night. A few residents had gone away early for the holidays, but virtually everyone else was on the premises. Even Mrs. Pendergast. She had the strength. Faith had watched her knead dough, and the muscles on her upper arms stood out like brand-new tennis balls. But Mrs. Pendergast!

Then there were the Hubbards. They were all there, yet it seemed unlikely they would deal with their employee problems in quite this manner. She suddenly remembered the way Donald had looked at Eddie at the Holly Ball. There was no doubt he was jealous. Could Eddie have been waiting for Charmaine and gotten Donald instead? Who else? Sylvia Vale would do anything for Roland Hubbard and Hubbard House. If she knew what Eddie was up to, would she have resorted to murder to get him to stop?

She scribbled away, stopping to tie Ben's loops of spools. He insisted she put one on. She got him some cookies and milk, a shameless bribe to leave her alone for a while longer.

At the top of the next page she wrote "Leandra." She was sure whoever had pushed her had wanted something in her purse. John Dunne hadn't ridiculed the idea either when she'd mentioned it to him on the phone. But what? It would have had to be something small enough to fit in Leandra's bag, which was big, but not more so than a breadbox. The bag wouldn't have held a three-volume novel or a baby, for example—however Ernest and important. The classic item would be incriminating letters, but she didn't think those were the kinds of things kleptomaniacs took, although she was by no means expert on this point. She made a note to ask Tom what he knew about the subject and then consult the Aleford library.

She turned a page and wrote "Charmaine." Dunne continued to be almost positive she had staged the attack on herself. That meant she was trying to divert suspicion away from herself, which revived the theory that Eddie was lying in state waiting for her. But what had she told Donald? Going out for some fun on a snowy evening, darling, don't wait up? She made another note reminding herself to find out if Donald's room had a bath attached or if an occupant would have to leave for his or her ablutions.

She leaned back in the chair and pulled Benjamin onto her lap. He had looped all the rest of the spool necklaces around his own neck. "Ben's a beautiful Christmas tree!" he chortled.

"You're *my* little tree," Faith said, and hugged him, mindful of the disparity of her actions and thoughts. While her arms twined around her adored son, all she could think of was whether Dunne had been able to trace the knives yet. She'd forgotten to ask him. She also wanted to know if they'd determined whether Eddie had been tied up before or after death. If after, it could have been an attempt to make it look like a woman did it—Eddie didn't seem to be the type to let a man tie him up for fun and games.

Ben struggled to get down, and as she got up to follow him, she was uncomfortably certain that she was a lot closer to the why of Eddie Russell's murder than the who.

Just before she started to put together the *risotto coi funghi* they were having with broiled bluefish for dinner, she called Millicent Revere McKinley. Millicent would know whatever there was to know about James Hubbard, and Faith was trying to fit him into the puzzle. So far there didn't seem to be a place for his piece.

Ben was watching "Sesame Street," which providentially popped up on the screen at all hours of the day, and Faith dialed the number, confident that she had a way to make Millicent talk.

"Hello, Millicent? This is Faith Fairchild."

"Oh?" Millicent managed to convey serious doubt with the interjection—as if perhaps it were someone pretending to be Faith Fairchild, God only knew for what reason.

"Yes," Faith declared emphatically. "I wanted to ask you something, and I also happened to remember you had asked me for my grandmother's recipe for the sherry nutmeg cake you enjoyed so much at our house."

Enjoyed so much that she had devoured three large pieces. Faith had a sneaking suspicion that Millicent, bearer of the local WCTU torch, had a weakness for any potent potable confections. She'd also tossed back several helpings of a soufflé Grand Marnier at a Sunday dinner once.

"Of course, I'd love to have the recipe. So handy for the holidays." Millicent appeared to be weighing the question. She knew this wasn't a case of altruism but your basic tit for tat. Faith had politely but firmly told her the recipe was a closely guarded family secret when she had asked for it. This was partially true. It *had* been a family secret until one of Faith's cousins had submitted it to a contest in *Family Circle* magazine and, as third runner-up (twenty-five dollars), had it printed in the December issue a few years before. But with Millicent it always paid to have something in the arsenal, and Faith knew a good weapon when she saw it. Now the time had come to use it.

She brought out the Howitzer. "I'll be baking several later this week, and if you're pressed for time as we all are about now, I could make an extra one for you and tuck the recipe in with it."

Millicent fell. "That would be lovely, dear. So thoughtful of you. Now what were you saying about a question?" There wasn't even the suggestion of a quaver in her voice. Millicent was indomitable even in defeat.

"When we were talking about the Hubbards the other day, you mentioned Donald and Muriel. I wondered if you had known James, the youngest?"

"Is this in connection with that shocking Eddie Russell business—in which I hear, incidentally, you've been rather intimately involved?" Faith had expected Millicent would make a comment like this. She had no doubt that Millicent blamed her for the whole thing, casting the shadow of scandal on such a noble edifice.

"It might be, yes. But I merely wanted to know a bit more about James Hubbard. If you know, that is."

Millicent knew.

"It almost broke poor Roland Hubbard's heart when James ran away. He was only sixteen. He'd been a worry to his father for years. Couldn't seem to settle down like the other two. Always skipping school to go fishing or whatever. Maybe if his mother had lived, things would have been different. He was a sweet boy, never rude. But he just wouldn't listen to anyone."

"Where did he go?"

"I believe he went south someplace, Florida. The family never talked about him, of course, but every once in a while some friend would get a postcard from him, and then we'd know where he was and what he was doing."

Faith could imagine. She knew from Tom that Hattie Johnston, the former postmistress, who had retired the year before Faith had arrived in Aleford, had had her own rules

when it came to the U.S. mail. A postcard was public information and people who wrote them knew they would be
read; otherwise they'd write a letter, which was sacrosanct.

"What was he doing? Did he stay in Florida?"

"I don't think I ever heard for sure what he was doing
there—at first something with show business, I think. In
later years he managed to get some training, and he
worked as an aide in various hospitals. Mostly out west and
in the south, but I did hear that he had come back to
Massachusetts about two years ago."

"Anything else you can think of?"

"I asked Donald how James was when I heard he'd
come back, but Donald said they knew nothing about it
and that if James wanted to see them, he knew where to
find them. I don't think any of them have been in touch
since he went away originally. Roland felt it was up to
James to make the first move."

Millicent apparently thought she had given good
value, and the tone of her voice changed slightly. "Would
I be able to count on the cake for some friends I'm having
for tea on Friday?" She didn't issue an invitation.

"Absolutely," Faith answered. "And thank you for all
your help."

"Anytime, Faith dear. Now I must be going. Good-
bye."

Faith said good-bye and replaced the receiver. Anytime, ha. Unless Millicent wanted to start whipping up
soufflés, in the future it would be back to groveling on the
carpet if Faith wanted any information.

As she drove into Boston the next morning, Faith had
a slight twinge of guilt over not having revealed James
Hubbard's whereabouts to John Dunne yesterday. But it
disappeared immediately as she turned up the volume on
the radio and swiftly flicked through several oldies sta-
tions—New Englanders seemed particularly partial to
them, and when she drove up from New York, she didn't

have to look at the signs to know she had crossed the border. Whatever station she was tuned to immediately began to play "Time in a Bottle." Now she located WGBH, the PBS station, and Robert J. Lurtsema's plummy tones filled the air. He was giving a weather report and it sounded like Shakespeare.

Miraculously she found a parking space on Cambridge Street, walked up to Anderson, and started climbing the hill. She had no trouble finding the Winthrop Chambers. It was an old hotel that had been converted to a rooming house. There was a wreath on the door. Someone had stuck a Celtics pennant in it. She walked into the lobby. It didn't look like Hubbard House. There were two ancient Naugahyde club chairs and a scarred coffee table heaped with overflowing ash trays, old newspapers, and magazines. The windows were so dirty that it was difficult to see outside. No one appeared to be around, and just when she was wondering if she'd have to go buy a clipboard and knock on doors pretending to be doing a survey on wash-day detergent preferences, a door behind the desk opened and a man came out.

"Looking for somebody?"

"Yes. Is James Hubbard here?"

"You the same person who called yesterday?"

"Yes, I am."

"He said to tell you he'd be in the market."

"The market?"

"Yeah, he's selling Christmas trees down by Faneuil Hall. He said he'd be looking for you."

"Thank you very much."

"No problem. Merry Christmas."

Faith walked over the hill to the Faneuil Hall Market-place—the old Haymarket. There had been a market in this spot for three hundred years. The long stone warehouses stretching toward the waterfront, once occupied by meat and dairy wholesalers with names like Capone and Sullivan, were now filled with stores like The Sharper Image,

Ann Taylor, The Gap, and small boutiques selling things in the shape of hearts, stuffed animals, and every possible kind of earring yet devised. The food vendors offered a vast variety of comestibles—pizza by the slice, fruit kebobs, egg rolls, oysters and clams on the half shell. There were still pushcarts, a quaint reminder of the old days, but instead of the strident cries of "Open 'em up! Open 'em up! Best beans in the market! Best in Boston!" that had echoed in the streets, most of these carts were indoors and sold whimsical rubber stamps and *tchotchkies* made of dough.

It wasn't as hard to find James as she had feared. There were only three men selling trees in the square in front of a large glass-enclosed florist's shop. Two of them appeared to be in their nineties and were probably in their sixties. The one who looked like sixty would have to be James, aged thirty. The five-year-old in the sailor suit sitting on the steps at Hubbard House was now wearing two tattered coats one on top of the other, ancient running shoes, unlaced but not, Faith suspected, as a fashion statement, and a wool cap pulled low over his forehead. James had seen a lot of hard times.

She walked over to him. "James Hubbard? My name is Faith Fairchild. I live in Aleford and I've been doing some volunteer work at Hubbard House. Do you have some time to talk to me?"

James looked at her blearily. Faith was uncomfortable. The contrast between the two of them was enormous and even obscene—she was wearing a warm, clean, Thinsulate-lined coat. Her boots matched her purse and she had on a bright, spanking-new blue wool hat and muffler. She exuded the smell of Guerlain's Mitsouko, which she'd sprayed on after her shower that morning. He gave off a ripe aroma composed of cigarette smoke, the rancid grease of fast food, rum, and his own unwashed body. She wouldn't be surprised if he asked her with words or a look, "Who the hell do you think you are, lady?"

Instead he said, "Hubbard House? You're working at

Hubbard House? Wouldn't do that if I were you. Place is dangerous." His speech was slurred. He looked over her shoulder as if expecting to see someone else with her. "You came alone? She didn't come?"

"I'm alone, yes," Faith answered, "Who were you waiting for?"

"Never mind," he said. "So what do you want with me?" He didn't say this in a belligerent tone, merely one of curiosity, even idle curiosity.

"I wanted to talk to you about Eddie Russell."

"Eddie? Good old Eddie. Got me away from the place. We joined the circus." He laughed, and the laughter ended in a fit of coughing. He reached into a pocket and took out a pack of cigarettes. He lit one. He didn't have any gloves on, and his hands were so chapped they were bleeding.

"The circus?" Faith asked.

"Yeah, we were kids. The circus came to Lowell and we went up to see it. Stayed around and ended up going along. The old man was pretty p.o.'d. Said if I didn't come home, he wouldn't have anything more to do with me. That was okay. Eddie moved on, but I stayed with the circus a long time. Nice people. Nice places. Warm places. Not like friggin' Boston."

"So you never saw Eddie again."

"Why are you so interested in Eddie? You got a thing for him?"

Faith realized James didn't know Eddie was dead.

"No, I'm married—happily. I'm just interested, that's all." She hoped James' alcoholic stupor was thick enough to make this less-than-satisfactory explanation seem plausible.

"Yeah, well Eddie and I are buddies. We go way back. Joined the circus together, did I tell you that?"

"Yes, you did. Have you had any good times together lately?"

It was time to try to move James toward the present.

He looked at her cagily. "Why don't you bring Eddie down here and we can all talk."

Faith thought quickly. Standing in the cold trying to parry his questions was not going to get her anywhere. Knowing that James had run off with Eddie and remembering that Millicent had said James had returned to Massachusetts two years ago, which was when Eddie had also come back, convinced her that James and Eddie had been buddies who stayed in touch. James had worked in hospitals, moving around. Had he been Eddie's inside man—supplying whatever the customers wanted? She decided to try to get James to go someplace warm for a cup of coffee. Maybe he'd talk more and let something slip.

"It's terribly cold here," she said. "Could you take a break and have a cup of coffee with me?" There was a place called The Bell in Hand across the street and down the block.

He smiled. He must have been good-looking at one time, but now several teeth were missing and his blue eyes were so bloodshot, they looked purple.

"Never turn down a free cup of coffee, especially from a beautiful lady. But I gotta stay here a while. Come back in a half hour. I can go then."

Faith spent the next thirty minutes wandering around the marketplace. She bought a pound of the chewy black and red raspberry candies Tom liked so much and went back to the stand where they were selling trees. James was in virtually the same position as when she'd left. She wondered if he was doing any business.

He saw her approach and called to one of the other men, "Hey, Billy, keep my place, will ya? I'm going to get some coffee."

"Bring me a cuppa?"

"Sure," said James, and he followed Faith to the curb. The traffic was brutal as usual, and as they waited for a break, James unaccountably started talking again.

"Thought you were Muriel when you first came. Best

sister a man ever had. Like a mother. Never had a mother, did you know that? I mean I had one, but she croaked."

"I'm sorry. That must have been very hard."

"I don't even remember her. Muriel does. Muriel tells me about her."

But Muriel hadn't told him about Eddie Russell. Or maybe that was what she had been calling about.

"Do you see your brother Donald often?"

James started to laugh, then his eyes filled with tears, "Dumb bastard. Wouldn't even write to me. Told Muriel I had to come apologize to Dad. Dad! He's a looney and that's his nuthouse out there. They don't know. I stay away. I'm not crazy."

He reached out to grab Faith's arm to pull her across the street and darted into the break between cars. He missed her arm but kept on going. She started to follow, then saw a shiny new black Cadillac Seville bearing down on them with no intention of slowing down.

"James!" she screamed, drawing back. "Stop! There's a car coming!"

He turned and waved at her to come, giving her a lopsided smile.

The car hit him head on. The driver didn't even stop to look.

9

Faith dashed after the car to get the number from its license plate. She had been stunned when she had first arrived in Boston by the aggressiveness of its drivers and the apparent total lack of logic in its street signs, but this accident went far beyond a rude gesture. Or it was no accident.

The plate was obscured by layers of dirt, but she thought one number was an eight and another a two. It was a Massachusetts plate. She ran back to James. He wasn't moving. A few bystanders had gathered around him, and one was directing the traffic into a side street. Someone said a woman had gone for the police. Faith bent down close to him. There wasn't any blood that Faith could see. He'd been thrown almost to the other side of the street and was lying on his back; one arm was twisted underneath. She took off her coat and put it over him.

"James," she said, "James, it's going to be all right. Help is coming."

She had no idea whether he could hear her.

He opened his eyes and stared at her.

"Stan," he slurred.

"No, no, don't try to stand up. Just stay still. An ambulance will be here soon." She could hear the wail above the Christmas carols on the loudspeakers outside the market. She knelt down next to him. He looked very young; his eyes were pleading with her.

"Stan," he repeated, then seemed to make a colossal effort. "Stanley."

It was a name. One of the men who had been with him selling trees? Billy was approaching, and Faith stood up and called to him, "Could you get Stanley? Is that the other man's name?"

He came closer. "That's Patrick. No Stanleys around." He crouched down over James and said tenderly, "Hey, pal, hang on. What do you want? Some of this?" He reached into his pocket and took out a bottle. James closed his eyes. The loudspeaker began to blare "Santa Claus Is Coming to Town."

A police officer was pushing his way through what had now become a crowd.

"Clear the way here. Stand back." He bent down over James' supine figure. His back was to the crowd. He turned and asked over his shoulder, "Anybody see what happened?"

Faith stepped forward. "Yes, I did. He was hit by a car—a black Cadillac Seville, fairly new I'd say. It had Massachusetts plates and I think two of the numbers were eight and two. It was coming from there"—she pointed back toward Government Center—"and it never slowed down. It went toward the waterfront down North Street."

The ambulance had arrived, and suddenly there was

activity everywhere. The policeman stood up and walked over to Faith. "You happen to know who he is?" There was no reason not to tell. "Yes, his name is James Hubbard. He was living at the Winthrop Chambers on Anderson Street. His family lives in Byford. His father, Dr. Roland Hubbard, is the director of Hubbard House, a retirement home there."

The cop looked at her quizzically. "He a good friend of yours?" His inflection indicated his incredulity.

Faith was freezing. Her coat was being loaded along with James into the ambulance. She was in no mood to stand on the street corner chatting with one of Boston's finest about her taste in friends.

"I know the family. Look, can I give you my name and how to reach me? I really have to get home to pick up my little boy."

"Okay." He took out a pad. "We'll be in touch with you, and you'll have to come back and sign a statement. You've been a big help," he added. "Lots of people don't want to get involved in things like this."

Well, she was involved, Faith thought. Involved right up to her ice-cold neck. She took the card with his name and number and ran back toward Cambridge Street. Not only did she have to pick up Ben or have him suffer that worst of all fates, being the last child waiting for his mother, but her meter was about to run out. When she got to the car, she looked at her watch and shoved another quarter in, then went down the street. There was a phone by the curb, but she pushed open the door of a bar, The Harvard Gardens, in search of one with some warmth. She had to call John Dunne immediately.

"Stanley," James had said. "Stanley," and there was only one Stanley in this case, or rather two—senior and junior, but she was putting her money on Stanley Russell Senior. The bad husband with "flash," Dr. Hubbard had said. Her mind raced. It all fit together neatly. Eddie didn't have the brains for something big—witness his little blackmailing schemes and general gaucheness. No, somebody else was directing the drug business—overseeing the hospital thefts, the street sales, and—if someone began to look like a liability—arranging "accidents." But would he kill his own son? And why? Faith could imagine that James' obvious addiction was creating problems. He probably talked too much and was certainly eating into profits, if he was still employed by Stanley at all. When Faith had walked in on Muriel, she was saying "You've got to go—" Where? To the police? To get help?

By the time Faith found the phone through the hazy smoke in the bar, she was sure that Stanley Russell had tried to kill James, or have him killed. What connection it had with what had been happening at Hubbard House she wasn't sure, yet there had to be one.

Surprisingly, Dunne picked up his own phone. She told him briefly what had happened.

"What's the name of the cop who took the information?" She gave it and the number to him.

"I was on my way to Hubbard House when you called. Turned up some interesting stuff, and I wanted to ask some people a few questions. Now we've got some more to ask. Want to meet me there? The police probably already called them, but you might want to tell them what happened in more detail, and I'd like to be there when you do. By the way, Faith, just to be sure. The car was definitely aiming for James Hubbard, right? It wasn't by any chance trying for you?"

Faith was stunned. "Of course not. Who would want to kill me?"

"Simply a thought. So you want to meet me in Byford, say in half an hour?"

"Yes," Faith agreed readily, dismissing the choice of targets from her mind. It merely muddied the waters. What this case definitely did *not* need was more options. Especially now when it seemed everything was coming to a head, and she had no intention of being left out, if that was what John was suggesting. This Safety First attitude was a bore.

Of course, she was gone for that half hour. James could have called someone. But whom? And why?

She hung up the phone and dug into her purse for more change. Please, Pix, she prayed, be home. God was good and she was.

"Pix, something important has come up and I have to meet Detective Lieutenant Dunne at Hubbard House. Could you pick Ben up from school and hold on to him until I get home?"

"Sure, but he'll have to come with me while the Evergreens finish decorating Peabody House for the Christmas tea tomorrow."

"Won't he be in the way?" asked Faith, picturing Ben festooning himself with tree lights and ornaments under the eyes of the garden club members and the Peabody House residents.

"Of course he'll be in the way, but you know how much the people there love to see children. I'll manage. Now go off to whatever you and Dunne are up to and happy hunting."

In another life she must have done something especially wonderful to end up in this one with a friend and neighbor like Pix, Faith thought. If the Millers ever moved, she'd have to go too.

No one in the bar had looked up when she had come in and no one looked up as she left. Out on the street it was as cold as a witch's—she paused mentally; she was a minister's wife after all—finger, and she hugged herself to keep warm as she sped to the car and its heater.

It didn't take long to get to Byford, and she was there before Dunne.

She waited in the parking lot and thought about the case. She'd been right. James Hubbard *was* the key. He must know all about both Russells' operations. If it hadn't been so obvious that he didn't know Eddie was dead—and was also clearly unable to negotiate a trip to Byford even in good weather—she might have put him on the list of possible murder suspects. She'd decided to add Stanley Russell Senior. He might not have had much paternal feeling for a son he hadn't watched grow up, especially if that son was starting to cut into his profits or threaten him with blackmail. Eddie was certainly dumb enough to do that. Wasn't that what Scott Phelan had pointed out—that he was stupid enough to get himself killed? If Stanley himself hadn't wielded the knives, someone in his employ might have. But the timing and locale didn't make any sense. Why not just wait for him to try to cross the street in Boston? Under ordinary circumstances, the car would have been long gone before anyone had tried to get the number. It was Stanley Russell's very unlucky day that Faith was there watching.

She thought some more about James. He knew about the Russells. What else did he know about Hubbard House? Maybe Dunne would be able to question him today. And where was the lieutenant anyway? She looked at her watch. She wanted to know what he knew and was willing to trade information. She looked in her rearview mirror, saw his car pull up, and stepped out to meet him.

He looked at her outfit—a black wool jersey DKNY skirt and top—chic, but chilly. "Where's your coat?" he asked.

"Gave it to James. Have you heard how he is?"

"Yes. He's dead, Faith. I'm sorry."

Faith began to shiver even more. The little boy in the picture was dead. The man she had been talking to only an hour ago, the man who was looking forward to a hot cup of coffee, was dead.

"Do you think the Hubbards know?"

"Not yet. I asked Boston to hold off. But the family does know he was hit, and Roland Hubbard went in to the hospital. Muriel and Donald are here keeping everything going. Charmaine's here too, probably getting in the way."

Faith thought of Dr. Hubbard, driving in to see the son he hadn't seen for sixteen years. What was he thinking? And when he arrived, it would be too late. Too late to say anything, or hear anything. It was heartbreaking.

"You were right, incidentally. Stanley Russell does drive a Cadillac, plate number MBA 802, although at the moment he says he wasn't driving it today."

They entered through the front door of Nathaniel's house. Sylvia Vale was outside the office. She had been crying. She didn't seem surprised that Faith was there.

"I'll tell Muriel and Donald you're here," she said, and disappeared into the office.

"You haven't told me your news. What was so interesting that you had to come here to ask more questions?" Faith realized she'd gotten sidetracked by James' death and what she was sure was the involvement of Stanley Russell.

Dunne looked down at her and with a trace of smugness said, "We traced the knives."

Traced the knives! That meant they had the murderer!

Donald and Muriel arrived together. Charmaine was a few steps behind. They looked as if a tiny spark would send them flying to kingdom come.

"Is there someplace private where we could go to talk?" Dunne asked.

"How about my office?" Donald was clearly trying to speak in a nonchalant tone, as if Dunne and Faith were coming to consult him about hangnails or persistent dandruff, but the words came out in four terse bullets.

They followed him through the annex hallway into the other house. Muriel was behind them and Charmaine was lagging far to the rear. Faith thought they might lose her before they reached their destination, but at one point John Dunne whirled around—thereby creating a small vortex— and swept her up to the rest of them with his firm eye.

Donald reached in his pocket, took out his keys, and

opened the door. Faith stepped inside and was mildly shocked. Donald was evidently a devotee of the Bauhaus as opposed to the Adam school, the period to which the house belonged. He had retained the cherry wainscoting, as well as the long windows with their hand-blown glass panes that offered wavy views of the front lawn. Everything else was a minimalistic compilation of chrome, leather, black, white, or glass. The single note of color was a huge abstract portrait of Charmaine, in the style of Soutine, which hung in solitary splendor on one wall.

Donald automatically went to the other side of his desk and sat down. Faith took the chair in front. Dunne brought two chairs from the rear of the room and placed them next to Faith's for Muriel and Charmaine; then he went over to the wall and leaned against it next to Charmaine's portrait, where he could see them all.

Faith knew she was supposed to wait for Dunne to start, but he appeared to be in no rush, and it was all she could do to keep from saying something. She looked at Donald, Muriel, and Charmaine. Only Muriel was not visibly tense. Charmaine was chewing her thumbnail. Donald was tapping the top of his desk with a pencil. But Muriel—Muriel seemed to have gone someplace else. Her eyes weren't focused on the room or anyone in it. She sat absolutely still.

Dunne spoke in a deceptively mild manner. "When did you last see Stanley Russell, Charmaine?"

So he was starting there.

She lost the color in her face, which highlighted the artificiality of her blusher and foundation. She looked as garish as a hooker.

"I don't know anyone by that name," she answered defiantly.

"He knows you."

She looked startled.

"I may have met him once in Florida with Eddie. I think Eddie said Stanley was his father's name, so that may

176

have been who the gentleman was." Charmaine had dropped her southern accent and was trying Katherine Hepburn. Dunne wasn't buying it.

Donald was staring at her. It was hard to read his face—resignation, disappointment, fury. Muriel had turned her gaze to the windows. She wasn't even there.

"I believe you have seen him since then. Seen him in Boston both with and without his son present. Is this true?"

Donald spoke up. "My wife doesn't have to answer these questions without a lawyer present."

Dunne nodded. "That's true. I merely thought she'd like to help us out here. Two people are dead and another in the hospital barely hanging on."

"Two!" Charmaine looked wildly about the room, as if expecting more bodies to materialize—or someone gunning for her.

The door did burst open, startling the rest of them. Francis Coffin doddered in, followed closely by several of his men.

"Have I missed it?" he shouted, then pulled a piece of paper from his pocket and waved it wildly.

He walked into the middle of the room and faced the desk. "Donald Whittemore Hubbard, I have a warrant for your arrest for the murder of Edsel Russell on December sixteenth. You have the right to . . ."

John Dunne heaved a sigh, straightened up, and walked toward Donald, who appeared to have been turned to stone. It hadn't exactly gone according to plan, but it was too late now. Dunne placed his hands on the pristine surface of the glass-topped desk and leaned forward.

"We found out who bought the knives, Donald."

Donald's face crumpled. Charmaine started shrieking. Muriel stood up, went over to her sister-in-law, and slapped her across the face. Charmaine shut up instantly. Then Muriel sat down again in the same pose. The room was quiet. She reached up and fingered one of the earrings she was wearing. They had been hidden by her hair, and Faith noted how incongruous they looked with the rest of Muriel's prim outfit and indeed with Muriel's face—dangling gold peacocks with tiers that moved provocatively as Muriel turned to Dunne and said in a level voice, "Put the warrant away. Donald didn't kill Eddie. I did."

Sun streamed in through Faith's living room windows on Thursday morning. There had been a light snowfall during the night, and outside everything looked deep and crisp and even. John Dunne was sitting next to the Christmas tree with a cup of coffee and a huge cinammon roll, one of a dozen he'd brought with him in a large sticky sack. Tom had left reluctantly to keep an appointment. Faith had kept him up half the night with the story of Muriel's confession, but there were still some holes that only Dunne could fill in. Tom's last words had been "Take notes if necessary. I don't want to miss a thing. Promise?" Faith had promised. It was nice to have a husband who shared one's interests. Ben was in front of the TV with the sound turned low watching Big Bird wait on his roof to make sure Santa would be able to fit down the chimney. Faith hoped it wouldn't give Ben any ideas.

"Sure you won't join me?" John cajoled. "Best bakery I know around here, almost as good as the one on the Grand Concourse my mother used to go to when I was a kid."

Faith shook her head. Maybe she'd have one later to keep him company, but now all she wanted was information, not sugar-covered fingers.

"Will you ever forget the look on Coffin's face? I thought he was going to pass out of the picture for good right there," Dunne said appreciatively.

To say that Francis Coffin had looked dazed and confused was an understatement akin to saying the Minotaur's labyrinth was tricky. Francis seemed to stop breathing for a moment, then shook his head. "No, sweetheart. It's your brother . . ."

Muriel was annoyed. "I killed him. Tied him up. Two knives, one to his chest, one to his windpipe. Now leave Donald alone."

Donald made a grab for his senses. "Muriel, what are you saying? Neither of us had anything to do with this. It's a ghastly mistake. They were my knives, but I have no idea how they got there."

Muriel stood up and stared at Donald. "Et tu?" her expression said. "Donald, I killed Eddie. There's no mistake." And no mistaking the ring of pride in her voice.

"I'm calling a lawyer, Muriel. Sit down and don't say a word." Donald reached for his phone, "insanity defense" written all over his face.

She watched him dial. "Tell Mr. Horton to meet us at the police station. I assume that's where we're going? Unless you'd like me to tell you about it here? It's certainly bound to be more comfortable." Her calm was staggering.

"Why not here?" Faith said, her one and only contribution to the events of the afternoon.

"Why not?" Dunne agreed, and read her her rights.

Muriel nodded in acknowledgment. "Then tell Mr. Horton to come here, Donald, although I don't know why he's bothering."

She hadn't waited for the lawyer's arrival, despite her brother's adjurations. Muriel wanted to tell her story, and she wanted to tell it right away.

"Eddie and I were lovers. We have been since he came here." Muriel flung a scornful look at Charmaine. "This may surprise you. We were going to be married. He never cared anything for you. He was just flirting, so no one would suspect about us." Charmaine appeared dumbfounded, then started to say something, caught Donald's eye, and thought better of it. Muriel continued. There was no stopping her.

"We used to go to his apartment, but we liked the guest room too. The bed was so big." She smiled dreamily. "When he told me we had to stop seeing each other, that he was going away, I knew he'd meet me one last time. I was good; he said. The best he'd ever had."

So it was love twisted into jealous hatred, Faith thought. As Muriel talked, she began to look almost pretty. What kind of a person uses a woman like Muriel? Eddie Russell—and Faith was pretty sure she knew why.

And so did Muriel. "You're all thinking I killed him because he was leaving me. As if I'd do something like that." She sounded genuinely indignant. "No, Eddie had to die because he was doing terrible things. James told me. He had done them to James. Started him on drugs. He stole my keys to the medications room and made copies. James told me. Eddie denied it, but I knew it was true." She was beginning to sound drugged herself. Her voice assumed a flat tone, and the words blended into one another. "He was hurting Hubbard House. He was hurting all of us. He was hurting Daddy. I had to stop him from hurting more people. I had to stop him from destroying Hubbard House."

No one heard the door open. Muriel had them mesmerized.

"I didn't know the knives would be missed. There were a lot of them—and so many other presents for your Scouts, Donald. And how else could I have done it?"

A voice called from the doorway, "Be quiet, daughter. That's enough."

They all turned to see Roland Hubbard filling the doorway. He looked like something out of William Blake's Prophetic Books—larger than life, if not of some other world.

Muriel fell sobbing hysterically to the ground. "I'm sorry, Daddy. I'm very, very sorry."

He walked over, knelt down, and gently put his arms around her.

After a few minutes, Dunne spoke to Roland Hubbard and the three of them left the room. Everyone else left too after that, and the last words Faith heard as she got into her car, her eyes brimming with tears, were Francis Coffins:'

"Do you mean to tell me his *sister* did it? That mouse? Come on!"

Faith decided to join John in a cinnamon roll.

"So what happened at headquarters? And what about Leandra? I can't imagine Muriel had anything to do with that. Although I had narrowed my choices down to Donald and/or Charmaine, I never suspected Muriel. It just shows how clothes can create an image."

"She's only being charged with the murder of Edsel Russell. Leandra Rhodes regained consciousness yesterday and the first thing she said to her husband was 'Somebody pushed me.' That was another thing I wanted to talk about with the gang at HH, before Francis screwed things up—or didn't. I can't make up my mind."

"How did *he* get the warrant?" This had been nagging at Faith since Francis Coffin had swooped into Donald's office.

"Another snafu. It wasn't ready when I left, so I arranged for someone to follow me, and he thought I was bringing Donald into the Byford police station for questioning. So of course when he appeared there with a warrant, Coffin was like a puppy seeing his first red meat and took off before anyone could check it out."

"Okay, that clears that up, but what about Leandra?"

"I think it probably *was* Muriel who gave her a shove. When she gave us her valuables at the station, she handed over a silver locket with a picture of the two of them inside, and maybe it's what Leandra had appropriated—something that linked Eddie and Muriel as more than faithful servant and gentle mistress. Muriel seems to be someone who has been tuning in and out with greater and greater frequency lately, and I'm betting that in one of her more lucid moments, she began to feel a little desperate about getting caught for the naughty thing she did. We'd talked to a lot of the Hubbard House people, and you were right—Mrs. Rhodes never leaves home, or anywhere else, without her bag. The only way for Muriel to get it would have been to snatch it."

"I'm so glad Leandra is going to be all right. She is, isn't she?" And, Faith thought, how typical that Leandra's first words should be right on the mark. No "Where am I? Who am I?" for her. Just straight to business.

"She's going to be in the hospital for a long time while those bones mend, but they think she'll be fine. However, unless Muriel confesses or Leandra remembers something more about her attacker—which I doubt, otherwise she would have said—that incident as a police matter is shelved."

"I know we're wandering all over the place and I want to know what else Muriel said, but do you think Charmaine thought Donald did it and that's why she staged the phony attack on herself?"

"More likely she thought we'd trace the knives and think she did it, but possibly the other. He is her husband, and she may have figured she wouldn't be invited to many A-list events if hubby was doing life. She recognized the knives right away, as Donald must have. He's on the area Scout council and every year gives the local troops gifts of knives, compasses, fancy canteens, whatever. We didn't have any luck tracing the knives through the local Army-Navy stores, so we began to check the distributors—see if anyone we knew had ordered them by mail. Donald had placed a large order with Gutmann several weeks ago."

"Poor Muriel wasn't very smart about all this."

"Oh, she was. If it hadn't been for the knives, we wouldn't have had much to go on." He smiled and took another cinnamon roll. "Want to hear how she did it? It's pretty funny in a weird sort of way."

Faith waited politely for him to finish the roll, which took several seconds.

"She went to the guest room stark naked under the robe she was wearing in case she bumped into anyone. He'd been asking her to get into a little bondage, and she

182

hadn't wanted to, but this time she said she would—told him it was a bon-voyage gift. The cords were his. He had a lot of stuff like that in his room. To continue—she told us she went into the bathroom, to pee I guess, and saw your watch and toothbrush by the sink, so she knew she had to kill him and get out of there quickly. She was pretty annoyed about that. I think she blames you for her not getting one last good lay. Although of course at the time she didn't know it was your watch. Just figured it must be someone stranded by the weather. She didn't know where that someone was—and wouldn't she have been surprised—but she ran from the bathroom, threw her robe or whatever off so she wouldn't get blood on it, and stabbed him before he had a chance to think what hit him. Then she ran back to her room. She had taken a towel from your bathroom in case she needed it, but she didn't. None of the blood on the other towels matched Russell's, incidentally. Lot of unsteady shaving hands at Hubbard House. Anyway, she put the towel with the rest of hers in her own bathroom. She never got a drop of blood on her and didn't leave so much as a hair on him. She used those thin disposable rubber gloves, which she flushed down the john back in her room. Pretty good thinking and a whole lot of luck, all in all."

"And she knew exactly where to put the knives from her nurse's training. But why two? One for her wrongs and one for James'?"

"Nothing so poetic. The first one in the windpipe was to shut him up and the second was the insurance. She said she was pretty sure one would do it, but she was afraid to take a chance."

"Was her father there during the confession?"

"No, he waited outside. It was just the lawyer, Muriel, Sully—Detective Sullivan, that is—and me. Fortunately we managed to lose Coffin on the way."

Faith felt very tired. "I'm going to make some more coffee. Want some?"

"No, much as I'd like it. I have to get back to the store.

Somebody found a body in the woods near Ashby when they were looking for a Christmas tree to cut down."

He went over to Ben, who was sufficiently in awe of Dunne to look away from "Sesame Street." Dunne patted him on the head. Faith hoped it would not stunt his growth. "Say hi to Santa for me, kiddo."

At the door, he gave Faith a kind of hug. "Put it behind you now. It's over. It's sad as hell, but it's got nothing to do with you. Throw a log on the fire, make Tom some wassail, and be merry."

"I will," she promised. "It's just that it's been so involved and it seemed relatively simple at first." At first—Chat's call seemed months ago.

"You did a good job, Faith. All the bad guys are rounded up. You'll probably get some sort of citation from Boston for getting Stanley Russell's license plate number. They've been trying to nail him for years and now they've got him on vehicular homicide, hit-and-run, you name it. He must have been pretty desperate to shut Hubbard up to take a chance like that. Whether we'll ever establish any connection between him and our friend Charmaine I doubt. In any case, there'll be no more blackmailing of the elderly by any of them. Hubbard House is safe."

She closed the door behind him. He was right. This was where Howard Perkins' initial suspicions had led, and she knew he would have been pleased that the place he had grown to love was battered and bruised, but not broken. Chat, who was arriving on Saturday, would be pleased too. Everyone was pleased, so she should be pleased as well and she would be if only she didn't feel so terrible.

The show was over. She flicked off the set, grabbed Ben before he could protest, and tried not to feel guilty at how often she had been resorting to the electronic babysitter lately. "Time to make the gingerbread house, my little gumdrop."

***

184

The Hubbard House Christmas party was held right on schedule. Faith had been fairly certain it wouldn't be canceled. She hadn't lived in New England for this long without learning a few of the mores, and one of the biggies was "On with the show, keep dancing even though the ship has struck an iceberg, and above all, don't let the sun catch you crying."

She planned to stay for only a short time—nibble a cookie, drink some punch, then race home to watch Tom watch the Celtics. It was amazing how frequently they seemed to play. When she told him her plan, he approved, except for the racing part.

"It's getting cold out, and the roads may ice up. And—"

"I know, I know. No more snowbanks. No more bodies. Don't worry, darling. See you soon."

She left him happily ensconced in what they called the "comfy chair"—virtually the only one in a parsonage filled with an orthopedic army of straight-backed, hard-seated varieties bequeathed by Tom's predecessors. Ben was snuggled in Tom's lap and Faith was sorry she had to leave.

As she drove up the winding drive, the two houses sparkled ahead—lighted from top to toe. Inside, someone had completed the decorations started earlier in the week. There was an enormous tree in the living room covered with gold balls, a few discreet strands of tinsel, and small white lights. A large silver bowl of holly sat on the mantel and more sprigs of holly were tucked on top of the pictures on the wall. Faith could hear the sounds of merriment from the dining room, left her coat in the closet, and hastened in. A fire was crackling in the large fieldstone fireplace at one end of the room, and Faith felt drawn by its warmth.

Mrs. Pendergast, resplendent in a long dress of royal purple velvet, was presiding over the punch bowl. Faith was relieved to see it wasn't eggnog. One cup a season was plenty and she always had that at the Millers', where Sam ladled out a robust version for all the neighbors on Christmas Day.

"Faith, I'm so glad you came. Have some claret cup? It's one of Dr. Hubbard's family recipes." She handed her a brimming cup.

"Thank you and Merry Christmas, Violet. Your dress is beautiful."

"I wear it every year and have only had to let it out three times. It's my favorite color. Now do you think Mother knew somehow and named me after it, or did I get to like it because of the name?"

It was one of those metaphysical questions Faith preferred to avoid.

"Probably both," she answered, and took a sip of punch. "It's delicious."

"Now I want you to go over to the buffet and try my cream puffs—Dream Puffs, I call them. Even if you don't eat anything else, have one of those. I know you young people are always on a diet." She eyed Faith's slender figure, not in her red Mizrahi tonight but in a Scott McClintock Little Women update—midnight-blue velvet bodice and puffed sleeves with a short, full taffeta skirt. Faith thought it was very regional and felt she ought to have had a fitted coat, tippet, and muff to match for the sleigh ride home.

She left Mrs. Pendergast, got a Dream Puff—there was no way to avoid it—and strolled over to the windows. The lights in the room had been dimmed and candles were everywhere. Winston's and Sylvia Vale had done beautiful things with white roses, red amaryllis, boxwood, more holly, and yards of gold and silver ribbon. Carols were playing softly. The whole effect was of a beautiful stage set. Faith expected the woman sitting on the window seat to turn and start singing "Have Yourself a Merry Little Christmas" to Margaret O'Brien. The figure turned, but it was Julia Cabot, not Judy Garland, and she didn't sing but waved. Faith sat down next to her.

"Merry Christmas, Faith. Ellery will be down in a moment. He always has trouble with his studs and insisted I go ahead."

Most of the men were in black tie, elegant, courtly, and like the women in the pretty once-a-year Christmas gowns, very well preserved.

"Merry Christmas, Julia." Faith paused. It was hard to know what to say next. Since she had walked into the room, she'd had an odd sensation that none of the events of the past week had occurred. That Eddie, Leandra, Muriel—and maybe even James, the prodigal, would come through the door and it all would have been a dream. Something to mention briefly in the golden glow of the room, so whoever you were speaking to could laugh incredulously at such a phantasm and make it disappear.

Julia didn't laugh. She spoke into the pause. "It seems so odd to be here like this, yet there isn't anything else to do but go on. This is what Roland wants—and all of us agree. He spoke to Ellery and told him what had happened and asked that he tell everyone else. Poor Muriel. I had no idea she was so unhappy."

Faith hadn't considered things from this angle, but of course Muriel was unhappy. Living in such isolation. Easy pickings for someone like Eddie Russell.

Julia continued. "Some of us knew about James. I did, because Ellery mentioned once that there was another child. Roland lost two children on Wednesday. I don't know how he can bear it."

"Where is he tonight?"

"Sylvia said he would look in later for a few minutes. She was able to convince him it wasn't necessary for him to be here all the time. That people understood."

"I was glad to hear that Leandra is going to be all right."

"Yes, I saw her yesterday. She's demanding to come home, so I'd say she's mending fast. I think I'd like to be like her—or like her in that way—when I grow up."

"Me too," Faith agreed, and the two women laughed.

Faith recognized some of the Pink Ladies from the Holly Ball. Denise wouldn't be waltzing in tonight, but she was going to be all right. Tom had been to see her on Tuesday and she had called Faith just this morning. Joel was staying with Joan and Bill Winter, Denise's neighbors, and visited her every day. The thing she had feared most—that he would hate and reject her—had not happened, and they were both going into therapy. She told Faith it was going to be the happiest new year of her life.

Faith finished her Dream Puff, aware of Mrs. P.'s eagle eye from across the room. She saw Sylvia Vale and excused herself from Julia to say merry Christmas. A few minutes more, then she could leave.

As she crossed the room, something that looked like a Christmas package all wrapped up in shiny paper and ribbons swooped down upon her.

"Mrs. Fairchild! So glad you could come, and I do hope we can keep you on our roster of volunteers?" It was Bootsie.

"I am going to be busy starting my catering business again, but I would be happy to help out if you get stuck." Faith was beginning to count the days until Mr. Dandy—not his real name, she suspected and hoped—of Yankee Doodle Kitchens left for Florida and she could hang her toque out.

"That's so kind of you." Bootsie lowered her voice and slipped her arm through Faith's, drawing her to one side, and enveloping her in a slightly nauseating cloud of Beautiful. The woman must bathe in it, Faith thought. Like mother, like son.

"And I'd like to thank you and the reverend for being so good to my boy. He's been having a hard time lately. Girl trouble, I suspect, but then a mother's always the last to know." Faith was fairly certain this was true in Bootsie's case.

The woman was still talking, and suddenly Faith's ears

opened wide and it was all she could do to stop herself from bursting into the Hallelujah Chorus. "I'm not supposed to mention anything until he's had a chance to talk to your husband, Tom. I hope I can call him that. I always think of him that way, since that's how Cyle speaks of him. Maybe Reverend Tom, but that sounds like one of those TV shows. But Cyle has begun to have doubts. I know you'll be as shocked as I was, though I did wonder in the beginning when he had been an economics major why he wanted to go into the ministry. He's going to take some time off and think about it all."

Faith wanted to get this straight. The torrent of words, the perfume, and maybe the combination of Dream Puffs and claret cup were starting to make her feel sick. "Are you saying that Cyle is dropping out of divinity school?"

"Well, maybe not permanently, but for now, yes."

Hosanna.

Faith pried herself loose from Bootsie and went to find Sylvia. She definitely had to go home, or lie down, or find a bathroom, or throw up. The only other time she ever remembered feeling like this was before Ben was born.

She stopped dead in her tracks and did some counting. My God, she thought, I'm pregnant! She had never had morning sickness, just night. Her joy was slightly clouded by the memory. Then she felt happy—what a Christmas present for Tom—conflicted—what about the business?—strong—I'll manage—and terrified. She looked for a chair, then decided she'd better go call Tom to come get her. It was early and he could pop Ben in the car. There was no way she could drive feeling like this.

She left the room, which was now filled with all the residents, volunteers, family, and friends. There was plenty of laughter, and couples were starting to dance.

Tom answered on the fourth ring. It must be a close game.

"Honey, I'm sorry to bother you, but do you think you

could come and pick me up? I'm not feeling well. A bit mal de mer."

"Faith! Do you think this could be—"

"Possibly." His elation leaped over the wires, but the room was beginning to spin and she wanted him to come quickly. "In fact, more than possibly. We'll talk about it later. I'm going to go upstairs and lie down until you come. I'll come down in, what, about twenty minutes? No, thirty—you've got to get Ben into his snowsuit."

"Oh, darling, this is the best news. I can't believe it. I won't keep you. Go take care of yourself and we'll be there as fast as we can. I love you."

"I love you too."

Faith hung up the phone and staggered to the elevator. She'd go into the annex and find an empty room. The guest room had lost whatever appeal it might have once had. First she got her coat. She seemed to be freezing.

Upstairs nothing was stirring, not even a mouse. She opened a door and peeked in the darkened room. Something white and filmy was silhouetted against the window. It was hovering over the bed.

Farley's ghost!

She started to back out of the door and run.

The ghost stood up. It wasn't Christmas Past.

It was Roland Hubbard.

Roland Hubbard in a turn-of-the-century nurse's uniform complete with wimple.

10

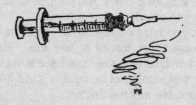

Dr. Hubbard raced to the door, grabbed Faith, pulled her into the room, and pushed her down in a chair by the window. He had a syringe in his hand and was clearly not indulging in just a little harmless cross dressing.

"What are you doing here, Mrs. Fairchild?" he hissed angrily.

"I was feeling a—"

"Shhh, we don't want to wake the patient."

Faith lowered her voice to a whisper. It wasn't hard. "I was feeling a little sick and came up here to lie down, but I'll go to another room. I'm sorry I disturbed you."

She attempted to get out of the chair. He pushed her back down and kept his hand flat against her sternum. It was hard to breathe, and she thought she might be sick.

"What to do? What to do?" he was muttering to himself. He looked over at the sleeping figure in the bed. "The angels will come another night, my dear Geoffrey."

The first shock had worn off, but Faith was still having trouble believing what she was seeing—Dr. Roland Hubbard, eminent physician, dressed as a nurse and nuttier than the fruitcake Mrs. Pendergast was pressing on one and all downstairs. James had said Hubbard House was a nut house and James had been right. Only she would have preferred to verify this knowledge second, third, or tenth hand.

"Dr. Hubbard," she whispered in what she hoped was a reasonable tone, "please let me up. You're hurting me."

The pressure on her chest lightened, yet he didn't remove his hand. He looked about the room and darted over to the sink for a towel. She jumped up, but he caught her before she could reach the door.

"Now, you must do exactly as I say," he scolded her. "I don't want to be forced to use this." He waved the syringe in her face and she could see it was full—full of something that would not be terribly good for her, and he should know. He was the doctor.

He was tying the towel as a gag around her mouth before she had a chance to say—or whisper—anything to warn him.

There was nothing she could do. She threw up. Dream Puffs, claret cup, the angel hair pasta with shrimp she'd had for supper—all came forth, most of it in the sink where he rushed her immediately, but some on herself and the floor. The room instantly took on that horrible odor parents have nightmares about—the odor preceded by a certain cough and cries for help, galvanizing the most deeply asleep mother and father to instant action. Faith's own mother was miles away, but Dr. Hubbard was doing his best to substitute.

She'd assumed he would be infuriated, but he was almost tender. He handed her a glass of water to rinse her mouth, helped her off with her spattered coat, and gave her a fresh towel.

"Feeling better?"

She looked at him in astonishment. It was Nurse Jane Fuzzy Wuzzy come to life.

"Yes, thank you."

"Can't use a gag," he said to himself—or one of them. "Come on, then. If you make a sound, I'll use this." He held up the syringe again. Faith nodded. She had no intention of joining the angels.

They moved out into the corridor after Dr. Hubbard had opened the door and looked cautiously up and down. Everything was dark.

He pushed her along past the elevator and opened a door leading to the second floor of the next house. She walked as slowly as she dared. When Tom arrived and didn't find her in the living room or at the party, he'd come upstairs to look. It was too soon to expect him, but the knowledge that he was on his way was keeping her from total terror. She considered telling Roland she might be pregnant, but decided to keep this news in case she needed to make a last desperate plea. Total terror began to manifest itself at the thought, and she closed her eyes and took a breath. Tom. Tom would be here soon.

They were near the staircase. Pale streaks of the waning moon caught the pattern of the oriental carpet tread. The chandelier glowed softly, and Dr. Hubbard was guiding her with a sure hand.

Please, Faith prayed, not the guest room.

It wasn't. They descended the stairs.

It was going to be his office.

He opened the door and turned on the light, then reached into his pocket for his keys and locked the dead-bolt at the top.

"Sit down," he said in his normal volume. It sounded so loud, Faith was sure someone must hear it.

He took a seat on the other side on the desk and

appeared to be lost in thought. Finally he pulled his chair in and leaned forward, bringing the fingertips of both hands together. She was ready for the prognosis.

"Unfortunately, it is sometimes necessary in life to sacrifice the needs and well-being of one person for the greater good of the community. When it is a young person such as yourself, a decision like this assumes tragic proportions. But you do see that I have no choice."

Faith didn't see at all.

"I'm not sure I understand what you're talking about, Dr. Hubbard. Or, in fact, what is going on here at all."

"Faith," he replied sorrowfully, "put simply, you know too much." He should have looked more absurd in his outfit, but the solemn surety in his voice overshadowed all else.

She tried to reassure him. "I don't know anything. You've been under a great strain, which explains the way you're dressed, but—"

"Do you have any idea how much it costs to keep Hubbard House going, young lady?"

She was more than willing to change the subject—only she wasn't sure this was what was happening. Still, so long as he was on one side of the desk and she on the other, she was safe from that booster shot lying conveniently close to his hand on the desk blotter.

"No, I don't."

"A great deal of money." So this wasn't going to be an itemized rundown of all it took to keep Hubbard House going: Q-tips, baked beans, vitamin C pills. Faith was a little disappointed.

"For years we have sought to keep afloat with our fees, private donations, a grant here and there, whatever the government can occasionally spare. It hasn't been easy."

"I'm sure not," Faith murmured. Where was Tom?

"Not easy at all. But no one is turned out, and we have not relaxed our standards. Not for a minute."

Faith thought of the flowers from Winston's. Maybe a few less posies and a few more pennies saved?

"We have established a certain quality of life here, and I intend it to remain that way so long as I'm here. Although Donald, of course, feels as I do and will carry on after me."

Faith nodded. She didn't feel sick anymore. Just scared. She was pretty sure where this line of thought was going.

"That's why I had to do it." He stood up, remembering to grab the syringe, and went over to his wife's portrait. "A wonderful woman. The best wife any man could have had. She would have agreed with me completely." He swung around and looked Faith squarely in the eye. "I had no choice, don't you see?"

"Absolutely, whatever you did I'm sure you thought was for the best."

"It *was* for the best. I only picked people who were very close to leaving us anyway. In a few instances they were individuals who had expressed a wish to be relieved of their sufferings. And months would go by when I didn't have to make any night visits at all. But this fall has been bad. Contributions down. Expenses up. Of course it's a hard time of year in any case, lots of flu, pneumonia. Nothing odd about a ninety-four-year-old dying peacefully in his sleep.

"Farley thought I was a ghost. He would insist on keeping his window open and then kicking his covers off. I always checked in on him." He gave an affectionate laugh and reached up to remove his cap and veil. He unbuttoned the uniform, and Faith was obscurely relieved to observe that he hadn't deemed it necessary to wear ladies' undergarments as well. He had his own shirt and trousers on underneath. "This was Mother's uniform. In case someone did wake up before the morphine took effect, I wanted them to be comforted and not startled."

Not startled! At the moment Faith could think of few things less startling than seeing Dr. Hubbard in Florence

Nightingale drag with an empty syringe in hand bending over one's bed.

"It was a painless and rapid method, a simple overdose."

"These then were residents who had left bequests to Hubbard House?" She asked more to keep the conversational ball rolling than from any lack of certainty, since as long as the ball was in play, the game wasn't over. She hadn't watched all those basketball games for nothing.

"Not all of them, of course. That would have been foolhardy. I had to help some on as a little window dressing, so to speak. Though until poor Farley fell into your bouillon, we haven't had an autopsy here for years. It's not the sector of the population that calls for them, you know, especially these days. There's barely money in the state for homicide victims."

Faith wasn't interested in the always-dismal state of the state's coffers. "Farley!" She was genuinely indignant. Then there had *never* been any question of its being her bouillon.

"Oh no, my dear. Completely natural, although the morphine would have been hard to detect if it had been me. No one would have been looking for it, you see. No, Farley was his own doing. Nothing to do with either you or me."

Faith rubbed her eyes. She was very tired, and sitting with a madman discussing which of them might have killed someone wasn't alleviating her weariness. She suddenly thought of Howard Perkins. The start of this whole business. Had he been visited by this angel of mercy killing too? She had to know—or she'd never be able to face Aunt Chat again. Oh, that she could face her now!

"What about Howard Perkins?"

"Howard Perkins? Did you know him? Charming man and with us for such a short time. He should have moved here years earlier. It's very difficult for me to understand why anyone would want to stay in New York, but then he would go on so about his beloved opera and the museums. What about him?"

"Did you—rather, was he . . . ?" Faith searched for some polite equivalent to "murder him."

Roland caught her meaning. "Oh no, he had a very bad heart. Besides, he was leaving everything to some woman in New Jersey, and I certainly wouldn't have used him as camouflage when he had joined us so recently." Dr. Hubbard sounded offended at the kind of thoughts Faith had been harboring.

Her lassitude increased. She was almost beginning to relax. Tom would arrive, find her, and the good doctor would join his daughter in a nicely furnished padded cell.

Then Roland's next words sent a megadose of adrenaline coursing through her veins and any notion of fatigue disappeared at once.

"But we stray and time is passing quickly. I must put in an appearance at our little party, and this could take a while. I really am so very, very sorry that I have to kill you."

He went to the closet and put on his coat, then reached up on the shelf and took a gun from an ancient Wright's Arch Preserver shoebox.

"It will be much nicer for you if you cooperate and I can see you out the normal way, but I'll bring this just in case."

Normal? Just in case? Did words have meaning anymore?

Faith began to think rapidly. She had no idea where they were going, but it was obviously outside. How would he explain her lack of a coat? Once again she was going to freeze because of one of the Hubbards. But she had underestimated Roland.

"I'm going to give you one of my overcoats. You notice I say 'give' and not 'lend.' I don't expect that I will get it back. I'll explain that I gave it to you to wear home, since yours was soiled. This was after I came across you being ill in one of the rooms. You insisted you were fit enough to drive and I didn't like to quarrel with a lady. Of course, I should have insisted, but then you are so stubborn."

He was rehearsing and Faith's mind was suddenly blank. He was going to kill her and there was nothing she could do about it. If she screamed, no one would hear her, and he would kill her "normally" or not, before she could expect help in any case. She looked at him as he courteously held his coat out for her. He was over six feet and fit as a fiddle. There was no way she could overpower him.

"Best give me your keys now, my dear. I'll be driving at first."

She took them out of her prized Judith Leiber bag, which still swung from her shoulder. It had been an engagement present from Hope, and Faith had followed suit and given her one also. Hope! The wedding! She had one more fitting for her matron of honor dress! It wasn't your whole life that flashed before you in terminal moments, but ludicrous and totally inappropriate bits and pieces.

Dr. Hubbard unlocked the door and was reaching for the knob when a knock came.

It was Tom. It had to be Tom. She was safe.

Hubbard opened the closet door and shoved her inside. The same closet she had ducked into a week earlier. The same closet she'd been able to duck out of. A key was pushed into the keyhole, obliterating the light from the room. She heard it turn with a disheartening click. She started to scream and pounded on the door with all her strength. Why wasn't Tom coming? What could be happening? It seemed like hours and her screams were getting hoarser and hoarser.

The door opened at last and she rushed straight into the arms of—Dr. Hubbard.

"Dear Sylvia. Worried about me and wanted me to know I was missed. It sounds like a lovely party, but I told her I wasn't quite up to it. Of course she understood." He looked at his watch. "I just might be able to get back for some of my claret cup if we hurry. My great-grandmother's recipe. I do hope you had some."

Faith was sobbing.

"This closet was the strong room. Tinned on the inside, you know. And these doors are very solid."

He opened the door to the hall, closed it firmly behind them, and poked the gun in her back. It was obviously the signal to start walking, and she did.

They started down the corridor toward the rear of the house. He walked, as he always did, with a measured tread, head erect. His long overcoat billowed out behind him like the robes of some crazed medieval king.

Near the stairs Faith turned to him and said beseechingly, "Dr. Hubbard, I am going to have a baby." She was crying so hard she could barely get the words out.

"Are you, my dear? Congratulations are in order! How unfortunate that it should come at a time like this."

There was no hope whatsoever.

He steered her to an outside door that she remembered led to stairs going down to the parking lot. She stopped crying. This was time not for Niobe but for one of her relatives—Athena or Hera.

At the top of the stairs Faith silently kicked off the high heels she had been wearing. The cold from the icy ground shot painfully through her feet to her legs. She walked on tiptoes, so he wouldn't notice the sudden change in her height. It was excruciating.

"Mind your step here, it's treacherous. We certainly have had a cold winter, haven't we?" Roland sounded as though he were escorting her to the prom and worried she might turn an ankle.

Faith didn't reply. It was one thing for the murderer to be so civilized; she the victim didn't have to follow suit. And she'd be damned if talking about the weather would be her last act.

It wasn't.

At the bottom of the stairs she took off, sprinted a yard

or two ahead of him, tore off the coat and threw it over his head—she was close enough to aim correctly, but far enough away so he couldn't grab her. Then she sped off away from the lampposts toward the darkest part of the shrubbery.

"Faith! Faith! Come back here! You can't get away from me!" He was enraged. The last words were clearer, and presumably he'd gotten out from under the coat, but Faith didn't turn around to look.

There was a series of paths and small terraces that sloped down from the parking lot alongside the steep front driveway. She headed for these and the direction of the main road. Going down the drive itself would give him a clear shot, and she had no doubt that he would use the gun now, no matter who saw or heard. He was beyond whatever reason he'd managed to retain.

"Faith!" he screamed at the top of his voice. He wasn't far away.

She left the path and ran closer to the drive near the mountainous rhododendron bushes, bordered by Canadian hemlocks. There was only one thing to do. She dove into the center of the largest clump and ducked down in the middle of the branches. They were covered with snow and ice, and as she pushed through, they rattled like castanets. The sharp needles of the hemlocks cut into her face, bare forearms, and legs, but her whole body was so numb from the cold, she could scarely feel the pain.

"Faith!"

She held her breath as he came closer and closer. The branches were silent. He was only a few feet away. Thank God she had worn the dark-blue dress.

"You can't hide from me. I know you're in these bushes someplace."

She let out the breath slowly and took another. She was in a tight fetal position and dared not try to make herself yet smaller. The slightest movement would start the branches clacking together.

"Be reasonable, Faith! It's cold out here. I've changed my mind. I'm not going to hurt you, dear." His voice, calm now and almost convincing, came from farther away. Then there was silence. All she could hear was the hideously loud beating of her own heart.

Then a sharp crack followed by a regular thwacking noise. Dr. Hubbard had broken off a branch and was beating the bushes.

Thwack! Thwack! It was coming closer. She shut her eyes and pictured him bringing the stick down on her head with all his manic force.

Thwack! Thwack! He took his time. He was thorough. She opened her eyes. She wanted to see him coming.

She started to edge cautiously out from under the bush to one farther along, and as she did so she heard a car coming up the drive. Scarcely believing, she waited until it was almost even with her hiding place, then she stood up and broke through the branches the short distance to the pavement.

It was Tom. He stopped the car abruptly and jumped out.

"Faith! What's—"

"Get down," she screamed as she ran out of range to the driver's side of the car. "He's got a gun."

She flung herself next to Tom. "It's Dr. Hubbard. He's trying to kill me. He's killed all these people. We've got to get out of here!"

Tom didn't hesitate. Without standing up, he opened the back door and pushed Faith in, then got in the front himself and started the engine.

Faith pulled Ben from the car seat where he had been obliviously sound asleep and shoved him beneath her on the floor. He didn't like it.

Tom executed a rapid U turn and started down the drive.

A few feet away Roland Hubbard came leaping from

201

the bushes and froze in the car headlights like a deer straying at midnight from the safety of the woods. For an instant he stayed like that, then raised the gun to his temple and pulled the trigger.

11

Tom put down the phone. Faith was putting the finishing touches to a platter of small open-faced sandwiches she was preparing for a high tea she was serving before the Sunday-school pageant. It was Christmas Eve.

She raised an eyebrow. John Dunne did it so well, she thought she might give it a try too.

"You don't want to know."

Faith sighed. "I already do and it's the bell all over again. It goes something like this: 'How is Faith and, of course, dear little Benjamin? It's too bad she had to bring about the collapse of a fine old institution like Hubbard House, not to mention bringing Dr. Hubbard to ruin as well, why bless me, the man delivered half the town.' Millicent has this all down pat, am I right?"

"Essentially, although I think even Millicent is having a little trouble reconciling Roland Hubbard's rewrite of the Hippocratic oath with his otherwise impeccable reputation."

Aunt Chat walked into the kitchen with Ben trailing closely behind. She'd arrived that morning along with reporters from every major and minor news agency in the northeast. Chat had immediately appointed herself Faith's public relations person and handled them all with great aplomb. They were gone now, and for the last half hour she'd been sitting by the fire playing an intense game of animal dominos with Ben. She was flushed, whether from the flames or her probable triumph Faith wasn't sure, though if childhood memory served, Chat had never let Hope and her win either.

"It's time to stop talking about all this and start a little holiday celebration. I know I started the whole thing, but you didn't listen to me, and if you had, you wouldn't have gotten into the mess you did." She was hugging Faith tightly as she spoke, which took some of the asperity away from her words.

"But Chat, if I—we that is—hadn't done anything, Dr. Hubbard could have continued for years." She shuddered.

"I know, you silly girl, and that's why this whole thing is such a mess. You ought to be spanked, yet you probably saved a good many lives. Besides, you're too grown up."

Faith had heard from Julia Cabot earlier, and the reaction at Hubbard House the night before had been one of shocked disbelief accompanied by profound relief at having escaped alive. Geoffrey Gordon, who had been slated to join the angels, made a miraculous recovery and was leaving for the Riviera later that day.

Faith reluctantly left her aunt's embrace. After last night she had been spending most of her time hugging anyone in sight. But time and tide—or in this case hungry parishioners—wait for no one, and she had to get the rest of the food out. Tom was taking care of the libations—vin chaud, cider, and tea, definitely no claret cup. Or bouillon.

As she checked the phyllo triangles filled with ricotta and prosciutto browning nicely in the oven, she told Chat, "But there is a grain of truth in what Millicent is spreading all over town, though I will not admit it to anyone other than you two. Hubbard House was a wonderful place—save for that one little problem."

Faith felt a bit giddy. What was she saying? It was the perfect retirement home, except you might be killed in your sleep?

She continued, "Obviously it got completely warped in his twisted mind, but Roland Hubbard did create a fine community. Do you think it can possibly keep going?"

"I don't claim to understand this part of the world very well," replied Chat, which was more than modest—she tended to view New England with great bewilderment as a place that banned books, probably still believed in burning witches, and elected some of the most liberal politicians in the country with no apparent regard for consistency. "However, it's always been my impression that once an institution, always an institution here. I'd be willing to bet they won't even change the name, and in future only the most rude boor will ever mention Dr. Hubbard's peccadillo."

"Chat's right, and I have it on good authority. Cyle dropped by to tell me that he is taking a leave of absence, which news I was able to receive with a relatively sober face. Thank you, Faith." Tom kissed her and she kissed him back. They had slept very little the night before. In the midst of clutching each other and Ben in thanks at being alive, rejoicing at the news of the possible pregnancy, and starting Faith's circulation going again in various congenial ways, she'd almost forgotten Bootsie's blurted remarks. After she'd told him, Tom had leaped out of bed and done a jig.

"His mother had had a call from Leandra. It looks like the two pillars are going to indeed hold the temple up. The residents want to run Hubbard House as a cooperative and buy it from Donald, retaining him as chief physician."

Chat nodded, "You see, just as I said. His whole family turns out to be certifiable, but until he starts talking to the furniture—although even then it might be dismissed as eccentric—no one would think of not retaining him." She deftly grabbed Ben's hand as he was about to reach for a bottom one of the Comice pears Faith had arranged in a pyramid next to a large wedge of ripe Stilton. "No, no, sweetheart, that's for the company. Aunt Chat will get one especially for you."

Faith gave her a grateful look and took the tray into the dining room. The table looked very pretty. She'd covered it with shiny gold paper and put candles everywhere. She'd filled every vase she could find with greens and red carnations, then tied trailing gold moiré ribbons around the bases. The dining room had a fireplace too, and she went back into the kitchen to tell Tom it was time to light the fire.

She came in on the tail end of a joke. Tom, Chat, and Ben—who was joining in just to be merry—were in gales of laughter.

"Tell Faith," Tom said as he wiped his eyes. "She needs some comic relief."

"I told Tom that now there was absolutely no reason for you to feel guilty. Hubbard House was going on, and the next time Millicent said anything, you should look past her and say sweetly, 'I was merely finishing what I started two years ago—now I have the bats in the belfry.' "

Faith jotted it down next to the phone.

The Millers were the first to arrive, and Samantha promptly took charge of Ben and the children's table set up in the kitchen after first exclaiming how precious he looked. He did look pretty precious in navy-blue velvet short pants and a shirt with tiny trains embroidered on the collar that Chat had given him.

"What will I do when she discovers older boys?" Faith wailed to the Millers.

"Bite your tongue," said Sam. "Now *we* older boys"—he put an arm over each of his sons' shoulders—"want to know where all the edibles are."

Faith steered them into the dining room, where Chat was doing the honors—a teapot in one hand, her own mug of vin chaud in the other. Pix followed her in, and followed her out again as the front doorbell sounded. She had been there for several hours earlier, but still appeared to need to shepherd her friend around.

The parsonage filled quickly, and soon guests were happily munching and sipping. Millicent had arrived, and Chat was managing to keep her away from Faith by waving a plate of brandy snaps someone had brought in front of her face. Millicent wasn't a member of First Parish—she was a Congregationalist, as were her ancestors back to the flood—but she moved with ecumenical fluency from the functions of one religious institution to another, putting an oar in wherever possible—welcome or unwelcome.

Pix wasn't the only one attached to Faith, and she found that whenever she went into the kitchen to replenish supplies, she was accompanied by a dozen or so people who seemed not to want to let her out of their sight. This was terribly reassuring, though rather inconvenient. Tom and Charley MacIsaac had been among their number until Faith pulled them aside and swore she wouldn't even go to the bathroom without telling one of them.

The children were decorating gingerbread cookies under Samantha and Jenny Moore's watchful eyes. *The Nutcracker* was on the CD player and Faith took a moment to let the feeling of the holiday wash over her. It was Christmas Eve, a time of magic and promise. And despite a few scratches, she was here to enjoy it.

Two hours later she and Chat were sitting in the family pew waiting for the pageant to start. It was very cold out, and the few steps from the parsonage to the church had felt like the Iditarod. Faith hugged her coat close to her and moved an inch or two nearer to Chat's ample frame. The three Advent candles burned brightly on the altar. The choir began to sing "Silent Night" while the children walked down the aisle dressed in sheets, cut-down bathrobes, old drapes, looking for all the world like real angels, shepherds, kings, queens, and the Holy Family. Eight-year-old William Carpenter stepped forward and started to read slowly and clearly: "And it came to pass in those days, that there went out a decree . . ."

Ben was one of the angels and did not fidget too much until it was time for him to appear to the shepherds keeping watch over their flock by night. Faith thought of her own public debut, a nonspeaking role as a tree in first grade. She'd felt she was destined for better things. Ben seemed to be handling his first foray with an equal lack of stagefright. The only hitch had been when he had removed his halo during the processional, saying loudly that it itched him. Tom was watching his flock while seated to one side of the pulpit, and his eyes searched for Faith's as Ben's group started to sing "The First Nowell." There seemed to be a tear or two in his and she knew there were in hers. Chat squeezed her hand.

It was a lovely pageant, and Pamela Albright, kneeling unobtrusively in front of the children and gently supplying a line here and there, deserved a medal. The kings arrived and the congregation welcomed them with a rousing rendition of "We Three Kings." More than one dear friend of Faith's seemed to stumble over the "Sealed in the stone-cold tomb" line, and the lady herself skipped the verse altogether.

Near the end of the pageant the three Queens arrived, an addition Pamela had suggested after discovering Norma Farber's poem "The Queens Came Late." Samantha Miller stepped forward and read it now:

The Queens came late, but the Queens were there
with gifts in their hands and crowns on their hair.

They'd come, these three like the Kings, from far,
following, yes, that guiding star.
They'd left their ladles, linens, looms,
their children playing in nursery rooms,
and told their sitters: "Take charge! For this
is a marvelous sight we must not miss!"

Faith thought she would have felt the same way: not
wanting to miss anything. It was what life was all about. She
listened to the gifts the Queens brought—"a homespun
gown of blue, and chicken soup—with noodles, too—and
a lingering, lasting cradle-song." Then she heard the last
lines:

The Queens came late and stayed not long,
for their thoughts already were straining far—
past manger and mother and guiding star
and child a-glow as a morning sun—
toward home and children and chores undone.

Faith folded her hands over her for-the-moment flat
belly and said thank you, then stood up with the rest of the
congregation to sing "Joy to the World."

"How about Sophie?"

*"How about Sophie who? Sophie Tucker? Hagia
Sophia?"*

*Tom had been on the edge of sleep and he was tired. A
few hours after the pageant there had been the candlelight
service; then when they got home, Chat was waiting with
champagne, ginger ale for Faith, and some caviar from Pe-
trossian's she'd secreted in the back of the refrigerator. The
three of them had sat by the tree talking and savoring until
late. There was the Christmas Day service tomorrow and Ben
would be rousing them in what seemed like a few minutes to
see what Santa had brought.*

"How about Sophie as a name for the baby? Like a little

French schoolgirl? Or maybe Emma? Emma Woodhouse? Emma Bovary? Emma the Laura Ashley perfume?"

"What makes you so sure this is going to be a girl?"

"I don't know. It just feels like it's going to be a girl."

Tom rolled over and drew Faith close to him. "Well then, why don't we name her Pandora after her mother and be done with it?"